The Longest Road

The Whinburg Township Amish

Adina Senft

Moonshell Books, Inc.

This is a work of fiction. Names, characters, places, and incidents are a product of the author's imagination. Locales and public names are sometimes used for atmospheric purposes. Any resemblance to actual people, living or dead, or to businesses, companies, events, institutions, or locales is completely coincidental.

Book Layout ©2013 BookDesignTemplates.com
Cover design by Seedlings Online. Images from Shutterstock and the author's collection, used by permission. Edited by Leslie Peterson, Write Away Editorial.

The Longest Road / Adina Senft—1st ed.
ISBN 978-1535455374

For Christina Boys

*And with thanks to Special Agent John Fortunato,
Federal Bureau of Investigation,
and Leslie Peterson and Nancy Warren
for their help and insight*

And forgive us our sins; for we also forgive every one that is
indebted to us.
And lead us not into temptation; but deliver us from evil.

—LUKE 11:4 (KJV)

Prologue

Whinburg Township, Pennsylvania
November, thirteen years ago

"Look after your sisters," Mamm said from the kitchen door of the farmhouse, pulling her black knitted sweater around her against the chill outside. Behind her, the golden light from the kitchen lamps shone through her white organdy *Kapp*, making her look like one of the angels from the Bible. "Especially Hannah—you know Leah follows wherever she leads, including right off the edge of the hayloft."

And into the feed mixer. And once, this past spring, even into the breeding stall in the very back of the barn, where she'd gotten herself and poor little Leah locked in. It was a good thing they'd only put the mare in there or the *gut Gott* only knew what might have been left of Hannah and Leah by the time Dat had finally found them.

1

"*Ja*, Mamm," Samuel said. He was ten now, and while he didn't mind babysitting, he'd often thought it would have been nice if Mamm and Dat had started off their family with a girl, who could do the things older sisters were meant to do, instead of him. But you just didn't say things like that to Mamm or you'd get about a dozen reasons why not, right on your backside.

So he took their hands—six-year-old Hannah on his right and Leah, a year younger, on his left. That meant Hannah had to carry the basket, which was nearly as big as she was, but Mamm wanted lots of walnuts for the Christmas baking, and the trees up there in the old orchard had the best ones. It lay partway up Oak Hill, for which the little village of Oakfield on its other side was named. On this side was the town of Willow Creek, in Whinburg Township, Pennsylvania, where sometimes Dat would take Samuel to get feed or supplies or, better yet, to the mud sale in the spring, where they'd spend the day walking around looking at the equipment and talking to the other Amish men, including nearly everyone from their own church district.

Samuel loved a good mud sale. He liked all the different kinds of equipment that folks would buy and then bring to his clever Dat, who would convert them from electric to hydraulic or battery power for cash money. He liked the food the ladies sold at their tables, and he liked the fast voice of the auctioneer, who was his very own Onkel Orland from the farm down the road and Samuel's second most favorite person in the world next to Dat.

But mud sales were in the spring, and the fire auction and Thanksgiving were both done for this year, so the next thing to look forward to was Christmas, weeks away yet. Which was why Mamm wanted the walnuts. Once they'd hulled them, the nuts would have to dry, and then they'd all be cracking and shelling for several nights, but the reward would be her Christmas nut cake, which Samuel only got once a year and which he loved above all things.

The late November day was crisp and clear, and because all the leaves were nearly down in the woods, he could see the yellow leaves of the walnut trees from some distance away. They always seemed to cling longer than the ones on the poplars or maples, maybe because the old orchard was waiting for people to come and look after it and needed to fly a flag to help folks notice it way back here.

"Hey, there's Jebbie and Josiah Zook!" he exclaimed. "Looks like we won't have the orchard to ourselves after all. Come on, they don't know which tree is the best one."

Second row, third tree down. All three of the Riehl children knew it, since Dat had said it was the best one when he'd first brought Samuel up here. At one time Mamm and Dat had talked about buying the farm, but it had become so run down and tangled up in some *Englisch* family quarrel that they had abandoned the idea.

Samuel was kind of glad. They couldn't have the cows up here, he didn't think, because there was no pasture, and he would have missed the cows.

Jebbie and Josiah Zook were his best friends. When they all grew up and turned sixteen and got to drive to the singing in their own buggies, they were going to form their own gang. They'd call themselves the Squirrels and have so much fun that everyone would want to join them.

"What are you doing over there?" Jebbie called from the top of the fence next to the tree in the first row. That was just like him. Go for what was easy instead of what was good.

"Never you mind," Samuel called back. He'd never tell them which was the best tree. "But our walnuts are going to be better than yours, and you know what that means!"

"What?"

"Mamm's Christmas nut cake is going to be better, too!"

Howls of dismay followed this announcement, and Samuel laughed. It wasn't easy to put one over on the twins, and he should know. So he savored his victory while he climbed up into the tree and began to shake the walnuts off the branches. The little girls ran around on the ground, gathering them up and putting them in the basket. Mamm had made them wear their mittens, since the hulls stained clothes and hands something awful, but little Leah had already lost one of hers.

And here came Jebbie and Josiah, pelting through the trees. "We want some of those!" they crowed, and the girls scattered.

"Hey, no fair!"

He leaped down and was soon defending his tree against the invading knights, just like in his book about the castle where the king had been imprisoned. Then it was two on one, rough-housing and wrestling and laughing until he was nearly sick. They knocked over the basket, but that was okay—walnuts were easy to scoop up. Or the girls would do it.

"Hannah! Leah!" he called over his shoulder, breathless with laughter and holding Josiah off with one arm. "Pick those up!"

4

But instead of an indignant squeak of protest, since the boys had done the knocking over and if Mamm was here they'd be doing the picking up, too, he heard only Jebbie blowing snot out of one nostril—an ability Samuel envied something fierce.

"Hannah!" He struggled loose of Josiah's hold and took a quick look around the orchard. "Leah! *Wo bischt du?*"

The orchard lay still except for the flutter of yellow leaves. Had they got tired of waiting and decided to climb up and shake the branches themselves? Wouldn't he just catch *Druwwel* if one of them fell!

"Come on, you guys. I can't see the girls."

"Gut!" Jebbie pushed him. "You give, you lose."

"Neh, I mean it." They weren't in the tree. They weren't in any of the trees, because enough leaves had fallen that the grass was carpeted in them and he could see right through the branches.

And he could see something else, too. The sun had gone behind the shoulder of Oak Hill. They only had maybe half an hour before it got dark up here, and he for sure did not want to be walking down that trail through the woods in the dark.

"Hannah! Leah!" What had gotten into them? They knew better than to go wandering off— *Neh,* this was Hannah he was talking about. She was always sticking her nose into things to see why they worked (the feed mixer) and opening doors for who knew what reason—to see why they were closed, probably (the breeding stall). It would be just like her to see a deer track and go running off to see if there was a deer on it. And where Hannah went, there went Leah also.

5

With a groan, he turned to his friends. "I've got to find *mei Schweschdere* before it gets dark. Come on."

Something in his face must have told them that the time for horsing around was over, but still, Josiah couldn't resist getting in one last face-washing with a bunch of old wet leaves. Then they all loped through the orchard, calling the girls' names.

No one answered.

Maybe his sisters had gone to the top of Oak Hill to see how far they could see. It took the boys twenty precious minutes to go up and look, but there was nothing up there but rocks and the remains of somebody's campfire.

Maybe they'd come back by now and were picking up the walnuts. Samuel raced down the hill, but the basket lay on its side, right where Josiah had kicked it over.

Something cold and heavy settled in his stomach, prickling and clawing like it was a big eagle and his guts were its supper. He'd seen an illustration like that in the book he hadn't been allowed to take out of the library bus that stopped in Willow Creek and Oakfield on its way back to Whinburg.

"Here, help me fill this." He began scooping nuts into the basket. "Maybe they got tired and went home." It was the only thing he could think of. The only thing that made sense. Little girls didn't disappear off the face of the earth. Of course they'd gone home.

With a sense of relief, he said good-bye to the twins and jogged home, the basket getting heavier and bumping against his knees the whole way. When he staggered into the yard, he knew that Dat had come in from the fields because the barn door was open and Samuel could hear his deep voice inside. He always talked to the horses when he put them away.

The normalcy was a relief. The girls would be in the kitchen, chattering away with Mamm and no doubt telling on him. But since they'd run away and left him to carry in the walnuts, he wouldn't get in *Druwwel.*

At least, he hoped not.

Dat came out and saw him standing in the yard. "Samuel, are those the walnuts your mother has been waiting for?" Dat tousled his hair. *"Wo ischt dei hut?"*

His hat? He had no idea. He must have lost it in the orchard—probably when he'd gone down under the attack of the marauding knights.

He followed his father through the outside door down into the basement, where men removed their muddy, manure-covered boots before they so much as looked at Mamm's spotless floors. Then they climbed the inside stairs, and emerged into the kitchen.

"Samuel!" Mamm turned from the stove. "You're so late, I was getting worried. Look at that basket! We'll have the best nut cake ever this year." As Dat closed the basement door, she frowned. "Where are the girls?"

The eagle in Samuel's stomach took another poke at his innards. "Aren't they here?"

"What do you mean, 'aren't they here'? Of course they're not here. They were with you."

Samuel's lungs didn't seem able to expand enough to get a proper breath. "I thought they came home."

"Well, they didn't."

Dat knelt next to him. "Why don't you tell us what happened and we'll go look for them."

"I already did. I couldn't find them anywhere. That's why I came home—it's the last place left."

"They couldn't have just disappeared." Mamm turned off the gas burners under the pots on the stove. "What happened? Exactly."

Samuel's throat closed, but he cleared it and talked fast before the tears welled up and he cried like a little *Boppli.* "Jebbie and Josiah Zook were up there, too, picking, and they came over to our tree—the best one, Dat—and we were horsing around and Josiah knocked over the basket, and when I hollered at Hannah to pick up the walnuts I saw she wasn't there. So then we looked all over—we even went up to the top. And all around the fence, and all along the path, I was calling and calling. But they didn't answer. So I thought they must be here." He looked up into his mother's pale face. "They have to be here."

"I'll search the yard and the barn," Dat said, pulling on his jacket.

"I'll look over the house and cellar, just in case they came in without my hearing them."

But when his parents met again in the kitchen, from which Samuel had not moved, not so much as a toe, they shook their heads.

"One of them could have taken a fall, and the other is too scared to leave her," Dat said. He collected the lantern and two flashlights from the mudroom and would have taken the kitchen lamp, too, but Mamm stopped him.

"Neh," she said. "I'll leave this one in the window. If they're up on that hill and got their directions mixed up, they'll be able to see it."

Dat didn't argue, merely nodded and said, "Samuel, go across lots and get your Onkel Orland and his two oldest boys. Have them bring the most powerful flashlights they have and the megaphone he uses at the auction."

Samuel had never run so fast in his life, over the familiar fields, down into the creek, and up through the copse dividing the two properties. Coming back was even faster, for Onkel Orland had abandoned the idea of a buggy and had put bridles on the horses, riding bareback with Samuel up on the horse's withers in front of him.

What the bishop would have to say about that, Samuel wasn't prepared to speculate. Horses were for work and travel, not for riding on.

But Onkel Orland didn't care. He, his boys, and Mamm and Dat combed the hill half into the night. The next day, after not very much sleep, the bishop was informed—though probably not about riding the horses. Men from the neighboring farms joined in the search, and Oak Hill and the farms at its feet rang with the sound of the girls' names.

But they found not one thing except Leah's other black mitten, lying on a deer trail. Which only seemed to make everyone feel worse, not better.

Finally, after a pickup supper that Mamm was too upset to eat, the bishop came and sat with them at the table.

"The entire *Gmee* is praying for the girls' safe return," he said heavily. There were tiny sticks and bits of the wispy seeds called Old Man's Beard in his beard. Samuel would have found this hilarious at any other time, but tonight, he wondered if he would ever smile at anything ever again.

The bishop looked Dat in the face. "If I were Bishop Lapp over in Whinburg, I would tell you that this is an

Amish matter and advise you to trust in the Lord and keep searching until we find the girls. But I am not as … traditional as he, and much as I would rather avoid it, I believe it is time for us to ask for help from the *Englisch* sheriff."

Dat sat as if frozen to his chair. "You have lost hope, then? Is the God who brought them into this world not enough to bring them home to us?"

"It is not a matter of faith, Jonathan Riehl. It is a matter of using the resources He has given us. And I know that the *Englisch* sheriff has resources that reach into the world much farther than we can. Your chances of finding your daughters are greater if you accept that help as well as that of the *Gmee*."

"But … that would be going against the will of *der Herr*," Mamm whispered. Tears welled in her eyes, and Samuel wondered how she could possibly have any left. He had heard her crying after they'd come home, and that had made him cry, too, bundled up in his quilt with a pillow against his mouth so they would not hear.

"God's will, Rebecca? Or man's?" the bishop asked quietly. "If somehow human hands have been mixed up in this, we will merely be casting our net wider, giving our two little fish a greater chance to be pulled in."

Speechless, Mamm gripped Dat's forearm and nodded. Then, handkerchief pressed to her mouth, she went out of the kitchen.

The next day, the bishop came in his buggy and Dat and Samuel went to Whinburg with him. The man in the khaki uniform with the shiny gold star pinned to his chest pocket asked about a hundred questions, some of which Samuel didn't know how to answer. But Dat's grip on his hand helped him get out enough words to make the *Englisch* man with the steady gaze nod and write a lot of things down on his pad.

"We'll be in touch, Mr. Riehl," he said when they were ready to go. "We'll do everything we can to find your little girls. It'll be a challenge, without photographs or fingerprints or even dental records, but we've overcome greater."

But in the end, nothing happened.

Nothing except a whole lot of *Englisch* cars pulling into the yard later that week, and a van with a big satellite dish on the top containing two guys with black cameras on their shoulders. Dat shooed them back into it by leading the big Percherons he'd borrowed from Onkel Orland right up to them so that they had to scramble in or be trampled by the enormous hooves.

Nothing except the sheriff coming a month later in his black and white car, shaking his head and saying they were doing everything they could.

He came when Samuel was eleven, too, and when he was twelve, and when he was fourteen, calling it a *cold case*, whatever that meant.

The last time the black and white car had come, it was a different sheriff. But he hadn't come about the girls.

He had come about Samuel.

But Samuel wasn't there, because by then he had a job, and freedom, and *Englisch* buddies who knew how to party so hard he forgot the grief, forgot the shame of what he'd allowed to happen—even forgot who he was half the time. The farm might be his legal address, but these days, that house with the lamp still burning in the window was the last place in the world he wanted to go back to.

1

Pitt Corner, New York
August, present day

Megan Pearson swung her virtual sword with all the magical strength her character possessed, and the first head went flying off the hydra. Oops. *Satisfying, but wrong strategy, dummy.* This was no time to lose it—her entire quest team was counting on her and duh, everyone knew that if you took the head off a hydra, two more grew back.

She was gaming as Qu'riel, princess of the elves, lithe and blond and the most powerful character on the team. She had so many weapons that Joe had to carry some of them for her, and her skill at the first six levels had even given them all a bonus boost past the Forest of Mist and Doom. She was the character everyone else wanted to be, and Megan was proud of it. If they could just get past the hydra this time—

their third attempt—she'd get her gold circlet and a pantload of treasure points, which largesse she would share with everyone, just like a real princess.

Midori, her teammate from Japan who played as a tiger, went for the throat of the hydra, but one of the heads swooped down and bit her instead. *Ow!* She'd used up all her health crystals ... Midori was dead.

Megan remained the last player standing—Joe in Alabama, Casey in Scotland, and Raheem in Calgary had already bitten the dust because no matter what they did, they couldn't get past this level. Two minutes later the hydra did her in, but not before she caught a glimpse of the door behind the creature's back. A safety!

She pulled out her phone.

Megan: Safety behind hydra. Next time we don't fight, we evade or distract. Tuesday?

Tuesday was good. Any day was good, really.

Megan logged out of the game and cruised Facebook for a while, but nothing interesting was happening to anyone she knew. A lot of the kids she'd graduated with were sophomores in college now, and while there were still a couple of weeks left of summer vacation, they just weren't the same to talk to anymore. They'd read books she'd only seen in the library. They had problems like financial aid and where they would intern, while she lived in her parents' basement and worked at the local coffee bar while she waited for something better to turn up.

Sometimes she hung out with the crowd at work, but after a while the same old conversations got boring, unless a new movie opened at the Majesty or somebody got pregnant. Nothing interesting ever happened in Pitt Corner, a town so obscure that the impending arrival of a Walmart was the biggest news since the troops had come home—in the seventies. Pitt Corner was the kind of community that belonged in a Norman Rockwell painting, which was great if you were her parents and knew who Norman Rockwell was, but not so great if you were nineteen and going a little nuts with the smallness and sameness of it all.

Then again, maybe she ought to be thankful for the sameness. It meant they weren't on the move, packing up and heading out for another town, another job for Dad.

The pounding of feet on the stairs announced the arrival of her overachieving little sister, who approached every day as though it were a mileage marker on her way to some destination she'd mapped out years ago. The door flew open and sure enough, Ashley burst in.

"Are you still down here?" she demanded. "You haven't moved one inch since I left this morning. Please tell me you haven't been gaming all day."

"Okay. I won't tell you." Megan rolled off her chair and onto the unmade bed conveniently located next to it. "If you just came down here to criticize, you can take off." She stretched to pop the kink out of her back.

"I thought you had to work today."

"I called in sick."

Ash looked her over as though diagnosing illness. "Uh-huh."

"Hey, it was the only day we could all play together this week. We're in a bunch of different time zones, you know. *My* friendships are international."

She valued her friends enough to make sacrifices to be with them. They did the same. They'd never seen one another face to face, but they were making tentative plans to meet up at New York Comic-Con next year, if they could all scrape up the money. Which meant she'd probably have to ask for more shifts at the coffee bar. Which probably wouldn't happen because she kept missing the shifts she had. Maybe she'd quit and find another job.

Or maybe they'd go to Comic-Con the year after next instead.

"So you've told me like, fifteen times. Megan, you've got to get out of here and get some sun. And do some laundry. It stinks in here."

Okay, this was getting seriously annoying. "Are you quite done?"

Ashley gazed at her, her eyes pinched a little at the corners with worry. "No, I'm not."

Fine. Megan rolled off the bed altogether and reached for a jacket. "If you won't leave, then I will. Don't touch my computer."

"Do you *ever* think of anyone but yourself?"

Stung, Megan stopped herself from shouldering her sister to one side. "What's that supposed to mean?"

"I mean you're down here all day, you go to work when you remember to, and meanwhile, do you even see what's going on with Mom?"

"Mom?" What was going on with Mom? Everything had been normal for months. She went to work at Dress Barn, she came home, she made dinner. Sometimes she brought a plate downstairs. Sometimes, when it smelled good, Megan went up to get it. Megan tried to remember the last time she'd really looked at anyone in the family. The week was already a blur, the days smudging into one another. Sunday, maybe? When Megan had emerged at noon and Mom had made her eat a banana?

Ashley rolled her eyes. "I rest my case."

"You can come down off that high horse now. What are you talking about?"

Now her sister shook her head. "Where do you get these weird expressions? What is a high horse?"

Megan had no idea. It had just popped out. "Something somebody rides on because they're better than everybody else," she said, making it up on the fly. Made sense, right? "Now ... Mom?"

"Go up there and see," Ashley suggested. "Maybe it'll give you something to think about besides ... whatever it is you think about."

Enough was enough. Megan did push past her this time, stomping up the stairs in a put-upon way that somehow faded by the time she stepped into the kitchen.

"Mom?" She wasn't in the kitchen, which was weird, because it was after five.

Dining room, living room, bathroom. Nothing.

Finally, she knocked on her parents' bedroom door. "Mom, are you in there?" The rumbling sound of someone pushing open the slider came from behind the door, and Megan stepped inside. "You okay?"

Her mother was outside in their little backyard—eight feet of grass and a couple of rhododendrons that her father babied as though they were children, even though they were only renting the place. Mom was walking in tight circles, her

16

arms flailing as though she were having an argument with someone.

Someone invisible.

A bolt of cold fright shot through Megan's stomach. Had she had some bad news? If so, who from? Neither of her parents had extended family, and they kept leaving friends behind every time they moved.

If it was only bad news, that would be good news. Because at least it would be something external. Something that could be dealt with and solved. It was the *internal* stuff that frightened Megan the most—the things that went wrong behind her mother's eyes that they couldn't control, couldn't help ... and sometimes couldn't see coming.

"Mom, what's the matter?" She walked through the slider in time to see her mother clutch her hair and pull on it, which yanked it out of the long braid that hung down her back. "Did something happen? Should I call Dad?" School got out at three o'clock, but there were often staff meetings and things afterward that the admin assistants had to go to, and sometimes he didn't get home until six.

"No," her mother moaned and finally stopped pacing. She didn't turn around, though, just stared at the rhododendron as if she were looking past it, while her hands dropped to her sides. "Megan, can you go start dinner?"

"Me?" She was a terrible cook. She could make oatmeal with those packets, and boil an egg, but that was about it. Stoves and ovens freaked her out a little—the angry red mouths of them just waiting to clamp down on her hand or arm and burn the daylights out of her. The thought of making cookies and having to shove a tray in an oven one-handed while holding the door open with the other ... Well, needless to say, one batch had been the end of her baking career.

"Just go and do something. I'll be fine. Your dad will be home soon." Mom's voice sounded clogged, and she enunciated her words carefully, like a drunk. Or like someone at the end of her rope who was just hoping you would go away before the façade cracked.

"Okay. But no promises it will be edible." Megan rolled the slider shut and retreated down the hall. Pictures lined the walls, with her and Ashley on one side like a walk through time—cap and gown, braces, pigtails, little blond baby pictures. On the other side were pictures taken on various road trips and in various backyards, and the one attempt at a formal portrait of the whole family when Megan had been about eight. She'd kicked up a fuss and broken something belonging to the photographer—she didn't remember what—and the shot still showed the traces of tears on her cheeks.

To this day Megan hated that picture. Everybody smiling and happy except her, who had obviously just stopped crying.

After she'd called for pizza—she'd make a salad to go with it, so Ashley wouldn't complain about junk food—her dad came home. He tossed his car keys on the desk in the living room and looked around. "Where's your mother?"

Quickly Megan explained the weirdness, trying to sound mature and calm and feeling like a bad actor in a soap opera saying her lines.

Dad went outside, and she could hear them talking. Megan sidled over to the kitchen door, which also opened into the backyard, and cracked it a couple of inches.

"—can't breathe, Carl. My heart is going a mile a minute and my mind—there are blank spots."

"Jan, calm down. What do you mean, blank spots? That's never happened before."

"Just ... blanks. In my day. Where I can't remember where I've been or how I got there."

Her father said something about driving that Megan couldn't catch, and then, "Do you want me to go and get Lynnie?" Lynnie was her mother's best friend, who lived two houses down and was a retired RN. Their family had hardly ever gone to the doctor in the three years they'd lived here, because four times out of five Lynnie knew what was wrong or could patch you up with something out of her bathroom medicine cabinet long before you could get in to see somebody at Urgent Care.

"Yes. No. I don't know." She clutched her husband's jacket. "What if it's early-onset Alzheimer's?"

"I'm sure it's not. I'm sure it's just stress."

Megan frowned. It was never stress. Stress didn't put you in seventy-two hour hold every couple of years. On the good side, right now it didn't seem like they were going to pack up and move on a couple of hours' notice. Nobody was screaming or running the suitcases out to the car or watching the rearview mirror instead of the road.

Her mom had a nice, boring job working at Dress Barn. Was waiting on customers and moving racks around the floor stressful? Maybe so—some days at the coffee bar could be pretty stressful, if Izzy called in sick and Megan had to take over the counter. But she never got all weirded out about it and lost time. That only happened when she was gaming. She'd start at nine and two minutes later, she'd look up and it would be one in the morning.

"Maybe I'll go over there," Mom said at last. "But you'd better walk with me. It's not like before. My heart is galloping like I just had a fright."

The pizza had come and Megan and Ashley had already helped themselves when their parents finally came back. Megan warmed up a couple of slices and served some salad for her mom, who slid into her usual chair looking pale and not quite there.

"We weren't sure when you were coming back," Ashley said around a mouthful. "Sorry we didn't wait."

"That's okay." Her dad sprinkled chili flakes on his and took a bite. "Your mother needed to see Lynnie. Apparently she had a panic attack."

"Is that all it was?" Did that mean she was getting better rather than worse? "Are you okay?"

"She gave me some pills to calm me down," her mom said, and nibbled on a piece of tomato.

"The good stuff, I hope—Xanax? Or are you going old school with Valium?"

She'd meant it to be a joke, but her mother just stared at her.

"It's one thing to help your mother with her prescriptions," her father said in his Head of the Family voice, glaring at her. "But nobody else in this family had better be taking drugs—over or under the counter."

Ashley rolled her eyes. Megan just felt sorry for him, trying to have the *Just Say No* talk when they were years past needing it. She'd tried pot once or twice in tenth grade, but the dreams that followed were so strange and so intense it just wasn't worth it. But no pharmaceuticals for her, thanks—natural stuff was bad enough. "Sorry," she said. "Just trying to lighten things up."

"That's Megan, Miss Socially Oblivious," Ashley said with a sigh. "Mom, when are you going to see a real doctor?"

Their mother shook her head. "I'll be fine. If the pills don't work, then I'll talk it over with Lynnie and see what she thinks. But I'm sure it'll be fine."

That was her mom. The world could be burning down, and she'd say it would be fine, even if you could see explosions from here to New York City. Her sense of denial had been honed to a fine art, whether they were talking about having to move again or registering for a new school or the two of them were fighting while Megan and Ashley cowered in their room—if they shared one in that particular house. If anybody asked any questions, the answer was always, "It'll be fine."

Megan had learned not to ask questions and to simply deal with the move or the new school or whatever it was. She had to be the big sister, right? Though lately—since graduation a year ago, really—she hadn't been dealing very well. It was just easier to go down to her room and hide—er, hang out—online and promise herself she'd make a change tomorrow.

Besides, Ashley hadn't needed a big sister in a long time. And now that she was going to be a college freshman, it wasn't likely she was going to need one in the future, either. A hollow space yawned deep under Megan's solar plexus at the thought.

She must still be hungry. She reached across the kitchen table and helped herself to another piece of pizza, but the feeling never really went away.

2

Riehl farm
Willow Creek, Pennsylvania

Twelve slat-back chairs were pulled up around the big dining table in the kitchen. Three of them were always empty. Every time the family sat down for a meal, the sight of those chairs was like a hook in Rebecca's spirit—a tug—an urging to silent prayer.

Jonathan sat at the head of the table, with Rebecca at his right hand, close to stove and sink for the serving of food. Next to Rebecca were the two empty chairs and plates that had been set for every meal for the last thirteen years, and then, like stair steps of sixteen, thirteen, and ten, came Barbara, Melinda, and Katie. Daadi Riehl's place was at the other end, opposite his eldest son, and next to him Mammi Kate, for whom little Katie was named. The old folks took their meals with them in the evening, since they lived in the *Daadi Haus* on the other side of the garden now that they'd grown too old for farming. Between Mammi Kate and the chair at Jonathan's left hand that had been empty for five years came the little boys, Saul and Timothy, six-year-old twins who were going to become scholars next week, starting first grade in the one-room school down the road, much to their impatient delight.

Since moving into the *Daadi Haus*, Mammi Kate had taken it as her duty to manage the twins at mealtimes, for which Rebecca thanked *der Herr* daily. It was a full-time job looking after those two, and having brought up eight herself, Mammi Kate was a wealth of experience and wisdom—to say nothing of her hand of iron, which meant the little boys were much better behaved than little boys often tended to be.

When Rebecca had finished setting out the steaming bowls of mashed potatoes, chicken and dumplings, carrots in butter, and thickly sliced fresh tomatoes swimming in oil, she took her seat and bowed her head for the silent grace.

Thank You for the bounty of the earth during this busy season of putting up and putting by, Lord. Please watch over my missing children, wherever they are. Hannah will be a woman grown by now, and Leah not far behind—if they're alive—

Rebecca stifled the sinful doubt that wormed its way into this sacred conversation between her and God.

Protect and keep them, and bring them back to us if it is Your will. Yours is the power to keep and save. Be with our Samuel, Father, and work in his heart to clear away the noise and tumult of the world so that he can hear Your still, small voice in the whisper of the wind in the grass and the poplar trees, and feel the warmth of Your love in the sunshine. Bring him back to his place among us, I pray.

The rustle of sleeves and the long inhalation with which Daadi Riehl signaled that grace was said and he was ready for his supper caused Rebecca to send one final plea heavenward. Then she came back to herself to pass the potatoes and dish up chicken and dumplings for her family.

The plates in front of the empty chairs were not filled, of course, because that would be wasteful. But they were still set for every meal, as though at any moment Hannah, Leah, and Samuel would come in laughing, shake the weather off their coats, and pull up their chairs to tell everyone where they'd been.

Her *Englisch* friend Ginny Hochstetler thought Rebecca foolish for setting those places, meal after meal, and washing the dishes afterward. But after the first year or two, she had stopped her gentle suggestions, as though she realized that she was just wasting her breath. But her Amish friends knew—even Evie Troyer, the bishop's wife, did the same for Ben, the fence-jumper in their family. Rebecca could no more remove those chairs and put them elsewhere in the house than she could tell the rest of her family she wasn't going to feed them anymore. If she did, it would be like admitting that her eldest children weren't coming back. That she had given up hope. That she didn't believe God would be faithful in returning them as unexpectedly as He had taken them away.

Like the lantern that burned in the kitchen window every evening, summer and winter, those chairs would stay there waiting for her children until God in his wisdom and mercy did bring them back.

After dinner, while the girls did the dishes, singing one of the songs from the handwritten songbook that sat on the wide windowsill, Rebecca went upstairs to the room that had been Hannah and Leah's. She had never been able to remove the hand-carved Noah and his ark full of animals from the low dresser where they'd left it. Their clothes had gone to their sisters, since even Rebecca realized that when they came back, they would no longer be little girls of six and five. But the Nine Patch quilts she'd made still lay on the two twin beds, the rosy salmon color still as bright against the black and burgundy as it had ever been.

She crossed the room to the drying racks set up near the windows, where sliced apples were laid out on revolving mesh shelves in this warm south-facing room. She pressed her thumbnail into one of the thicker slices. Almost ready. Tomorrow night, she could gather them up and pack them away, ready to be used for *snitz* pie in January or February when the fresh apples in the cellar ran out.

Samuel had loved snitz pie. And her Christmas nut cake.

Her knees weakened and she sat on the end of Hannah's bed. That year, when it had happened, she'd given the entire basket to her sister-in-law Ruthie and had never made nut cake again from that day to this. The smell of walnuts made her sick.

Oh, the price the family had paid for those walnuts.

Someone tapped on the jamb and Rebecca looked up to see her mother-in-law, her eyes soft with sympathy and her face creased with concern, hovering in the doorway. "A blue day?"

Rebecca began to nod, then shook her head instead, the strings of her prayer covering moving gently on her chest.

"*Neh*, not so blue. More like a gentle lavender. I was just thinking about the girls—and how much Samuel loved snitz pie."

"Maybe that love will be what brings him home again."

Rebecca smiled, not because she really felt it but because Kate was trying to encourage her to do so. "I hope so. But we haven't heard he wants to—that is, if what Trout Silas says can be believed."

Trout Silas King had come by his nickname because of the size of the trout he insisted he'd caught long ago in Willow Creek, which everybody knew only contained brookies that never grew longer than a woman's forearm. But when Trout Silas wasn't at the creek, he made furniture in a shop out on the main highway, which put him in a good place to see a lot of people—farmers, tourists, Amish folk ... and Amish boys who had determined they were going to be *Englisch*.

Two weeks ago Silas had spotted Samuel driving a wreck of an old red car down the highway, heading for Whinburg. "Hardly know how it kept going, it was making such a racket and spewing smoke, but he was driving it as proud as if it were the latest from BMW." Rebecca's heart had sunk, and Jonathan had gone away into the barn shortly after waving Silas good-bye, and stayed there until well past dark.

Rebecca knew he prayed when he was with his cows, after the milking was done and the animals were settling in for the night. He prayed by the bedside with her, too, but in times of deep distress he sought the comfort of the cows, warm and companionable and unlikely to comment if a man were unable to hold back tears.

If Samuel had been driving a car, that meant he had gone to the trouble of studying for the license and having his picture taken, a thing forbidden by the *Ordnung*. *Thou shalt not make unto thee any graven image, or any likeness of any thing that is in heaven above, or that is in the earth beneath, or that is in the water under the earth.* Their bishop, Dan Troyer, had spoken the words from Exodus in the last Council Meeting, when the tenets of the *Ordnung* had been outlined for the *Gmee*. There were two Council Meetings every year, which all baptized members of the church were expected to attend, where everyone was reminded of the familiar standards of dress and behavior so that they could be transformed by the renewing of their minds, not conformed to the world.

A driver's license meant that Samuel had taken yet another step away from the faith of his family, another step into the swirling currents of the world. Rebecca's deepest fear was that he would be swept away altogether, maybe even to another state, and they would lose him for good.

It was one of her deepest fears, anyway.

She hardly dared admit what she feared for the girls, lest somehow the thought would reach the ears of Satan and he would make it come to pass. But that was her human nature talking. She must put her fears into God's hands and leave them there, and have faith that His care for Hannah and Leah was sufficient for them, and His power would overcome that of Satan.

She rose and took her mother-in-law's arm. "Let me go with you down the stairs. I don't want you to take a fall."

Kate *hmph*ed at the thought, but Rebecca noticed she didn't refuse the offer.

The next day, after barn chores at four, breakfast at six and family prayers, and after the ironing was done, Rebecca harnessed Midnight, their buggy horse, and led him out into the yard where Barbie was mowing the lawn with the push mower. Katie and Melinda were waist-deep in tomatoes, picking a couple of baskets full so that Rebecca could make tomato sauce later this afternoon.

She loaded three king-sized quilts into the back of the buggy, each carefully taped inside an extra-large white trash bag. "I'm away, girls," she called. "I should be back by noon."

"Will you bring me some of that yellow fabric?" Barbie begged, leaning on the mower, the front of her dress and her bare shins all covered in clippings. "It'll be on sale by now, and I'll have a new dress for next spring."

Rebecca couldn't help but smile at the persistence of her middle daughter. "I think we've had this conversation before," she reminded her gently. "Yellow is a worldly color. What would the bishop's wife say?"

"She'd say that God made all colors for the flowers, and delights in them," Barbie said with sixteen-year-old stubbornness.

"God may delight in them, but Bishop Troyer doesn't," Rebecca told her. "You're pushing it with the salmon pink you got in June. I thought we were going to get a visit over that for sure."

"Our cousin Susie wears yellow," Barbie grumbled, dragging the mower around so it faced in the opposite direction. "I don't see why I can't."

"Your aunt Ruthie has the say in her household, and I have mine," Rebecca told her, and climbed into the driver's side of the buggy.

She flapped the reins over Midnight's back and the buggy crunched down the gravel drive. The fabric store in Willow Creek had expanded into the adjoining shop when the junk shop that had been there had finally been cleared out, after five years of languishing with a dusty CLOSED sign in its window. Miriam Byler had a real head for business, and when she'd seen how much traffic their local quilters brought to the area, she had broached the idea of a co-op to be housed in the new space. While many of the Amish women sold their quilts out of their living rooms, with one or two pieces hanging on lines in the front yard to let the tourists know what was for sale inside, quite a number had seen the wisdom in putting a couple into the co-op so that the *Englisch* ladies didn't have to travel around the district with the maps that the tourist bureau put out. Their chances of the ladies finding their work in the co-op were much higher.

"It's one-stop shopping," Amanda Yoder, one of the *Youngie* who worked for Miriam, had said to Rebecca the last time she was in. "They can buy quilts on this side, and if they want to make their own, we have made-up kits, fabric, and findings all ready on the other side."

Rebecca loved quilting. Or rather, she loved piecing— putting together simple squares and strips and triangles, nice and orderly, to make something enormously complicated. It was a form of expression, she supposed, so she was always careful that her delight in the design didn't tip over into pride in her own work. How could it, when a quilt wasn't complete until the patient stitching of the other women during quilting frolics and on Sisters' Days had been added to create both practicality and art? Seeds, feathers, scrolls, flowers ... a quilt was not simply one woman's creation. It was a community project and represented the skills of many, unacknowledged and unknown except by themselves.

Miriam crooned in admiration when she unfolded the Rondelay that had taken Rebecca and Barbie a good bit of last winter to piece. "Oh, Rebecca. This is just lovely. Look at that leaf-green and those pinks!"

Rebecca had used *Englisch* fabrics, of course, with their showy patterns. She made some quilts in the Amish colors, but the more colorful ones sold faster because they fit in better in *Englisch* homes. At least, she and Miriam imagined that was the reason. The other two were a Blooming Nine-Patch and a Burgoyne Surrounded, both of which looked much more complicated than they actually were, and had given her many happy evenings of piecing while the snow of the winter that would not end had pummeled their part of Pennsylvania unmercifully right up until May.

"With Labor Day next weekend, I'm sure these will sell right away," Miriam confided. "I'm going to put the Rondelay on the bed display right in front of the door, and it will sell by Saturday, just you watch."

"What about Lizzie King's Log Cabin Star?" Rebecca said, smiling, with a glance at the quilt on the display. "I don't want to push her out of the best place. Trout Silas would never stop teasing me about it."

"I'm going to hang it behind the cash register on the other side," Miriam told her comfortably. "Everyone needs a little inspiration when they're buying fabric. I hope you'll drop in again next week. I know I'll have some money for you."

"I will," Rebecca promised. "And now I'm off to the dry goods store. Between the tomatoes and the baking, I need another twenty pounds of sugar."

Back in the buggy, her heart was light at the thought of the money the three quilts might bring in. With the markup Miriam would put on them, some *Englisch* tourist would need to hand over almost a thousand dollars—for the Rondelay, at least. The thought of the lion's share going into her and Jonathan's perpetually empty savings account was like a warm breath of spring on a winter day.

Her next project was a quilt for the fire auction in March, the annual fundraiser for the local volunteer fire department. She and her girls contributed to that every year, as did most of the women. Rebecca was lost in thoughts of how she might design the pattern, watching the asphalt scroll past Midnight's glossy black rump, when a flash of red caught the corner of her eye.

A beat-up red car sat parked in front of the single gas station in Willow Creek. No one was in it, which meant the driver was inside paying for his gas.

Without a second thought, Rebecca guided the horse into the station, where, unlike most of the other local businesses, there was no rail for tying him up. She made do with looping the reins around a hose for putting air into tires.

Then she walked over to the red car and waited.

Samuel came out counting his change. He didn't even look up until he reached the driver's door, when he must have seen her shoes and skirt. Startled, the blue eyes so much like her own flashed up and met her gaze, and she smiled.

32

"*Guder mariye*, Samuel," she said, and throwing caution to the winds, she reached out and hugged him. Oh, he was so thin! Who was feeding him? She could feel his spine like a row of rocks beneath the soil before he seemed to realize what the hug might reveal, and pulled away.

"Good morning, Mamm." He looked over at the buggy, obviously seeing that there were no little heads outlined in the rear window. "Are you here by yourself?"

"*Ja*, I came in to deliver some quilts to Miriam, and to get some supplies at the dry-goods store. Trout Silas told us he'd seen you in your car, so when I spotted it, I thought I would stop."

He walked over to greet Midnight, who whickered in recognition as Samuel rubbed his nose and patted his neck. It wasn't lost on Rebecca that he had put the horse between them. "How's my boy?" he murmured to the horse. "You're looking good."

And you are not, my son. "How are you, Samuel?" She might have said *Wie geht's?* in the language of home, but since he had not returned her good morning in *Deitsch* a moment ago, she took her lead from him. She would not do anything to make him get into that car and drive away from her.

"Fine," he said. "Working up at the RV factory over Linwood way."

"Ah," she said. "You would need a car to get there. It must be every bit of thirty miles." Too far for a horse and buggy to go there and back in a day, but hardly anything for a car.

He nodded.

"And where are you living?"

Again his gaze met hers. "Why? So you can tell Dat and he can come over and yell at me? If so, I'd rather be shunned."

Is that what he thought of them? The crack in Rebecca's heart widened just a little. "*Neh*, my dear one. Dat has shed many a tear over you, out in the barn with the cows. And you know you are not under *die Meinding*. You never joined church, so you cannot be. But your family and friends would be free to welcome you, if ..."

"If I came back and told Dat I'd be Amish again." He gestured to his jeans, worn to a lighter blue at thigh and knee, and his *Englisch* shirt with its pearly snaps down the front. "It's not going to happen, Mamm. I've made my choice and I'm sticking to it."

"Isolating yourself from your family? Samuel, please don't let what happened to your sisters keep you away from God—and church—and us. It was not your fault. It was God's will. He has a larger plan that we just can't see yet. You mustn't separate yourself from us as some kind of penance. Only God can judge. You mustn't judge yourself—that would be prideful and a sin."

For how many years had she wanted to speak this truth to him and had kept it to herself? And yet here, in a grubby gas station parking lot, the words spilled out of her as though she had no control over them. Perhaps she didn't. Perhaps the Holy Spirit had given her the words when it was God's will that she speak.

But he had not taken it so. His face clouded. "I'm not doing penance, Mamm. I just want to live my own life, not Dat's life, that's all." With a final pat for Midnight, he walked back to his car.

She could stay there, her hand on the horse's neck, and let him go. But she could not. "Samuel, please."

He wrenched open the door and stood there, eyes blazing with pain and stubbornness. "What do you want from me, Mamm? I'm doing okay. I know that's not good enough for you and Dat, but it is for me."

"You are always good enough for me, my son, my heart," she said in *Deitsch*, but he did not hear her. He had already slammed the door and started the engine. In a cloud of blue smoke, he pulled out of the gas station and accelerated away down the road, leaving her standing in the hot sun, the tears drying on her cheeks.

As she untied Midnight, backed him around, and climbed into the buggy, it occurred to her that there must be gas stations much closer to the RV factory or wherever he was living than this one in Willow Creek. What brought him over so far? Was their community calling him back in a way that he wouldn't admit to himself? Was he hoping for a glimpse of friends and family—torturing himself with what he wouldn't allow himself to have?

She hoped so. Oh, how she hoped so. If guilt and rebellion had driven him away, only love could draw him back.

And if there was anything Rebecca knew how to do, it was love.

3

Pitt Corner, New York
August

Megan's mom didn't go to work the next day, even though her shift was clearly marked on the kitchen calendar. Her shifts and Megan's were the only things on there—no birthdays, no dinner dates, and in the past, no school tournaments or anything that might be construed as a life. Megan had asked her about it once, and Mom had just tapped her temple and told her, "It's all up here."

Maybe it was. Or maybe all those empty squares were telling a different story.

Something balled up in Megan's stomach—something it took her a minute to recognize. Anxiety? No, restlessness. Impatience at an existence that looked like everyone else's, but wasn't. Not even remotely.

THE LONGEST ROAD

If you don't like it, leave.

Maybe she should. But how? She couldn't rent an apartment on the pittance she made at the coffee bar.

Go to college and live in the dorms, like Ashley plans to.

Right, and parade her bad grades in front of everyone? She probably couldn't even get into the local community college the next town over, where you had to have a 3.0 GPA. Maybe she shouldn't have been so focused on gaming in high school, and done a little work instead. Maybe she should have figured out sooner that while she had the highest point score of anyone on her quest team, that probably wasn't going to get her on the dean's list—or anywhere else. But gaming comforted her. It gave her friends.

So move in with a couple of people. Rent a room.

She was already living with a couple of people and renting a room. Sort of. Megan did the housework when she remembered to. That was a little like trading labor for rent. And despite what Ashley had said, she didn't live in a stinky mess. She liked things neat. But you couldn't make a career out of that.

You say they're boring? You're about the most boring person you've ever met.

Right, well, Qu'riel wasn't boring. Qu'riel kicked butt and took names. Each of her favorite games gave her an identity and something concrete to accomplish. But Qu'riel was her favorite.

A videogame character? Really? A bunch of pixels?

At least I'm somebody when I play somebody. Just ask Midori and the others.

Are you even listening to yourself?

Annoyed at the naggy little voice in her head, Megan rolled off the bed, picked up the laundry basket, and went through to the laundry room, where she found a big pile of stuff that Ash was clearly planning to take to school week after next.

Well, labor for rent, here we go. She began to sort lights from darks. Though Megan wore mostly black, Ashley didn't, and sometimes her gold and pink and green wardrobe got its own load.

A thump sounded through the ceiling, as though someone had fallen out of bed or slammed a door really hard.

Megan poured in a quarter cup of concentrate, closed the washer lid, and started the cycle. "Ash? Is that you?" Her sister wasn't in the habit of slamming doors, but there was a first time for everything.

Ashley stuck her head out of her room. "Is that me what? Are you doing my laundry?"

She sounded so amazed that Megan frowned. "Thought I might as well do my stuff, since your pile will probably empty the water tank. You didn't just drop something, did you?"

Ashley gave her that drop-shouldered, *What foreign language are you speaking now?* look. "No."

Well, that was weird.

"I'm going to check. Maybe Mom knocked over a lamp."

Ash followed her up the stairs, muttering, and down the hall to their parents' room.

"Mom? You okay? I thought I heard something fall." Megan pushed open the bedroom door, feeling an odd sense of déjà vu.

"Holy crap," Ash said behind her, then pushed her out of the way. "Mom? What's wrong?"

Their mother was curled up on the rug, the sheets all dragged down off the bed with her, crying as though her heart was about to break. A stab of fear tore through Megan and she flung herself down next to her sister.

"Mom? Did you hurt yourself? Ash, is there blood?"

Megan actually glanced up at the olive-green ceramic lamp, but it was sitting on the nightstand the way it always did. Nothing was disturbed. Only their mother, having a complete meltdown in the middle of the carpet. This was worse than the other times. Way worse. Why had she been delusional enough to think things might be getting better? Denial clearly ran in the family.

"No blood." Ash had her hands under their mother's armpits. "Help me get her up on the bed."

Janet Pearson weighed far more than Megan ever would have expected. "No," their mom moaned. "Leave me alone. I just want to die."

What? Xanax wasn't supposed to do this, was it? "Mom, of course you're not going to die. Don't say that. Did you take another pill by mistake?" Megan was always the one to count out the pills into their plastic container marked with the days of the week. Had her mom snuck another one later?

Tears trickled out of the corners of her mother's eyes before she scrunched them shut, as though she couldn't bear the sight of her own daughters. "It's never going to be right." Her voice cracked. "I might as well be a murderer."

Another shock of fear zapped through Megan's stomach, worse than the first one. "Mom, you're scaring me. Ashley, call Dad."

Ash looked up, her face a pale oval in the gloom of the bedroom. It was eleven in the morning—why was it so dark in here? "We can't," she said. "They're all on some kind of staff retreat before the term starts. He didn't even take his phone."

How stupid was that? "Mom's sick and he didn't bother to take his *phone?*"

"They weren't allowed." She gazed anxiously at their mother. "Maybe we should call nine-one-one."

"No-o-o!" Mom practically shrieked. "No hospitals! Not again!"

"It's okay, it's okay," Megan put both hands on her shoulders, pressing her back onto the pillows. "Can you tell us if you took an extra pill? I won't be mad, I promise. Is that what's wrong?"

Her mom burst into fresh tears, rolling over and curling up. "No! I can't tell. I can never tell. You're dead. You have to stay dead."

Megan felt the chill as all the blood drained out of her face. Ashley's hand closed around her wrist, her fingers as cold as if she'd been carrying ice cream. "Go into the bathroom and get one of those other pills. This isn't like before. She's—she's having a psychic break of some kind."

Megan was so frightened she didn't even ask her sister how she knew about any other pills. She just went into the bathroom and found the bottle with its use-by date already a year old. It took two tries before her shaking hands could catch one of the pills, and the glass rattled against the sink as she filled it.

But when Megan offered both to her mom, she pushed it away so hard that water slopped onto her nightie. "No.

Nightmares. I never even saw her and she's in my head constantly. It's the pills, I know it, bringing her back." Quick as a snake striking, she slapped Megan's hand and the pill flew out of it, dropping with a *clickety-click* behind the nightstand.

"Who, Mom?" Megan said. "Who's in your head?"

"Go away."

Ashley had about fifty psychology books on her shelves and she hadn't even started freshman year. This was her department. *Do something,* Megan mouthed at her over their mother's shaking shoulder.

You're the oldest, Ash mouthed back. *What do we do?*

No Dad. No grandparents. They had one person left. "Run over and get Lynnie, and I'll stay with Mom."

Ashley ran out of the room. Megan had no sooner arranged the sheets and a blanket on top of her mother, awkwardly patting her as she did so, when she heard the screen door slam a second time.

That was fast. What a relief. Lynnie would help. She always knew what to do. She—

"They're not home," Ashley said, falling through the doorway breathless from running. "The car's gone and no one answers the door."

The bottom dropped right out of Megan's stomach. What were they supposed to do now? What was Plan B when all you knew was how to handle Plan A?

"How is she?" Ash knelt next to the bed, softly brushing Mom's hair away from her temples. "Megan, she's asleep. Come on, let her rest. Maybe I was wrong. What do I know? Maybe she just had the mother of all nightmares."

Wouldn't that be nice if that were all it was? Megan had her share of weird dreams of horses and enclosed spaces and ovens that came alive, but they didn't make her fall out of bed crying and saying things that didn't make sense. But Mom was sleeping now. She wasn't injured, so maybe the best thing they could do for her was just to let her sleep.

They tiptoed out and Megan stopped in the hall. "Maybe we could call the night nurse." Mom used to do that when they were younger, before there was a Lynnie to do the job. At least, she thought so. Sometimes Megan didn't trust her memories of the past. Sometimes what she thought was a memory just turned out to be a dream. Maybe it was inherited.

Besides, did they even have a medical plan?

"And say what? That she fell out of bed?"

"You said psychic break. That's more than falling out of bed. More than a nightmare. And those things she said—they didn't make sense."

Ashley threw up her hands. "I told you, I don't know. Call the night nurse if you want, but I guarantee they won't tell you anything useful."

Megan pictured herself trying to explain this to someone who talked young mothers through how to nurse a baby or what to do if a kid shoved a Lego up his nose. What would she say? That her mom was talking crazy? Megan's mind had gone so blank with fear she couldn't even remember half of what she'd said—except the murder part.

That she and Ashley were supposed to be dead.

Cold settled deep in her stomach. Maybe they'd better keep that to themselves, or the guys in white coats would come for sure.

In the kitchen, Megan put the kettle on and got down the chamomile tea. Ash looked at her curiously. "What are you doing?"

"Making tea. What does it look like?"

"I didn't know you even drank tea."

"Mom does. This stuff is supposed to be calming. I feel like something calming. Want some?"

"I think I will. Should we take her a cup, too?"

"When she wakes up."

With the tea made, Megan couldn't sit at their second-hand, Formica-topped kitchen table and relax with it. So she leaned on the counter, the cup between hands that still shook a little. This was weird. It was the first time she and Ashley had had a conversation longer than two sentences in weeks.

She was just about to ask her something innocuous, that wouldn't start a fight—*how are the plans for school coming?*—when *boom!*

Glass shattered like an empty scream.

Startled out of her wits, Megan dropped her mug on the linoleum, and tea splashed her legs and Ashley's pants.

Megan grabbed Ashley's arm before she let loose a scream, but there wasn't time to splash on cold water or even grab a towel. "That came from the bedroom!"

"I don't want to go!" Hands over her ears, Ashley fled into the living room.

"Call nine-one-one!"

She didn't know if Ash would do it or not. All she knew was that something bad had happened in Mom's room, and there was no one here to help.

GottGottGott—

Her brain gabbled like a chicken while her hands trembled and the contents of her stomach felt like they were going to come up any second. She pushed open the door to her mom's room.

The window had been completely blown out. Shards of glass lay everywhere.

Oh no oh no she was faking it we never should have left her alone oh Mom oh Gott—

She didn't want to see what was on the other side of the bed.

But she had to. Had to. In case there was hope.

Megan rounded the footboard.

Her mother lay curled up on the other side. Glass winked in her nightgown. Dad's shotgun lay on the carpet beside her. The air smelled burned.

Slowly, Megan knelt. Reached out. Her icy fingers closed around the stock of the shotgun and she pulled it out of reach.

Stupid. She's never going to pick up anything ever again. She's dead. Oh Mom. Please don't leave me behind. I didn't mean to be bad. No no no—I can't look. I can't do this. Oh Mommy Mom Mamm.

With a groan, her mother's body convulsed. Then seemed to collect itself. Hands pushed on the carpet.

She sat up.

Megan lost her breath. Her eyes felt stretched wide and dry by horror.

Their gazes locked. "I missed," her mother said.

4

Pitt Corner, New York
Four days later

For about the millionth time, Megan wished she had Qu'riel's strength and savvy. Instead, all she had was … nothing. She had nothing inside—no strength, no knowledge that might help, not even a dose of attitude that would help them get through this.

And their dad's face, drawn and gray as he sat across the breakfast table from the two of them … Megan swallowed and gazed down at her oatmeal.

"We know they can't keep her," he told them as he attempted to swallow hot cereal. "Once the seventy-two-hour suicide watch ends without incident, they have to release her. I'm going up to get her this morning, and when we come home, I'm depending on you girls to help her get settled."

"Why, where will you be?" Ashley said, alarm making her tone shrill.

Neither of them was handling this well.

"I have to go to work. The term has started—you know that—even though the students don't start until next week." He spread his hands in a weird helpless contrast to his take-charge tone. "If we're going to be a single-income family, I can't risk too many days off. Too many people want my job."

"But—what do we know about caring for her?" *Suicide watch.* Megan's throat closed and wouldn't let her say it.

"She's your mother," he said gently. "First and foremost. You know how to show her you love her, don't you?"

Did they? Ashley and Megan looked at one another, and Megan could practically see the questions forming in the air between them. Did they really know? Maybe Ashley did. She was huggier than Megan. Maybe because she'd figured out how to please their mom and Megan never could get the hang of it. No matter what she did, Mom always seemed to expect something else. Something more. Maybe that was another reason gaming was so satisfying. You knew what you had to do and it worked and nobody stood there *expecting* things that you didn't know how to give.

Okay. Never mind. Their house had been made safe— after the police had come and she'd been admitted to the mental illness wing of the county hospital, Dad had gone through it like a dose of salts. The shotgun had been taken away, the Tylenol, even the toilet-bowl cleaner. The glass had been vacuumed up and a sheet of plywood nailed over the window. They needed kitchen knives to make meals with, so he'd put them in his desk drawer, which had a lock on it, and given Megan the only key.

They were taking no chances.

Except that two days after Dad had brought her home again, Megan turned her back for two seconds to pet a neighbor's dog as she and her mom were taking a walk, and Mom walked straight out into traffic on the busy four-lane boulevard.

Megan didn't even remember getting her home, she was so freaked out. But Ashley met her in the yard and together they got her into the house.

"I can't take this," Megan rasped, collapsing on the nearest chair, shaking like a quivering aspen. "Mom, there has to be a reason why you're getting worse. There has to be a way for us to help you."

Mom sat next to Ashley with her feet neatly together and her hands on her lap. She could have been at the Junior League—except the Junior League would never allow sweatpants and a T-shirt. Tears welled in her eyes. "I can't tell."

"What does that mean? Tell what? Don't you know why you want to kill yourself instead of—of—" She forced the words out. "Living with us?"

Ashley took their mom's hand. "Meg, it's a chemical imbalance in the brain. That's what the drugs are for."

"It is not!" she said, and the tears welled up and over, as uncontrollable as a summer storm. Yes, she knew she needed to keep it together. But how? "She just doesn't want us anymore," she finally got out between gasps for breath.

"That's not true." Their mom's lips trembled, but she pushed the words out anyway. "I've wanted you right from

47

that very first day—so pretty, so neglected. You needed me so much, my sweet girls."

Wait—what?

"Neglected?" Ashley looked cautious, as though expecting another fit of crazy words that made no sense. "Did they do something bad to us in the maternity ward? When we were babies?"

So totally off topic. Maybe they were all going nuts. Saying random things that didn't track, as though this were the Mad Hatter's tea party and they'd all just fallen down the rabbit hole.

"Mom? Who neglected us? Not you. You've always taken care of us."

Their mother began to rock back and forth, her hand slipping from Ashley's and her arms wrapping around her middle. "You'll hate me."

Show her you love her. Easy for Dad to say. First chance he got, he was out of there, leaving two unprepared teenagers in charge. Love. Okay. Love was something you did, not something you said, right? They used to have a fridge magnet with that written on it.

Megan hesitated, then got up to sit on her other side, all three of them squashed together in the love seat. "We could never hate you, Mom," she said softly. "We love you. Now maybe you should—"

"You didn't at first. And you wouldn't again. Not after I told."

"Of course we would." Ashley's voice was soothing. Soft. Maybe she was practicing for when she was a shrink. At this rate she was going to have lots of experience. "We'll always love each other, won't we? Like you always said, no matter what happens, we're a family and we stick together. Right, Megan?"

"Right," she said. "You can tell us anything, Mom." What had the doctors told them to say? "We're your safe place." She didn't feel like anyone's safe place. She needed one herself, and who was going to see that she had it?

Nobody.

"Safe place," their mother repeated. The rocking slowed.

Either they were getting through or she was about to do something unpredictable. Megan tried to brace herself in case her mother jumped up and did goodness knew what— bolted for the door? Headed for the overpass across the freeway? Her insides twisted and chilled.

"You won't hate me?" Mom sounded like a little girl looking for reassurance. "Even after?"

"Of course not," Megan said, slipping her arms around her waist and squeezing. "If you have something to get off your chest, you can tell us. Don't leave it inside where it can hurt you." That was good. Qu'riel might have said that to a wounded teammate. Megan took her mom's hand.

"Because they were neglecting you," Mom said. "If nothing else, I've saved you from that. Dressed practically in rags, so thin your little ribs were showing. The first thing we did was take you to McDonald's. It was like you'd never been there before. You've had a real life. A healthy life. That I gave you."

"Of course we have," Ashley said.

Megan was silent. *I have no idea what she's talking about. Should we call the hospital? Call Dad and ask him to come home?*

49

"We took you," Mom said softly. "That day. You were lost in the woods and we found you. We took you both in our arms and—" She squeezed Megan's hand back, finally. "You looked so much like my Megan that it was almost like … almost like it was meant to be."

This was bad. Her own mother didn't know who Megan was, and she was sitting right next to her. "Mom, I'm Megan," she said softly, though she felt sick, like the cheese she'd nibbled on for lunch was going to come up. "Your daughter."

Her mom nodded. "Yes. You're Megan. Now." She wasn't far enough gone that she didn't see the confusion on Megan's face. "She died when she was three, you see." She turned Megan's hand over and traced the life line with one finger. She tilted her head in the direction of the hallway. "She's there, in the baby pictures."

"Those are our baby pictures," Ashley objected.

"They are, after you came. But before, there was only her. My little Megan Alice, named after my mother."

Cold snowflakes of dread landed on Megan's skin, starting at the top of her head, trickling down the back of her neck and then out along her arms. This was bad. This was really, really bad. "I don't understand. What—what— Are you saying those pictures are of a different girl? They're not me?"

Rabbit hole. Falling. Falling down the hole.

Her mother nodded. "We told you there was a gap because you both had the measles when it was picture-taking time. One year it was chicken pox. But you didn't. There was only her. And then the two of you."

No. That wasn't true. Megan dropped her mother's hands and got up to look.

In the hallway, the picture gallery hung where it always did in every house they rented. Mom packed up the frames so carefully every time they moved, and they helped unpack and hang them every time they found a new place to live. It was what they did, even when sometimes they hadn't had so much as a kitchen table to eat on. All along the row, here they were: Megan at one, her curly blond hair barely enough to put in a barrette. Megan at two, in curly pigtails and a pinafore. Megan at three, sitting with a teddy bear. Then Megan and Ashley, smiling at the camera, one five and one six.

Wait a minute. How had she lived with these pictures her whole life and never noticed what was missing? Shouldn't there have been another baby in the two- and three-year-old pictures? She and Ashley were a year apart.

Where had Ashley been for five years?

Megan peered at the toddler in the three-year-old picture. She'd spent her whole life believing that was herself. How could it not be?

Where is Ashley? You don't take only one kid to the photography studio. You don't have measles two years in a row.

How could that not be her? But she choked on the question and couldn't ask. She had the weirdest sensation of splitting into two people—of looking into the little portrait as though it were a mirror, and standing outside of it.

Two people. Not one.

"We found you in the woods," Mom said sadly. "We think you were six—you were so underfed you could have been five. We gave you a home. A good life. That wasn't so bad, was it? We did the right thing. When I got so sick the first time, Carl always told me I did the right thing. He's so good to me. He's never refused me anything."

Megan took the picture down. The picture of the girl who wasn't her. Her lips felt numb as she walked back into the living room. Ashley's skin had gone pasty white—nearly green.

Megan held out the picture. "If this isn't me—then who am I?" Was this the reason she'd never really felt she belonged? That she never quite measured up to what Mom wanted? Because she wasn't the real girl?

She was only a substitute?

No wonder she loved gaming. Playing a part. Being someone else.

She was someone else.

Her mother's mouth opened, then closed.

"You found us in the woods? Like Hansel and Gretel? Did you make it up? Mom, answer me. If we're not your children, then who are we?"

Her mother looked up, tears welling in her eyes. "You promised. You promised you'd love me no matter what. You said."

"Mother, who are we?"

Janet Pearson's face crumpled and she shook her head helplessly. "That's just it. I don't know," she wailed.

Megan looked at the picture in her hand, the little blond with curly pigtails.

Looked at her own white face in the mirror over the fireplace. At her blond hair with its purple streaks, that had never held a curl in its life.

THE LONGEST ROAD

And then she dropped the little eight-by-ten portrait as if it had burned her. It smashed on the tile floor of the entry-way and the glass over the familiar little face shattered into a million pieces, so that she couldn't see it anymore.

5

Whinburg Township, Pennsylvania
September

The town of Whinburg was so small that once they crossed the state line, Megan and Ashley had to stop at a gas station and buy a new map in order to find it. Megan wasn't quite sure how they were going to find the family they'd been taken from, but Mom had remembered the name Whinburg and a creek with willows along it. That was all they had to go on. That and Megan's overpowering need to get away from her mother, her father, and Pitt Corner as fast as possible. To try to make some sense of a life that—crazy and unsettled as it was—she'd always thought of as hers.

Ashley snapped the map open while Megan finished texting Casey and Raheem, who couldn't seem to understand why she'd skipped their game date last week, and kept putting them off this week, too.

> Megan: Parental difficulties. I'm handling it, but need some time. Catch up with you guys later.

Which was sort of the truth, and no way could she go into all of it now anyway. She pocketed her phone and started the car.

"I still don't know why we're doing this," Ashley said. "Digging around in the past to find something that might not even be there."

"Don't you believe what Mom said?" How could she not, when the proof was hanging right there in the hall?

Megan pulled out onto the county road, where a sign informed them Whinburg was five miles away. Great. They could have saved the three bucks the map had cost and bought coffee instead. One cup at the motel this morning had definitely not been enough.

"It doesn't matter whether I believe her or not. There's nothing wrong with my life that hunting down people I don't know is going to fix."

"We came from somewhere, Ash. Somebody."

"*If* you believe what our *very ill* mother said during a breakdown. Which I don't. Which any reasonable person wouldn't."

Megan wasn't feeling particularly reasonable, to tell the truth. "I believe that our childhood proves what she said. All those moves and crappy apartments? Neither of them holding down a job that they couldn't leave? That time we all threw our stuff in the car when you had your school recital the next day and left town and you didn't get to sing? Remember that? Mom and Dad spent more time watching the rearview mirror than the road, like they knew someone was chasing them."

"Maybe they were speeding."

"They were running. Because they had two little girls that didn't belong to them. Think about it, Ash. It all fits." There was something comforting about having something fit, finally, even if it was an out-there explanation for their unsettled childhood. Even if it made her feel sick to her stomach with a toxic mix of revulsion and anxiety. "We were supposed to trust them. But all those years, they were hiding that they stole us. Kidnapping's a crime, Ash. What's going to happen to them now?"

"You're thinking about it way too much—and making up half of it. Leave me alone. I need to talk to Keenan." And she called him again and that was that.

They'd had variations on that same conversation half a dozen times since they'd announced that they were going to Lancaster County to retrace their steps and … and Megan wasn't sure what. Bring balance to the Force? Mom had promptly freaked out, and by the time Dad got her calm again, and Megan had talked Ashley into going again, they were already a day behind.

Megan still thought it was a scary, insane idea, but something inside her—something that lived right under her breastbone and prodded and poked and nagged—had compelled her to pick up the car keys and stand firm behind her decision to go.

Ash still wasn't over it.

"Maybe it's stupid," she admitted at last as the sign welcoming them to Whinburg passed, and she slowed to pass a square gray buggy drawn by a glossy black horse. "But I have this weird feeling that we have to try."

"Why?" Ashley picked at the margins of the map.

Here be dragons. That's what the maps in *Quest of Qu'riel* had written on the edges. And the maps had proved to be right.

"What's it going to do for you? Or for them, if we find them?"

"I don't know," Megan admitted. "Give us closure? Or them? If they're out there, they probably think we're dead."

"That's exactly what Mom said, and it's creepy," Ashley said, staring out the window, probably so she wouldn't have to look at Megan. "You'd better get me back to New York by Monday. I have to—"

"—get the train to school on Tuesday," Megan finished along with her. "I know. And you will. After all, how long can this take? Look how small this place is—everyone probably knows everybody's business."

They cruised the main street of Whinburg, taking in the Amish people as they went about their business at the feed store, the pallet shop, the fabric store. There were lots of tourists mixed in, being sucked into restaurants with cheesy names like The Amish Kitchen and the Whoopie Pie Haus designed to do just that.

What the heck was a whoopie pie? Sounded like something from a trick and joke shop.

"They're all dressed exactly the same," Ashley said, gazing out the passenger window. "Except for the colors. Wow—look at that lady in the crosswalk. That's about the ugliest shade of taupe I've ever seen. At least her apron and that shawl thing cover half of it."

It was a little weird that they'd never seen Amish people before. In all their moves, all the road trips their family had taken, they'd never gone anywhere near a place where the Amish lived.

Megan had a feeling she now knew why.

"But those girls have better taste." She pointed to a little group of teenagers all dressed in turquoise, with a different kind of apron that tied in the back. "Maybe they're all sisters."

"Nice shoes," was all Ashley would say.

Personally, Megan thought their tennis shoes were practical for walking around town in. What did Ash expect, black patent stilettos?

She pulled up next to the girls and rolled Ashley's window down. "Ask them if they know where there's a creek with willows."

"Me? You ask them." Ashley slouched and folded her arms, forcing Megan to lean down and call past her.

"Excuse me—can you help us?"

One of the girls walked over and leaned in. She was wholesome looking, in a well scrubbed, never seen makeup in her life kind of way. "*Ja?* Are you lost?"

Two of the other girls giggled, as though it was impossible to get lost in a place as small as this.

"I'm looking for a creek that has willows along it. Does that sound familiar?"

The girl looked puzzled. "Do you mean Willow Creek?"

"I don't know. Maybe."

"There are no willows here, but the town of Willow Creek is about eight miles south."

"Does it have willows?"

"I don't know—I never thought to look. I guess it might, if it was named for them, *ja?*"

Close enough. "Okay. Thank you."

"You're welcome," the girl said cheerfully as Megan rolled up the window.

Ashley was already on the case, as though she figured the sooner they got there, the sooner they could go home and get on with their lives. "Turn left at the light. Highway forty-six should take us right to it."

Megan wasn't sure what to expect as they rolled into Willow Creek ten minutes later. It was even smaller than Whinburg, but there was a fabric store, a nice restaurant called the Dutch Rest Café, a gas station, and a couple of food stores.

"What's that?" Ash pointed to a bunch of sheds in a square with cars parked around it. "The Amish Market," she read. "Pull in here."

Megan did. "Why?"

"Look at all these Amish people. Somebody has to know if two girls disappeared from around here thirteen years ago. Besides, I'm starving. It's lunchtime and that looks like a deli counter."

As it turned out, the booth inside the covered market was more than a deli—and it was cheap. They got sandwiches the size of skyscrapers and big frosty bottles of unlabeled, homemade root beer. Megan hadn't known you could make root beer yourself. The only kind she'd ever seen came in a six-pack from Safeway.

After they'd finished their sandwiches, Megan held up dessert. "Now I know what a whoopie pie is. Two cookies with frosting in the middle." She took a big bite. "Oh wow, Ash, you have to try yours." Her eyes closed in ecstasy. Soft pumpkin cookies with maple cream cheese filling. Dessert didn't get better than this.

Ash had gone with a more conventional chocolate one with white marshmallow filling, but even she had to admit that it was good. Maybe not enough to make up for missing her last weekend at home with her boyfriend, but still, good. She was going to college with him next week anyhow, so what difference did it make?

Feeling fortified and a little buzzed from the sugar, Megan looked around. "Where should we start?"

"I don't know. Let's look around."

There was a lot to see. Handmade furniture. Quilts up the wazoo. Kitchen stuff made by hand. Pottery. Herbs for both medicine and cooking in a stand run by a blond woman with a sympathetic face who was wearing a dress in a yummy shade of raspberry.

Megan loved raspberries. On impulse, she stopped at her counter.

The woman smiled. "Can I offer you some herbs for your kitchen? Or maybe a cure?"

"A cure?"

The woman nodded. "I'm a *Dokterfraa*—well, in training, at least. My creams and tinctures help people to heal." She indicated little jars of cream, and rows of brown bottles, all with pretty labels that seemed to have been drawn by hand. "And these are jars of cooking herbs. My husband makes the ginger jars, with a special kind of clay. You can use them afterward for holding other things."

Almost against her will, Megan's mouth twitched. "What I have, I doubt you can cure."

The lady's gray eyes clouded under a crisp white bonnet shaped like a heart. "Oh, I'm so sorry."

Now she probably thought Megan had something awful, like cancer. "No, I only meant I'm looking for someone. Maybe you know them. Amish people."

The woman nodded encouragingly. "I know everyone in this district, and a few in the Oakfield district as well. Who are you looking for?"

"I don't know their names."

She had the lady's full attention now. "But they are an Amish family?"

"I think so."

"But if you don't know their names ...?"

"Not very helpful, I know. All we—my sister and I— were told was that they were near Whinburg, and a creek with willows along it."

"That would be Willow Creek, then—this village." The Amish lady nodded. "But without a family name it's difficult to—"

"They lost their kids," Megan said in a rush. "Thirteen years ago. Two girls."

The woman's eyes rounded and she touched her mouth with the tips of her fingers, as though she wanted to hold back the first words out of it.

"Does that sound familiar?" Did she have to sound so desperate? This was a—a treasure hunt. A detective story. Not something so important it would make a perfect stranger look like she'd seen a train wreck and had just realized she might have known someone on the train. "Why are you looking at me like that?"

"There is a family …"

Ashley finally spoke up. "What's the family's name? Do you know where they live?"

"On Red Bridge Road. The name is Riehl. Jonathan and Rebecca Riehl."

"Real?" Megan's stomach was making this weird dipping motion, as though she were on a raft and getting seasick.

The woman spelled it. "Their two girls disappeared one autumn, when my boy Caleb was small. He'll be fifteen this year. I remember everyone searching the fields and woods for them. For weeks people looked, but they were never found."

Megan couldn't breathe. "What—what were their names?" she finally got out. "The girls?"

"The eldest was Hannah. And her sister was called Leah."

"Hannah," Megan whispered. "Hannah Riehl."

Ashley tugged on her arm. "Thank you," she said to the woman. "Mrs…?"

"My name is Sarah Byler. And you are?"

But Ashley was already dragging her away, the bustle of the market covering up her low, urgent words. "Come on, Megan. If you throw up in public, I swear I'll get back on the turnpike and leave you here."

She hustled Megan out into the hot sun, which didn't help much. "Give me the keys. What's the matter with you?"

"Give me a second." Megan leaned on the hood of the car, taking deep breaths. "Hannah Riehl. Leah Riehl."

"It might not be ... who we're looking for."

"Who we are. Hannah and Leah Riehl."

"Not ringing any bells," Ash said briskly. "It might not be—"

Us.

But Megan knew. The way a tuning fork knows the sound of *A* when someone strikes it. The way birds know which direction to fly in the winter.

"Come on, Megan. Buckle up and let's get this over with."

Hannah. Hannah Riehl.

*

The sound of an *Englisch* car's tires crunching on the long gravel drive turned Rebecca's attention from the view out the window over the sink, where she and Barbara were doing the lunch dishes, to the screen door. Who could that be? Had the *Englisch* taxi she and her sister-in-law Ruthie sometimes hired to take them on big shopping trips come today by mistake? For sure they had no relatives that she could think of who might be coming to visit—not at the busiest time of the year. Amish folk did their visiting in the winter, during wedding season, when the outside work was done.

"Mamm, we have company." Dishtowel in hand, drying a water glass as she went, Barbara peered out of the door.

"Who is it?"

"I don't know. Tourists. They look lost."

The driveway was a little long for people to come down deliberately, and they'd long ago stopped selling produce at the bottom of it. Rebecca wouldn't risk any more of her children for any amount of money, even when times were tight. She and the girls took the overflow of the garden to Orland and Ruthie's stand next door, and split the money each week.

She heard the double thump of car doors, and dried her hands. "Stay inside, Barbara."

"Why, Mamm?"

"You heard me."

She made sure the screen door was closed behind her as she went out onto the broad, shady porch with its swing on one end and its cheerful pots of begonias and marigolds on the steps. Two young women stood uncertainly in the yard, looking about them as though they'd lost something.

She reached for the *Englisch* words. "Can I help you? Are you lost?"

They looked at each other and began to cross the yard toward the house. The taller one—oh my, her hair! It looked as though she'd taken a hay scythe to it, and then dunked the ends in purple dye. The shorter one had dark hair cut short in a smooth bob that swung along her jawline. Both were dressed in jeans and T-shirts with sayings on the front that made no sense to Rebecca.

Her gaze locked with that of the taller one, whose jaw went slack.

"Is this the Riehl farm?" the short one asked. "We're looking for Rebecca and Jonathan Riehl, and the lady in the buggy on the road said they were at thirty-six twelve Red Bridge Road."

"I am Rebecca Riehl." She took a step back. The older one was staring at her so intensely it was a little frightening.

This was more than a tourist's curiosity about her clothes or her hair. Her gaze asked. Demanded. Needed.

"This can't be right," the shorter girl finally said to the intense one. "She doesn't recognize us."

"That's not surprising—it's only been thirty seconds."

What did they want? Who were these girls?

"Thirteen years and thirty seconds," the intense one corrected herself. "Give her a chance—if we even have the right place to begin with."

Rebecca's lungs seized up, the way the wood stove sometimes did when the fire demanded more oxygen than the flue allowed. She couldn't speak. She could hardly even think.

Her whole soul felt as though it was flying into the sky, begging, *Oh Lord, can it be? Can it be? Hast Thou brought them home to me, oh mein Gott, mein Gott?*

"Hannah?" she croaked. "Leah?"

So many times she'd thought she'd seen them, in town, on a train, in a passing *Englisch* car. A face turning away, a pair of little feet running behind her, and she'd whirled or followed, only to look into the face of someone else's child, someone else's joy.

She'd been searching children's faces for thirteen years. Why was it so difficult to believe that they might simply drive into the yard and demand to be recognized?

Without warning, her knees gave out and she sat abruptly on the porch stairs, the purple skirts of her house dress puffing around her bare legs. "I—I'm sorry, I—" She lost her train of thought, staring from one to the other.

"I'm sorry if we've given you a shock," the dark-haired one said. "My name is Ashley Pearson, and this is my sister Megan. At least, that's who we were brought up to believe we were. But we found out recently that—that—um, how can I put this?"

The other one—the intense one—seemed to find her voice. "The woman we thought was our mother told us that she and our father found us in the woods somewhere around here, and took us away. We're—we—well, we'd like to know the truth about that. But maybe we got the wrong farm. Since this clearly isn't ringing a bell, maybe we should just go."

"Neh!" came bursting from Rebecca's throat at the thought, and she reached for them, struggling to her feet. "Don't go." Her heart felt like a runaway horse, it was galloping so hard.

"Mamm? Ischt okay?" came from behind the screen door. *"Du bischt engschderlich."*

"Ja, ischt gut," she said. "Don't worry, I'm fine."

"Who are these *Englisch*?"

"I—I—Barbara, go out the back and fetch your father in from the field."

"Mamm?" Alarm tinged Barbara's voice.

"Just go, quickly." Rebecca turned back to her visitors. In English, she said, "Tell me what you know of that day."

The girls looked at each other. "We don't know anything. That's why we're here."

Rebecca pressed a hand to her heart. "The children I lost were six and five. How old are you now?"

"Nineteen."

"Eighteen."

"And your birthdays?"

"April twenty-first and August fourteenth."

That wasn't right. The disappointment rushed her like nausea used to in the mornings, with the babies. "Hannah was born at Old Christmas—January second. And Leah was a summer baby, July twenty-eighth."

"So we're not your long-lost children." Ashley's voice sounded flat. "Well, I guess that's that."

"That doesn't prove anything. My birth certificate is *hers*, remember?" Megan said urgently. "The first Megan. Who knows, maybe your birthday is completely made up, too."

Rebecca struggled to make sense of that, and gave up. A question much more urgent demanded to be asked. "Do you recognize me? I have not changed as much as you have. Perhaps there is something about me that you remember?"

"I thought so, when we first arrived ..." Megan's voice trailed away. "I got nothing. Geez. Some homecoming this is." Her lips trembled and she turned away, as though ashamed of her disappointment, and maybe a little angry that she was showing it.

Ach, there was nothing quite as painful as hope. *Hope deferred maketh the heart sick.* How could God bring these girls here without giving them any memories of her, their mother? Perhaps that was the truth, then. She was not their mother. This was another woman's joy. Somehow, the thought that there could be two women enduring pain like this made her feel even worse.

"You'll notice I'm not saying *I told you so*," Ashley said in a tone Rebecca didn't like.

"Please. Do not be unkind to your sister," she said. When the girl's eyebrows rose, Rebecca realized she had offended her. "I am sorry. I have three girls—three other girls—of sixteen, thirteen, and ten. Sometimes they disagree in just this way. I did not mean to be familiar. To presume."

Ashley looked as though she didn't know what to do with such an apology. But *demut*—humility—demanded it, so Rebecca had given it. She took the opportunity to gaze at the girl, to trace the lines of her face looking for the giggly, sunny remains of a memory. Not for the first time, she wished the *Ordnung* permitted photographs.

She was wrong again, as she had been wrong all those other times. Maybe she could go into the garden now, and let her heart break in peace, behind the sunflower plants where no one could see or hear.

But no. There must be some way to find out the truth. The *gut Gott* had brought these girls here for a reason. A loving God would not toy with them in this way. He was a God of truth, of justice. She must hold to that with all her strength.

"I feel like a new mother," Rebecca finally said, casting around for the first words that came to mind, "looking at forehead and chin and eyes for family resemblances."

"Awkward," Megan murmured.

Rebecca heard it, though she had a feeling she wasn't supposed to. "I am sorry if I have made you feel so." Then she hit on a solution. "Please. Come in and I'll make some coffee. Maybe you like blackberry pie?"

"Love it," came out of Megan's mouth like a shot, leaving her looking surprised at herself.

"So did Hannah." Rebecca smiled, welcoming this tiny clue with trembling gratitude. "The summer she was three, she got into all the blackberries I had picked for jam. Such a mess! I was surprised she wasn't sick—but she had a stomach like iron."

"So does Megan," Ashley said. "She eats the most disgusting combinations of things—like peanut butter and celery, or ketchup on roast beef."

"I like peanut butter on celery—it's a *gut* snack," Rebecca said. "Come in the house." She took a deep breath, half of her wondering how she could say such mundane things when she wanted to fall to her knees and plead with Heaven. *Please, oh Lord, please.* "Let us see what else we can remember."

Oh Lord, reveal the truth unto me. Reveal it unto them. And then show me how we are going to live if we are divided one from the other by the world, the flesh, and the devil that these girls might have called by the name of mother.

6

The smell of the kitchen distracted Megan and gave her something else to think about besides this mistake of a trip.

Fresh-baked bread sat cooling on the counter—a dozen loaves at least. Someone had been drying canning jars, because an abandoned dishtowel lay beside them. On the stove, a big black speckled canner was steaming, and from across the room Megan could smell the tang of the fresh tomatoes piled in a cardboard box. Above it all floated the scent of coffee and cinnamon.

The tidal wave of scent washed over her, and when she surfaced, she could see.

"I've been here before," she said, almost against her will. Half of her didn't want to belong to these people. The other half desperately wanted to belong somewhere, or at the very least to know *where* she belonged, even if she didn't choose to stay there.

How confused was that? She was still two people, when all she wanted was to be one. To stop playing a role. To have a place that was hers alone.

An Amish farm wasn't the place she would have started with, but it was all they had.

Rebecca shut the fridge door with her hip. Her hands tightened around the glass pie plate before she set it carefully in the middle of the big table. "We've lived in the district for twenty-five years—since the year after I was married, and on this farm for twenty. Does anything look familiar?"

"It's the smell. Bread and coffee and cinnamon. It's like a memory I haven't had since … the last time I was here."

"Scent memory comes from the oldest part of our brains," Ashley said.

"Do you remember it?" Megan asked her, pulling out a chair. Ashley shook her head as she sat next to her, and at a sound from Rebecca, they both turned.

"Why did you sit there?" the woman whispered.

For a second, Megan was confused. "Where? Here? Sorry, is this someone else's chair?"

Ashley half rose, as though she thought she'd be ordered out of it.

Rebecca's eyes shimmered, and finally a tear trickled out of the corner. "That is your chair, Hannah," she said, sounding choked. "We have kept your places for thirteen years. Every meal. Every prayer. We have left that chair for you, and the one next to it for Leah, just as you are sitting in them now. It is a sign from God."

And before Megan could even move, Rebecca had flung herself to her knees between them and folded her into a hug—a real hug, oh my, it was like falling into pure love and comfort. Rebecca was bawling like a child, her shoulders heaving as one arm pulled Megan closer and the other pulled Ashley in.

She gasped out words Megan couldn't understand— sprinkled with a couple she did. *Mein Gott—denkes—ach, meine Dechder.* And as though crying were contagious, Megan felt her own throat close and hot tears spurt into her eyes.

Could it be true?

Did she want it to be true?

Was truth a choice?

All she knew was that Mom—Janet Pearson—never hugged like this, as though you were the most precious gift she'd ever had. Janet hugged as though there were someone standing behind you, waiting for her turn.

Someone she wanted instead of you. And now Megan knew who that had been.

The back door banged open and Megan and Ashley both jumped back, their chairs clacking against the ones set next to them.

"Rebecca?" A big man in a straw hat, his brown pants covered in dirt, with patches of sweat beneath the arms of his blue shirt, practically leaped across the kitchen to help her up. *"Liewi, was ischt? Bischt du okay?"*

A waterfall of Pennsylvania Dutch made his eyes widen, even as he hugged her to him and gazed over her shoulder at Megan and Ashley, still pinned in their chairs.

"Can it be so?" he breathed in English, and Rebecca stepped to one side, her arms still around him, so that he could see them. "Hannah? Leah? Has God brought you back to us?"

"We brought ourselves," Ashley said, "when our mother told us."

Another waterfall of Dutch, and now a girl sidled in the door, and another, and another. Two boys pounded up the steps and suddenly the kitchen was full of kids, all staring and murmuring among themselves. A little blond boy pointed at Megan's hair and said something that made the two younger girls giggle, which netted them a couple of sharp words from Mamm.

Mom.

Rebecca.

What was happening to her brain? Words were getting mixed up. Megan couldn't understand anything they said, and yet once in a while she caught something. But *Mamm* and *Mom* sounded the same, right? That was nothing to go by.

Now Rebecca seemed to have got to the part about the chairs, and Megan wished she'd never sat here. And now there were two more faces at the door—old faces. Who was this, now?

It was like someone had rung the bell to come in, and everyone had heard it but her and Ashley. They all sat around the table, leaving a chair empty next to Jonathan, and the old lady put the pie she was carrying in the middle of the far end, in front of the boys.

Okay, then. In the midst of a crisis, you have pie.

Good plan. It made sense. Unlike just about everything else.

"Do you remember your grandparents?" Rebecca palmed the tears from her face with both hands. She got a pitcher out of the fridge and collected a knife from the drawer. The oldest girl—Barbara?—had already set the table with forks and pie plates, and was making more coffee.

"No," Ashley said. "But I don't seem to remember very much. Megan, do you?"

Megan tried to, but the faded, wrinkly faces, one under a straw hat and the other under a snowy, heart-shaped bonnet, didn't look familiar at all. She shook her head.

"These are my parents, Mammi Kate and Daadi Riehl—Timothy Riehl," Jonathan said. At least, Megan assumed this was Rebecca's husband. No one had introduced them. But she could see that he had inherited his mother's brown eyes. And so had the middle girl. The twins each had their mother's full bottom lip, along with a matched set of dimples.

Megan had Rebecca's eyes, too. And the cheekbones.

Not the dimples.

It was just as Rebecca had said—like looking at a newborn for the family resemblance. For proof she belonged to this family and not some other.

The youngest girl had sleek brown hair like Ashley's. Where had that come from? Rebecca was a blonde. Megan had been too, originally.

She had to stop doing this. Especially since silence had fallen and everyone was staring at them.

Rebecca seemed to shake herself awake and began to dish up pie. She poured cream on it and handed the plate to Megan, who dug in.

When Jonathan cleared his throat, she stopped with her fork halfway to her mouth. "It is our custom to wait until everyone has a piece, and then to give God thanks," he said. "I hope you will join us in this?"

Hot color flooded Megan's face as she dropped her fork, making a couple of droplets of cream splash onto the red-and-white checked tablecloth. Ashley's shoulder bumped hers in a way it hadn't done since they were little. It said, *It's okay. I'm here. One for all and all for one, right?*

When everyone had a piece of pie, except for the empty plate and fork in front of the empty chair, they bowed their heads simultaneously. Silence fell. When no one spoke, Megan glanced around furtively, but even the little boys had their eyes tightly closed, their palms pressed flat to their faces. In seventh grade Megan had had a friend who went to the Pentecostal church. They said grace before every meal, but her dad said it out loud—a groan of a prayer that took so long that lunch often got cold by the time they were allowed to eat it. When they transferred to the high school for ninth grade, the girl had gone to a Christian school and Megan's sole exposure to the customs of religion had gone with her.

With a sigh, Jonathan raised his head, and everyone seemed to kick into action at once. Forks clanked on china, which was Megan and Ashley's cue to pick up theirs again and eat.

The blackberry pie melted on her tongue, rushing to every sugar-based pleasure center Megan possessed. It was all she could do not to groan aloud in her own personal prayer of thanksgiving. "This is really good," she finally managed. "The best I've ever had."

Rebecca smiled, a little watery, but still a smile. She glanced at Barbara. "This one made it. I am glad she did a good job."

"Me too," Megan said, already nearly finished. She sipped coffee and added more cream. "Thanks."

"If you want to learn how, maybe I can teach you," the girl said shyly. "Pie is easier than cake or bread."

Ashley snorted into her coffee mug.

"Does it involve ovens?" Megan asked over the rude sound. No need to tell this kid who obviously could bake complicated things like cake and bread that she could barely boil water. "Because I'm not very good with those."

Barbara looked mystified. "How would you bake it without an oven?"

"I don't know, but if it's possible, then I could make a pie. I don't like ovens or stoves. Even space heaters creep me out."

"That's because when you were four, you were helping me make snitz pie to take to a wedding," Rebecca said softly. "We had half a dozen baked already, but when you went to put in the last one, you looked back at me and didn't realize how close were your hands to the element. You burned the backs of them, dropped the pie all over the floor, and screamed and screamed until we could get your hands wrapped with burdock leaf and B and W ointment."

The last part went right past Megan. She was still catching up on the first part. "I burned myself in the oven?"

"Yes. And then, I suppose because you were afraid, you were nervous around the woodstove. Your hands had barely healed before you burned yourself again, poor *Maedel*."

"That woodstove?" Megan nodded to the big cast-iron beast, sitting all cold and innocent over there by the door on its low hearth of bricks.

"*Ja,* that one."

The vision she always had, of an oven looking like a big orange mouth ready to devour her arms and hands if she put something in it—it wasn't a vision. Or imagination. It had really happened. Of course an oven would look huge and hungry to a four-year-old. Of course the pain would make her hesitate ever to go near one again. And if she were made to, of course she'd bumble around it and get burned again.

"Wow," she said, almost to herself.

"You remember it?"

Megan nodded, slowly. "I thought I'd dreamed it, or made it up. But it was real." She looked past Rebecca to the kitchen stove, looking cool and white and normal. "That's the same oven, too, over there?"

"*Neh*, that is a new propane oven that we put in ten years ago, but the old one stood in the same place."

Megan flicked a glance at Barbara. "Thanks for the offer of the lesson, but I think I'll pass."

Barbara only smiled a shy smile, got up, and within a minute or two had brought a couple of plates of chocolate-chip cookies, a bowl of applesauce, and a heap of whoopie pies. Megan wasn't sure what surprised her more—the amount of stuff that came out of fridge and cupboard, or the fact that a sixteen-year-old was serving them all without a word or any instructions, as though it were normal.

Megan couldn't remember the last time she'd seen Ashley do anything remotely like this. Or, if she were honest, herself either. Serving other people wasn't very high on the to-do list at home. It was something she got paid to do at the coffee shop.

"Thanks," she told the girl—*my sister?*—and helped herself to a whoopie pie. "These things are addictive."

Oh, yum. Chocolate, with orange filling. She wasn't going to need supper at this rate. In fact, she'd cheerfully give up supper and just eat pie for the rest of her life.

"So, then," Jonathan said, "what are your plans?"

Megan looked up in surprise, as did Ashley. He hadn't said a word since finishing grace.

"Plans?" she repeated. Did he mean, like, long-term? Ash was going to college. Megan didn't have a clue what she was doing past the last bite of this whoopie pie.

"Ja," he said. "Will you stay with us?"

"Stay?" Okay, she had to stop sounding like a parrot. "You mean, for the night?"

He gazed at her for a moment. "Yes, for the night. Or for longer. Until we are certain."

"Certain of what?" Ashley swiped a couple of cookies.

"I am already certain," Rebecca said softly. "And I think Hannah is, too."

Don't call me that.

But isn't that what you want? Your own name? To not be a substitute anymore?

She must have twitched, because Ashley said, "We don't know enough yet. Sometimes memory can play tricks on you. Her thing about ovens might not be because of that pie incident at all. It might have come from a nightmare. Mom says she used to have them a lot."

"If she had been taken from her home and family, I imagine so," the old lady said from down at the end of the table.

"Hey!" Ashley exclaimed. "Can we set some ground rules here? Rule number one—no bad-mouthing our parents, okay? They did the best they could."

Silence fell, and Megan could imagine them all thinking, *Sure they did—after they took somebody else's kids.*

"Please do not speak to my mother in that tone," Jonathan said. "In our home, the children have been taught respect for their elders."

"I was taught that respect is mutual." Once Ash got the bit in her teeth, she didn't let go.

Bit in her teeth? Seriously, Megan—more horse references?

"In an Amish home, respect is earned by our willingness to serve others, and by obedience," Jonathan said heavily. "And by showing respect, particularly to the wiser among us. If you are going to stay, that is a good beginning."

Ashley's face was turning red, and if he wasn't careful they'd all get a lecture on equal rights and freedom of speech. Gently, Megan pressed her foot on top of her sister's.

"I think we both get that," she said. "I'd like to stay. Just for the night. Thanks."

"We've kept your room just like it was," the third girl said. Megan had already forgotten her name. No, wait. It was the same as the grandmother's. Katie. "Would you like to see it?"

"Sure," Megan said when it was clear Ashley wasn't going to answer. "Maybe you could give us a tour." She smiled, and the girl smiled back. It was like looking into a mirror. Megan's mouth got that same triangle shape when she smiled.

Lots of people's do. Look at Dennis Quaid.

"You go," Rebecca said. "Barbara and I will take care of the kitchen."

Megan took another whoopie pie for good measure, and knocked back the rest of her coffee, which was as good as any she'd ever made herself at the shop. Considering it came out of a metal pot on the stove and not a multi-thousand-dollar machine, that was saying something. Because—wait—

"You guys don't have electricity, do you?"

That was what was missing from the kitchen. Overhead lights. And shiny appliances. And pretty much every labor-saving device that had ever been invented, except for the fridge and stove that ran on propane.

"No," Katie said. "But we don't miss it, except sometimes in the summer. When it gets really hot, Mamm wishes for air conditioning. But Dat got a swamp cooler and hooked it up to the generator, and that works *gut*."

Goot. Good.

At the top of the stairs, it was warm, all right, but clearly not enough to warrant the swamp cooler. She and Ashley followed Katie down a short corridor and into a room at the end. "We have the dryer set up still, because we didn't know you were coming," Katie said apologetically. "Dat will take it out after we empty it."

Dryer? As in a clothes dryer? Were they movable?

Megan followed her into the bedroom and stopped just inside the door.

The smell of apples. Two beds. Two quilts in a familiar pattern. And—

"Noah," she said, rounding the end of the nearest bed and picking up one of the animals on the dresser between them. "And the ark." She turned. "Ash, do you remember—"

But Ashley was over by the window, inspecting what had to be the dryer, a setup that looked like a revolving display case without glass. Megan put down the horse figure and joined her.

"After we pick the apples, we slice them up and dry them for snitz pie," Katie explained. "This room faces south and west, so it's good for drying. Sometimes we make peach leather and hang it overtop, see?" She mimed hanging a long strip of something over the dryer, like laundry. "It's really good in our lunches in the winter."

"You go to school?"

"Sure," Melinda said, crowding into the doorway behind them. "Except for Barbie. She finished eighth grade a couple of years ago. I have one more year, and then I'll keep my work journal for a year, and show it to the teacher every month."

"I don't get it," Ashley said. "Aren't you supposed to be in high school?"

Melinda shook her head while Katie toyed with Noah's animals. "We go to eighth grade, and then a year of technical classes, or an apprenticeship. Girls work at home, and boys learn a trade. You write up what you learn in your journal, but after a year you don't have to do that anymore."

"Eighth grade?" Ashley repeated. "That's it? What grade are you in?"

"I'll be going into eighth next week. I'll be one of our teacher's helpers. With the little ones," she explained, looking as if this was a big deal. "Saul and Timothy will be starting this year, so they will have to do what I say." She grinned, and Megan saw she had a bit of an overbite. Megan had one, too, before three years of braces. She'd bet a hundred bucks there were no braces in this kid's future.

Two blond heads poked through the doorway and one of them said something to Melinda, who translated. "My brother Saul wants to know if you have a bag and can he carry it up."

Everybody was serving around here. It was like living in a Bob Dylan song.

"We do, but they're locked in the trunk."

"I'm not going to stay," Ashley said suddenly, in an undertone so the kids wouldn't hear. "This is freaking me out."

"They're just kids, being nice."

"Let me rephrase—*you're* freaking me out."

"Why?" Megan had never understood why she had the rep for drama. Ashley was the queen of that department, especially when she got going on one of her favorite topics.

"I don't feel comfortable when we don't have any proof we belong here. It seems like you're jumping in way too fast. This isn't our family, or our life."

"I think it is, Ash. I remember stuff." She gestured at faceless Noah and his little animals. "Like there's only one horse, because you chucked the other one in the stove by mistake."

"You just made that up."

"Ask Rebecca. I bet she knows."

"And she'd tell me I did, because she's desperate for us to be her kids. She'll say anything, whether it's true or not."

"Mamm doesn't lie," came a small voice from behind them. Megan had completely forgotten about the three kids over by the door. "Lying is a sin."

"Way to go, Ash," Megan murmured. Then, to ten-year-old Katie she said, "Of course she doesn't. Look, you boys, we'll go out and get the bags later, after your sisters give us a tour of the house."

"And the barn?" The sparkle hadn't yet come back into Katie's eyes, but she still gallantly played hostess. "We can show you the horses, and the pigs, and the chickens. I gather the eggs."

"Maybe we can help you, then," Megan said recklessly. She'd never touched an egg that hadn't come out of a carton, but she'd do it if it meant the life might come back into Katie's face.

And it did. Katie smiled, and Melinda waved them across the corridor. "Okay. Let's finish the tour quick. This is Mamm and Dat's room, this is ours, and that's the boys' room."

Except for the patterns on the quilts, which were all different, the rooms were equally austere. A dresser. A hooked rug. A row of hooks along the wall with white bonnets and black aprons, or in the boys' case, shirts, hanging from them. The three girls shared a room with bunk beds. No TV, no stereo, no iPods or tablets or earbuds—not even a portable radio.

What did Amish kids do for entertainment? Read the Bible?

Megan supposed that if they were really going to stay the night, they'd find out. But wow. Where was the nearest Wi-Fi connection? And how in the heck was she going to charge her phone when the battery ran down? Maybe she could live without *Quest of Qu'riel* for a couple of days, but there was no way she was living without her phone. She snuck a quick photo of the twin beds and Noah's ark and animals while Ashley and the kids were clattering downstairs and out the kitchen door.

The barn was huge and, like the house and the other buildings on the place, was painted white. All the houses were painted white, now that she thought about it. Maybe red and yellow and green paint was a sin, too.

Inside, it smelled strongly of farm animals, and she was hard put not to pull up the bottom of her T-shirt and cover her nose. They were introduced to the buggy horses, and shown the two buggies. "One for the whole family, and a market wagon with a flat in back for Mamm when she goes shopping," Katie explained. The chickens were the first thing that Ashley didn't badmouth or roll her eyes at. She crooned to them and practically had to be pulled away to tour the hayloft.

Megan was talking over her shoulder to Ashley when Katie cried, *"Achting gewwe!"*

One of the boys grabbed her hand and she stopped dead in the hay. "What? What's the matter? Is there a rat?"

The little boy gabbled at her in Pennsylvania Dutch and Katie took a deep breath. "You almost fell through the hay hole!"

Six inches beyond the toes of her sneakers gaped a hole probably eight feet across, with a drop of twelve feet at least. Megan gawked into it, and the dark seemed to fly out at her. She could swear the loft floor jerked, and she staggered back with a cry, tripping over a bale of hay and landing flat on her butt.

"Megan!" Ashley exclaimed. "Are you okay? Holy crap, you could've broken a leg!"

84

It was her nightmare come to life. Even now she could feel herself plummeting through the air, face first, and landing on a pile of hay so hard it knocked the breath out of her, like a monster was standing on her back not letting her breathe, and even when Dat rolled her over and massaged her chest, she couldn't take a breath, the dark moved in at the edges of her vision, it was going to eat her and she'd never see Mamm again—

"Megan!" Ashley shook her. "Talk to me! What's wrong with you?"

"Hay hole," she said, and gasped for breath. "I fell through the hay hole."

"No, you didn't. See? We're still in the loft."

"No, in my dream." She struggled up and sat on the bale over which she'd tripped. "I never knew what it was. But it was the hay hole."

Melinda sidled closer, but Katie and the boys were gone.

"Where'd the kids go?" she asked, to take the attention off herself and her stupidity. "Did they get bored?"

"They went to get Dat," Melinda said. "We thought you hurt yourself."

"Oh, great," Megan groaned. "That's all we need."

"Come on, let's get out of here," Ashley urged. "What's a hay hole for, anyway?"

"To feed the cows," Melinda said as though it were totally obvious. They walked outside, where to Megan's surprise they were at ground level. "We store it up here, but you throw it down to where the cows are through the hole."

"And meanwhile people fall through it and break their legs?"

"We all know it's there. Every barn has one."

The Amish had hay holes. She had a car. And Megan supposed that would be just as foreign and dangerous to Melinda as this barn was to her.

But why would she dream about it? It had been years since she'd had that dream, and yet with one look into the space, she'd been flung right back into it like it was happening all over again.

The little boys came pelting around the corner of the barn, their dad right behind them. He slowed when he saw the three of them on the big gravel ramp leading up to the doors. "The boys said you hurt yourself in the loft, Megan?"

He wasn't calling her Hannah, she noticed.

"I nearly fell through the hay hole, and lost my balance," she said. "I'm okay."

He had an odd look on his face, as though he had remembered he had something to tell her. "Our Hannah fell in one time," he said. "She was always running places and getting into things. She forgot the hole was there and was halfway across the empty space, I think, before she realized the floor had run out."

Like Wile E. Coyote in the cartoons. "I fell—she fell in?" Megan asked.

"*Ja.* Lucky for her there was a big pile underneath—I'd just finished tossing it down for the cattle. She had the breath knocked out of her, though."

"What about Leah?" Ashley wanted to know. "Hannah seems to have gotten into everything. What did Leah do?"

"Followed Hannah." He gazed at her, but it was like he wasn't really seeing her. "Even so young, Leah looked before she leaped. I supposed it was because so often Hannah was doing the leaping. She came to tell me that day, about

Hannah falling through. I was only in the dairy, so I came running and helped her get her breath back." His expression turned bleak. "It scared Samuel, though. It was his job to watch his sisters and he'd found a litter of kittens or some such. He sure got in trouble for that."

"Samuel?" Megan said. She didn't remember anyone at the table by that name. "Was that the dog?"

"Megan," Ashley muttered. "Duh. Empty chair."

Oh no, had there been a brother lost, too, that day?

But Jonathan's face had hardened, the faraway view of memory fading abruptly from his eyes. "Samuel was with the girls the day they disappeared. He was supposed to be watching them then, as well."

And without another word, Jonathan strode away up the ramp and vanished through the big, heavy sliding doors. Megan stared blankly after him, then met Ashley's gaze.

Had he died because of what he'd done—or not done—that day? Had he lost them, and then done something awful? Had he ... killed himself because of it?

Was that why his chair was empty?

*

Megan: Hi Mom.

Megan: We made it here safely. Hope you're OK.

Janet: Where are you?

Megan: At the Riehl family farm.

Janet: Is that them?

Megan: All the Amish folks know the story. They pointed us straight here. I think it's them.

Janet: All the Amish know? And?

Megan: They asked us to stay the night.

Janet: You're not, are you?

Megan: Why not?

Janet: They're strangers!

Megan: It's OK. They're nice.

Janet: Lock your door. Call me in the morning. I want to know you're OK. I want you to come home.

Megan: OK. We'll be fine. Bye.

7

"Hey, Riehl!" Samuel looked up from his tunafish sandwich to see one of the Amish upholstery installers jogging across the parking lot.

Ben Troyer nudged him. "Guess we're not shunned today, huh?"

No, they weren't shunned, even by the men working there who were full church members. At least here it wasn't like at home. He didn't have to be Amish to work here, didn't have to commit to a life he didn't want, in order to make a living. But that didn't mean he was buddies with everyone. There were some boundaries you just couldn't step over.

"That's too bad." He didn't stand, just waited there on the curb where he and Ben were having their lunch before heading back to the factory floor. As insulation men, they had a certain number of RVs to get through the line per day, which didn't leave a lot of time to linger even when they got a break.

"I guess you heard the news?" The kid jogged up, looking fit to burst.

"What news?" The Amish grapevine was always full of news, and now that some of the *Youngie* had cell phones, it was even worse. Of course, everyone knew that *news* meant *gossip*, and that was something Samuel had had enough of to last the rest of his life.

"About your sisters," the kid said. "You're Samuel Riehl, right? Jesse's cousin, who was on TV?"

"Yeah. But I ain't talking about him or my sisters. Bug off."

"Why not? Aren't you glad they're back?"

"Very funny." His appetite gone, Samuel packed up the remainder of his sandwich. He'd finish it on his next break.

"How do you know anything about it?" Ben asked. He'd never been baptized either, and with this much in common he and Samuel had taken to hanging around together when they'd first started working here, and last year had gone in together to rent a place to live. It was a single-wide in the trailer park and wasn't much, but at least it was theirs, Ben was quiet company, and people didn't bug him with stupid questions.

"My brother just told me that two *Englisch* girls were in the Willow Creek Amish Market this afternoon asking where your dad's farm was."

"So?" He couldn't imagine why anybody would ask that. They didn't sell stuff at the stand anymore. And two *Eng-*

lisch girls wouldn't want their washing machines or sewing machines converted from electricity to hydraulics anyway.

"*So* they were asking if there was a family here who had their girls taken away thirteen years ago. If that isn't your sisters, then who is it?"

His hands had gone cold, and he fumbled with the plastic bag holding the other half of his sandwich. "I don't know."

The kid stared at him, like he was expecting something else. Something more. "Don't you want to find out?" he said at last.

Samuel lost his patience. "It's none of your business. It's one thing to joke around, but maybe you'd better think about people's feelings before you say stuff like that."

"Aw, talking about feelings, now you hurt his." Benny got up and stretched in the hot sun as the kid backed away.

"Good riddance."

The kid turned and walked off, his arms swinging in a jerky way that told Samuel his feelings really had been hurt. Well, good. Maybe next time he'd think twice about butting into other people's business. Was that all Samuel was to him, too—the guy who'd let his sisters disappear? The cousin of the kid who'd been on that stupid reality show, *Shunning Amish*? Couldn't anybody give him credit for having his own life and just let him get on with it?

For days at a time he could forget he'd been brought up Amish. Forget his sisters. He'd drive back and forth to work, get groceries, pay the rent, all like a normal person. And then he'd see one of the guys from his old gang, the Woodpeckers, in a family buggy, his pretty wife beside him and a baby in her arms. Or he'd see a pair of girls walking along the side of the road in lime green or turquoise dresses, their arms linked, and an anger so black and scary would come on him so suddenly that he wasn't safe to be around sometimes. Once he had to pull off into the laundromat's parking lot because otherwise he'd have gunned the old engine and plowed the car right into an eighteen-wheeler, just to hear the crash.

Of course, then he wouldn't have anything to get to work with, not to mention he'd probably be dead, so he'd wrestled himself back under control. It had taken a good fifteen minutes, though, and he hadn't been very good company for anyone the whole rest of the day.

"You okay?"

That was Ben. He acted like he didn't care about anything, including himself, and then out of the blue he'd buy you a beer or ask if you felt like ice cream. It was one of the reasons Samuel hung around with him. Neither of them had too many other friends. Just ex-Amish like themselves who were trying to find their way, who weren't willing to join church and hadn't had any training in anything else.

"Yeah, I'm fine."

"Weird, huh."

"It ain't the first time. People tell me they've seen them, I tell them they're full of crap." He shrugged. "They always are."

"Yeah." Ben was silent for a moment. "What if it's true?"

"It never is." Samuel got up. "Come on. Break's over."

The rest of their shift was a race against the clock, dropping in the bats of insulation, nailing down the slats with the air nailer—*bam, bam, bam*, three to a side, on to the next one. It was exhausting work, and he hated wearing the breathing mask, but it paid well. Enough for the necessities of life, like gas and food and rent and paying off debts, and a little left over for savings and once in a while even some fun.

After having to pay for a new radiator for the car, he'd learned that having a little money set aside for surprises like that staved off a whole lot of grief when you didn't have a credit record or even a credit card. There was no need to know about stuff like that when you were Amish. But when you were living *Englisch*, life was a whole lot more complicated.

On the way home that night, they were more tired than usual The swing shift crew had been late, and while they'd pulled some welcome overtime, Samuel was so exhausted he could hardly see straight to drive.

"We ought to swing by," Ben said from the passenger seat. "Have a look-see."

"At what? Swing by where?"

"Willow Creek, man. See those *Englisch* girls."

Samuel swore at him so bad he ran off the road, and had to wrestle the car back into the lane before they drove into the ditch.

Ben didn't bring it up again.

The trailer park lay on the edge of Linwood, a place known for the RV factory and the Wal-Mart and not much else, about half an hour east of Willow Creek. One of the only benefits of living where they did is that they could come out on the little deck off the kitchen and see the fields instead of housing tracts and strip malls.

Samuel had thought that looking out at fields all too similar to the ones he used to work would bug him when Ben had suggested being roommates, but come to find out, it was kind of soothing, especially when the sun went down and the fireflies began their nightly show.

Hannah and Leah had loved chasing the fireflies. Daadi Riehl had of course had a lesson to preach about the difference between false lights and true, but like lots of things the Amish thought, it was all about the doctrine and not so much about actual biology. Maybe someday he'd tell his grandfather that the fireflies' lights were a chemical reaction designed to attract a female. That probably wouldn't fit so well into the lesson. But the likelihood of his talking to the old man was low, and of correcting his theology, pretty much zero.

Samuel nursed his beer and watched the fireflies, feeling the humidity in the air like a soft hand on his cheek. There'd probably be a thunderstorm tonight to break the heat wave.

Leah had been terrified of thunder. The three of them used to huddle together on Hannah's bed, watching the lightning and the rain, Samuel feeling like the protective big brother when the girls would squeak and hide their faces against his shoulder under the quilt.

He hadn't thought about that in years. Oh, he knew what was going on, why the memories were swirling in his head like mud in the current when you wade in the creek. He just wished that kid had kept his mouth shut about those *Englisch* girls.

He wished he didn't care. That he wasn't curious.

Because even if they were his sisters and they had come back, it didn't change anything. The girls were just as lost as if nobody knew where they were—because what were they going to do? Turn Amish and move back to the farm?

Wait. Samuel straightened in the lawn chair as a new thought occurred to him. If they did turn out to be Hannah and Leah, they were *Englisch* now. Even more *Englisch* than Samuel himself. So how would that work—for the first time having actual family on the same side of the fence as he was? Living like he was? And not feeling guilty and abandoned and ashamed, like he was?

Samuel's heart kicked up its pace a little, and he tilted the beer bottle. He'd only had three-quarters of it. He could still drive. Check out the old place. See if they were still there.

And if they were, what then? Pull up a chair in the living room and ask them how they'd been?

He snorted and put the bottle down on the deck.

Then picked it up and finished it off in three big gulps.

"What's up with you?" Ben came out with his own beer and settled onto the single step that led down on to the grass that became part of the field about ten feet away.

"Nothing."

"Uh-huh. You're having conversations with somebody in your head again."

Ben did it too. Usually when he thought he was alone, and it was usually his dad he argued with. Not that it got him anywhere—same as in real life.

"I was thinking about those *Englisch* girls."

"Uh-huh. Interesting subject."

"That would make, like, a third of the family who's not Amish."

"Figure you'd have some company, do you?"

"Maybe."

"So are you going to bite my head off again if I suggest we go for a drive?"

95

"How fast can you pound that beer?"

Ben grinned, and twenty minutes later they were rolling down the road. "You're not going to just drive in and say howdy, are you?" Ben asked after a mostly silent trip.

They passed the single stop sign in Willow Creek and turned down Red Bridge Road, so named because there had once been a covered bridge on it that crossed the creek. It had been torn down years ago, but the name stuck.

"*Neh*, are you kidding? If the gate across the Zook harvest track is unlocked, we can go in the back."

The Zook gate wasn't locked—wasn't even latched. Ben closed it behind them and climbed back in. A few minutes later, Samuel shut off the headlights and the car rolled to a stop along the wire fence dividing the Zook place from his dad's home field, which lay between them and the orchard.

"Come on." He didn't really know where he was going or what he'd do when he got there. But as they got closer, he saw what he'd never believed he'd ever see: an *Englisch* car parked against the rock wall that formed the wagon ramp up to the barn.

So, okay. His parents had company and they weren't Amish. That didn't mean anything.

And then, as they made their way through the apple trees, slipping from trunk to trunk and smelling the sweet scent of the ripe apples, Samuel slowed. Looked up. And saw two things.

The lamp in the kitchen window hadn't been lit.

His lungs seemed to collapse inward, as though he'd forgotten to breathe. He hauled in a lungful of air, and heard the swish in the grass as someone moved up beside him. "The lights are on in the girls' room," he whispered.

"The lights are on, but nobody's home," said a female voice, heavy with sarcasm, from the shadow two feet away. "Dude, what are you, a peeping Tom?"

8

The two guys were five or six years older than Megan, but she'd scared them as badly as if they were just kids with both hands in the cookie jar. The one closest to her jumped away and took half a dozen running steps toward the fence before he seemed to realize his companion was still holding his ground.

"'Dude'?" the non-running one said. "That doesn't sound very Amish. Who are you?"

"The one not spying on people?" A year of working behind the counter had taught her not to let guys walk all over her, and playing Qu'riel had taught her even more. It hadn't been easy, but at least these days, she didn't apologize first and ask questions later. After today, she was in no mood for any more surprises from people she didn't know.

But somehow these guys didn't feel like much of a threat. Maybe they were neighbors. They couldn't be coming around to see Barbie—that was illegal in Pennsylvania, wasn't it, with guys this age?

"We're not spying. We're enjoying an evening in the orchard, just like you."

"It's not your orchard."

"It's not yours either."

"I'm a guest here. Which brings us back to square one. What are you doing out here in the dark instead of knocking on the door?"

"A guest?" The other one had come closer, and from his tone, Megan had a feeling he thought he needed to make up for his aborted run somehow. "Since when do M—the Riehls have *Englisch* guests?"

"English? You mean, like you?" These boys weren't Amish—not that she was an expert. The only light was from the moon and the windows overlooking the lawn, but she could see they weren't wearing suspenders or hats, the way Jonathan and Daddy Riehl did.

"*Ja*, like us." He may have looked English, but he sure sounded Amish. *Ja* was definitely not the same as *yeah*.

"English who used to be Amish," she said. "Busy day for that."

The non-running one glanced over his shoulder, and the running one moved a couple of steps closer. "I'm Ben. And that's Sam."

"Sam? The Riehls had a kid named Samuel," she said. "I think he died."

"What?" Sam choked.

"Who told you that?" Ben sounded kind of amused, as if she'd got the answer wrong to a question he'd been thinking of asking.

"Nobody." Megan eyed his friend with concern. Sam was going to cough up a lung if he wasn't careful. "But everyone gets all weird when his name comes up, and they set a place for him at the table. Is that an Amish thing?"

"I don't think Samuel Riehl is dead." He whacked his friend on the back. "You okay?"

"Yeah," Sam gasped. "Close, though. I gotta get out of here."

"Okay." Ben watched him jump the fence one-handed and turned back to her. "Guy's got issues. Nice to meet you, uh—"

She stalled for a moment. "Megan." Not Hannah. Better to be the visiting English guest than the long-lost daughter, especially around strange guys who hung out in orchards after dark. "My sister Ashley is around somewhere. I think she was helping one of the girls put the chickens in."

"Kind of late for that. Chickens go in when the sun does."

"You guys *were* Amish, weren't you? I can hear it in your voices. And who else would know about chickens?"

"Ja," he said, with a little extra emphasis, as though he were mocking Sam from a moment ago. "But we're not now. What about you?"

"I don't know," she said before she thought, and then caught herself. "I mean, are you friends of the Riehls? Why were you out here, really?"

A tick of silence told her he was making something up, probably with more skill than she'd done. "Sam wanted to see if they were home, that's all. We were on our way to the door when we stumbled over you."

"Uh-huh." That was his story, and he was sticking to it, she supposed. Not very skilled at making things up, then.

100

Maybe that was an Amish thing, too. They didn't tell lies, did they?

"No need to tell the Riehls," he said easily. "We'll come by another time."

"Okay."

"Good night." He moved away, his boots making swishing sounds in the grass.

"How do you say that in Amish?"

"*Guder nacht*," he said from the fence. "And it's called Pennsylvania Dutch."

"*Guder nacht*, Ben."

From out of the dark of the neighboring field came, "*Guder nacht*, Hannah."

It wasn't until she reached the barn door that what he'd said sank in.

"He was reaching," Ashley said a little while later, after Megan had found her in the barn, hanging out with the chickens, and told her what they'd said. "Trying to trip you up."

"Maybe." The chickens seemed to have made themselves comfortable all over this part of the barn. They roosted on rafters, on hay bales, even one on top of an overturned bucket. "It doesn't smell as bad in here as I would have thought."

"That's because you came through the cow part and wiped out your olfactory cells. I thought I was going to lose my dinner."

"Compared to that, chickens aren't bad. Where's Barbie?"

"She went in for prayers. And then she had to put the little boys to bed. Apparently it's a major effort unless their dad has been working them all day to wear them out."

"Girl's got skills."

"If you can call it that. She's like somebody's mom in a teenager's body." Ashley pushed herself off a support beam. "I suppose we should go in. What do I do with this lamp?"

Megan had no idea. "Bring it in the house?"

Which turned out to be a good idea, because closing the outside door and finding their way across the chicken yard in the non-electric pitch dark would have been hard without it. Lamp or not, though, their trainers were encrusted with squashed chicken poop mixed with hay by the time they got to the back porch.

"Gross," Ashley said. "I'm leaving them out here. We can hose them off in the morning."

When they tiptoed into the house there was no one in the kitchen. Or the hall. But when they rounded the corner into the front room, the entire family looked up from where they were seated in a circle.

All those eyes trained on her made Megan halt in the doorway as though a door had closed in her face. "Uh …"

"We are waiting for you," Jonathan Riehl said quietly.

"Waiting …?" Ashley sounded as confused as Megan felt.

"At dinner we said we would wait, if you would like to join us for prayers," Rebecca said.

"Oh," Ashley said. "I thought you meant—well, if we didn't show, that you'd, um, just go ahead."

Good grief. Had the whole family been sitting here all the time she'd been out in the orchard and Ashley had been hiding—make that communing—with the chickens? Megan snuck a look at the six-year-olds, who were squirming like their rears were massively sore from those hard chairs.

"Sorry," she whispered, as though she was in church, though she'd never actually been in one. "I guess we misunderstood."

"The whole family takes part in prayer at the end of the day," Jonathan said. "And we begin the day with God as well. I hope you will not be so late in the morning."

Megan and Ashley slid soundlessly into the two empty chairs next to Barbie—did everyone do everything in order of age?—and Megan did her best to look as though she were paying attention.

Jonathan read out of a great big book that must be a Bible, in German. Then everyone slid off their chairs and onto their knees on the floor. Megan watched Barbie out of the corner of her eye, doing her best to mimic the kneeling and the clasping of hands. Their grandpa said a prayer into his chair seat, in English out of courtesy to her and Ashley, she supposed. And then everyone, even the twins, recited the Lord's Prayer in unison.

In one of Megan's schools—the one in Maryland, where Ashley was supposed to sing in the school concert—they had recited the Lord's Prayer before class and she'd had to learn it, like a poem for a recital. But that was a decade ago, and she'd forgotten all of it except for the rhythm of voices chanting in unison.

For Thine is the kingdom, the power and the glory,
Forever and ever, amen.

The floor was wood planks, uncarpeted, and was incredibly hard under Megan's knees. She wasted no time in scrambling to her feet, only to find out that the next thing on the program was going to bed.

"It's only eight o'clock," she whispered to Barbie as they climbed the stairs, while everyone was distracted by the departure of the old folks for their house on the other side of the garden. "How can you go to sleep this early?"

"Mamm and Dat stay up later," she whispered back. "Mamm does her sewing, and Dat reads, usually. Do you want to keep them company?"

Uh, no. "What time do you get up?" she asked instead.

"Four."

"For ... I don't know. Breakfast? School?"

"No, four. We get up at four o'clock."

Megan tripped on the last step and practically fell on her face on the landing. She grabbed the newel post and hauled herself up. "Four o'clock in the morning? What for? Do you have to catch a plane or something?"

"No." Dimples winked around Barbie's mouth. "We get up at four every morning. Dat and the boys milk the cows, and we girls wash the milk cans after Mamm pours the milk into the holding tank. The milk truck comes on Tuesdays and Fridays. While Katie gathers the eggs and the twins feed the poultry, and Dat lets the cows out to pasture, Mamm and Melinda and I make breakfast for when everyone comes in at six."

Megan didn't think her stomach would even be awake to accept food at that hour.

"I'll pass," Ashley said, hanging over the banister to listen. "Maybe a cup of coffee when I get up."

The dimples faded into disappointment. "You are not going to join us? If you didn't want to do the barn chores, maybe you could help me and Mamm in the kitchen. You don't want to miss breakfast."

"Or maybe we could head out and grab something at Starbucks on the way back to New York," Ashley muttered, shoving off the railing and going into the bedroom.

"Don't mind her," Megan said. Ashley hadn't been rude, exactly, but her own cheeks felt a little warm, as though she had been. "She was a sketchy about coming in the first place, and there's a lot to take in."

"Sketchy?"

Everybody in Pitt Corner used the expression; Megan had to think for a moment what it meant, exactly. "Undecided? Cautious?"

"About coming to see us? Why?"

"Well … I don't know. If we were wrong. If we invaded a stranger's house with our weirdness and they called the police or something."

"We would not do that." Barbara moved into the bathroom, where a Coleman lamp hissed on the vanity, and squeezed toothpaste onto a toothbrush—one of five lined up on the back of the sink.

What, no memorial toothbrushes for the missing three?

"Anyway," Barbara said around the toothbrush, "Mamm believes you are our sisters."

"What about Samuel?" she blurted.

Barbara spat and rinsed her mouth. "He is living *Englisch*. He works at the RV factory in Linwood and drives a car now."

"So he's not dead?"

Barbara's round eyes met hers in the mirror. "Why would you think he is dead? He's not, is he? Mamm only saw him a few days ago."

Megan felt foolish, making assumptions as serious as that and scaring the girl. "Hey, of course not. I'm glad, truly. That he's not." Time to change the subject. "There were some guys in the orchard just now—ex-Amish guys."

If she'd thought this would make things better, she was wrong. Barbara sucked in a breath through her nose and backed up a step, away from the sink.

"What ex-Amish? What were they doing? Who were they? Did you tell Dat?"

"Of course not. They weren't doing anything. Just looking at the house."

"You should have told Dat."

She ducked past Megan and ran downstairs, and before Megan could think, *Way to tattle, Megan*, Jonathan was standing in the stairwell looking up. "What is this about ex-Amish boys in the orchard?"

With a sigh, Megan trooped down the stairs and into the kitchen. "It's nothing. Just a couple of guys—Ben and Sam, their names were. They said they'd come to visit, and that they'd come another time."

Clearly mystified, Jonathan stared at her. "Sam? Came to visit? With Ben?"

"You know them?"

"It could only be our Samuel," Rebecca said softly, coming in with her hands bunched in her apron, as though she were drying them. Or hiding them.

"Your Samuel?" Well, that made zero sense. "Why didn't he just come in? Is he—" What was the word? "Is he shunned?"

Jonathan's eyebrows pinched, as if something hurt, or she'd poked him. "We call it being under the *Bann*, or *die Meinding*. But no. He was never baptized, so we do not shun him. He left his home to live *Englisch*, and while he does that, he separates himself from the will of God ... and from his family."

"Can't a person be in the will of God and live English?"

"If he is not willing to live Amish, then he is not willing for God's will," Jonathan said. "This is what we believe."

"What about everybody else who isn't Amish?"

"That is not for us to say. It is between God and the individual."

Which was a non-answer. "Samuel didn't want to be Amish, so he left?"

Rebecca blinked, hard. "He has had a difficult time with obedience. And forgiveness."

Megan wanted to ask, *Difficult how?* But she had a feeling she knew. Maybe getting up to milk cows every day for the rest of his life didn't appeal very much.

"He was with you—with the girls—the day they disappeared," Jonathan said at last. "He was responsible for you. But he was young. And when they're with their playmates, little boys forget."

"How old was he?"

"He was ten," Rebecca said softly. "When he came down Oak Hill without you, all the district came out to search. We searched for three days, but only found one of Leah's mittens on the path. Even the sheriff searched, but you were never found. Until today." Rebecca's eyes were wet, and her smile trembled.

Megan had been talking to her big brother out there and had not even known it.

The big brother who had been responsible for them.

Was that what had driven him away from his family? Not the cows, but living with the knowledge that he had been responsible for losing his sisters? Who could live with that? He'd been a little kid, for Pete's sake. His dad knew that, clearly, but had nobody explained it to him? Or was there a very subtle kind of punishment going on here?

Just who was having a difficult time forgiving whom?

How was Sam to know that Janet and Carl Pearson would be hiking around in the woods and find his little sisters, and in an act of denial the size of a river in Africa, would take them away to replace the little blond girl who had died? How could anyone predict something as crazy and horrible as that? Even if he had been there and seen them do it, what could a little boy have done? By the time he fetched help, the Volvo would have been miles away, heading for that McDonald's and another life.

She needed to find Samuel and explain that it wasn't his fault. Nobody should live with a guilt trip that big. As for the rest of it—the God stuff, the forgiveness—that was none of her business.

9

Gently, Rebecca pushed open the bedroom door and lifted the lamp. The golden light fell on the beds that had once been more than big enough for little girls, but now barely held the sleeping forms of the two strangers who were not strangers at all.

A bare foot poked out from under the quilt on the nearest one—Leah, in the bed closest to the door, as though unwilling to commit to sleep without the possibility of escape.

Rebecca had just come in from the barn, and the girls would be in soon to help her with breakfast, but she couldn't stop herself from stealing these few precious moments and gazing at her lost ones, like the man who had sold all that he had to buy the field where the treasure was buried, and couldn't stop himself from lifting the lid again and again to look at what lay inside the chest.

Leah. Ashley. The ashes of Leah. What fine features she had—the arched brows like a butterfly's feelers and skin as smooth as the porcelain of Rebecca's wedding china downstairs in the *Eck*. She still followed her older sister into everything, even when it was clear she had another life that meant more to her now than the one from which she had been taken. She had a rebellious spirit, though, and she wasn't afraid to speak up—or talk back, as the case may be.

What had her upbringing been like? What had it been like in the early days, for her little daughter who had been learning obedience and how to pray with her hands over her face and how to set the table and carry the dirty dishes to the sink to help her mother? What had these people, these Pearsons, thought when they had made that first meal and her little girls had covered their faces to pray? Had they told them not to do it? Or had prayer been outgrown and fallen into disuse, like their Amish clothes?

On silent feet, Rebecca crossed the room to the other bed. Hannah. She couldn't help the smile that flickered in the corners of her lips. Still a restless sleeper, still the one who kicked the covers loose and found them wrapped around herself in the morning. And every morning she would dutifully make her bed, tucking in the sheets that she would pull loose in her sleep again that night. She had learned to drive a car, like Samuel. Would that car take her away as his had done?

Her mind flashed to the shadowy orchard the night before. What had Samuel been doing out there? Even now, wonder and joy and grief spun inside her like clothes in the old wringer washer at the thought that he had come back to the home place on the very night that the girls had returned.

It was God's hand at work, gathering in, sweeping up the room to find the lost coins.

She wished God would make it clear what she should do. For last night, quietly behind their bedroom door, Jonathan had told her how uneasy he was about the situation.

"We don't know for sure that they are ours, *Liewi*," he had said, gently using the endearment to soften his words. "And even if we did, they may not want to stay. We need to go to the bishop and ask his advice. And above all, we need to pray on it."

It was her place to be obedient, to agree. And she did, in principle. But he was wrong, and she had to tell him so. "They are our girls, Jonathan. Who else would have such a fear of the stove but the girl who had been burned by it? And she remembered falling into the hay hole. None of the other children ever did, only Hannah."

"They could have heard stories. Or seen something on the television."

"Since when are stoves and hay holes on the television?" She had no idea if they were or not, but those events were specific to this farm, to this family. It wasn't a coincidence, or hearsay.

"I don't know if they are, but Becca, the point is this. After all we have endured, I couldn't bear it if what you hope for turns out not to be so. I couldn't bear your pain, if it's as big as your happiness now. I just couldn't."

He was a good man, and he loved her as much as she loved him. But his caution was more than she could stand, and she had blown out the lamp and lain silently in the dark, thanking God for the happiness and hope in her heart that was so much better than the cold despair she had been living with for thirteen years.

Now, in the cool predawn darkness, she set the lamp down on the bureau in front of Noah and his animals, and did for the first time what she had done every day all those years ago.

"Hannah. Leah. It's time to get up."

Leah didn't move. Hannah groaned and rolled away from her.

She squeezed her eldest daughter's shoulder. *"Liewi, kumm.* The barn chores are done, but maybe you might remember, we begin our days as a family together with God, with breakfast and then with prayers."

Hannah's eyes opened, and she squinted at the light. "What time is it?"

At the sound of her voice, Leah woke and stared around the room, as though trying to place where she was. Finally her confused gaze landed on Rebecca, bending over Hannah, and cleared slowly. Her brow pleated at the sight of the lamp, and the dark beyond the windows.

"It's five fifteen," Rebecca said. "I would love your help in the kitchen. Barbie and Melinda are still in the barn."

"I thought they helped you," Hannah said, falling back on the pillow. "It's still pitch black out there."

"Their father needs them this morning."

"So you need us?" Leah asked, in a tone that suggested she didn't believe it for a minute.

"Everyone on the farm has work to do," Rebecca explained gently, as though they had not learned this fact at her own knee when they were far younger than the twins. "Everyone has a job, from the chickens to the cows to Dat and me. We work for one another, to provide for one another, and to glorify God."

"I'll pass." Leah pulled the quilt over her head.

Hannah turned her head on the pillow to gaze at her sister, then looked up at Rebecca. The garish makeup had been scrubbed from her face, and she looked so young and vulnerable that Rebecca's heart squeezed. "You really need us?"

Rebecca nodded, not trusting herself to speak.

Hannah sighed, pushed the quilts aside, and swung her feet to the floor. "Come on, Ash. Time to earn our keep."

"No," came the muffled voice from under the quilt. "Ask me in about five hours."

"There will be no breakfast in five hours," Rebecca said gently. It had been quite a while since she'd had to deal with a flat refusal to do as she asked, but in this case, she oughtn't to be surprised. Had Jonathan been here, he would have told her she had no right to expect *Englisch* obedience to an Amish request, and he would have been right. But still ... she needed to begin the day with all her family gathered around the table. She was as hungry for that as she was for food. "It's bread day, so we have a pick-up lunch."

"I don't want to know what either of those are," Leah mumbled, but at least she pulled down the quilt enough for Rebecca to see her eyes, bleary and irritated.

"We make and bake the bread on Fridays. Monday is the washing, Tuesday is sewing, Wednesday is baking, Thursday shopping, and Friday is bread."

"What about Saturday and Sunday?" Hannah hunted in their bags for her clothes, and tossed a couple of items of underwear at her sister.

113

A bra landed on her face, and with a squeal of annoyance, Leah tore it off and flung back the covers. "Why should you care? We're not going to be here on Saturday or Sunday."

"The *Youngie*—the young people—will be playing volleyball tonight at the Miller farm just down the road," Rebecca said, removing the lantern and going to stand by the door as the two girls blundered between bed and bags, dressing as clumsily as though they'd never done it before. "Barbie has just begun to go places with the *Youngie*, so she could take you over there. And on Sunday, there is the singing."

"Singing?" Hannah repeated.

"*Ja.* They sing hymns from our *Ausbund*—our hymn book—and sometimes faster ones, like 'Be a Little Candle' and 'Amazing Grace.'"

"'Amazing Grace' is fast?" Leah mumbled, pulling a sweater over her head.

"You do not remember our hymns, maybe," Rebecca said, feeling yet another needle of pain in her heart. "They are sung slowly. Sometimes just one can take twenty minutes. But it is all in praise to God."

Reluctantly, they followed her downstairs and into the kitchen, where she poured two cups of coffee and pushed them into their hands. Hannah took milk, while Leah took hers black. After a few minutes, they seemed to perk up a little.

"What do we do?" Leah asked. "Hannah can't cook."

"Neither can you," her sister retorted.

"I suppose it's too early to call out for pizza."

"We do not have a telephone," Rebecca said with a smile. At least they were able to joke about it. She took bacon,

114

eggs, and tomatoes out of the fridge, along with a block of cheddar.

"No phone?" Hannah looked around, mystified. "How can you not have a phone?"

"There is a phone shanty out on Red Bridge Road, between our place and your Onkel Orland's," she told her. "And Dat has one in the barn, for business calls."

"It's okay out there, but not in the house?" Hannah said. "How does that make sense?"

Rebecca shrugged. "If I spent all day on the phone, talking with my friends and family far away, I would never get any work done. The *Ordnung* forbade telephones in the home nearly a hundred years ago."

"I need to remember to charge mine," Ashley muttered.

"We do not have electricity, either, remember."

At this reminder, Ashley's face went slack. "No power. No charge. Right. And I left my car charger at home."

"Where could we go for that?" Hannah asked, leaning a hip on the counter and curling both hands around her mug. She watched Rebecca pull out the big cast-iron frying pan and a couple of cutting boards.

"Maybe in Willow Creek, at the café. But they may charge you for it."

"Fine by me, as long as there's power. What are you making?"

"*We* are making breakfast. Take this cheese grater and cut two inches off the block. When it's grated, you can cut all these tomatoes in slices. Do you know how to make biscuits?" she asked Leah.

"I can make the kind that you whack on the counter."

Rebecca stared at her, a little shocked at the sudden violence of the words. "What?"

"You know, they come in a cardboard tube. You hit it on the counter and it splits open, and all the raw biscuits are inside. They're really good."

"We do not hit unsuspecting biscuits here. We do not hit anyone. We make them from flour and milk and baking powder."

"Then no, I don't know how." Leah sounded quite happy about it, and headed for one of the chairs at the table.

"I'll make them, then, and you can fry the bacon."

"How do I do that?"

Rebecca resigned herself to explaining to Jonathan why breakfast was late, but if she could teach these things to her younger girls when they had been barely old enough to see over the counter, she could teach them to these young women who did not know how to feed themselves except with a telephone. And if the bread didn't rise properly because they'd gotten started so late, well, they would eat heavy loaves and the girls would realize there was an order to everything a person did—and consequences, too.

When everyone came in thirty minutes later, the kitchen looked as though the pigs had got loose in it. The bacon was overdone, which was fine by the twins since they liked it crumbly. The scrambled eggs were runny in some places and brown in others, but at least they were edible. Hannah had forgotten the tomatoes under the broiler when she went for a second cup of coffee, but the chickens would enjoy them. The only unqualified success was the biscuits—and Rebecca always made a lot of them.

Melinda and Katie looked at one another across their plates and tried not to giggle, but failed miserably. But they kept their thoughts to themselves, as did Jonathan, so that they did not offend. Hannah and Leah looked as exhausted as though they wanted to go back to bed, and only picked at a piece of bacon and a biscuit with jelly on it.

"Who made you breakfast at your other house?" Katie asked when it seemed the older girls had finished.

"No one," Hannah said. "We don't really eat breakfast. I work at a coffee bar, so if I catch a morning shift, I just have a pastry there, usually."

"Don't you get hungry?"

"That's why God invented Cheetos," Leah said with a grin.

But Katie didn't grin back. She looked a little shocked. "God didn't invent them. Men did, in factories."

"I didn't mean literally," Leah said. "Of course he didn't make Cheetos when he got done with the plants and animals."

"God made me," little Timothy said in *Deitsch*. "He made you too."

When Katie translated, Hannah told him, "With the help of your mom and dad," with a smile.

"If you are all finished, we will return thanks."

"Is there more food?" Hannah blurted, looking around as though Mammi Kate had walked in with a bowl in each hand.

"We give thanks at the beginning of the meal, and return thanks afterward," Barbie explained.

For a wonder, the girls merely exchanged a look and settled back into their chairs as the other children did, too.

117

Jonathan wasted no time in his silent prayer, and before Rebecca had even raised her head, he had pushed back from the table. "I'll be in the barn. I'm expecting Jed Zook to come by about that augur."

The children looked stunned. The number of times their father had not gone in the other room to read the Bible with them could be counted on one hand. But today was different. Rebecca stepped in. "Saul and Timothy, help your sisters clear the table, and then wash your hands and faces. Daadi Riehl is expecting you to help him paint the fence."

To her surprise, Hannah began to pick up plates and silver, and take them to the sink.

"*Denki*, Hannah," Barbie told her, already running hot water.

"You're welcome."

"Her name is Megan," Leah said a little sharply, and Barbie turned in hurt surprise at her tone.

Rebecca laid a hand on her daughter's shoulder to let her know she hadn't done anything wrong. "Forgive us," she said. "It's difficult to know what to call you when we believe you are Hannah and Leah."

"Yes, well, it's a little weird for us, too," Leah said defensively. "I don't remember anything from here, even if Megan says she does."

"I was older." Megan set down the last of the dishes on the counter.

"That's where the drain tray goes," Saul informed her in *Deitsch*, but of course she would not understand him. "Look." He pulled it out and pushed the pile of dishes aside, and it was only Megan's fast reflexes that saved two mugs from crashing to the floor.

"I think we've caused enough chaos here," Leah murmured. "Time to go."

"Aren't you going to stay and help with the bread after the young ones leave?" Rebecca felt a clutch at her heart as she realized there was another meaning in Leah's words she'd missed at first. "You're not leaving, are you? To go back to New York?"

"No, not yet," Hannah said. "But we have some stuff to do. I'm sure the bread will manage a lot better if we're not here."

"What do you have to do?" They knew no one here, and none of the shops in Willow Creek or Whinburg would be open for hours yet—the Amish shop owners were getting their own families ready for the day, and had probably started even earlier than Rebecca had.

"Charge my phone, for one, and ... and track down some people." Hannah edged toward the stairs. "Excuse me. I need to take a shower."

"What people? Can I help you?"

Too late. They'd both vanished upstairs and here were her other children needing guidance and a calm mother who didn't look as confused and concerned as she felt at the moment. Once everyone had begun their day, she'd try again. Had she made a mistake in not treating them as Ginny Hochstetler treated her guests at the Rose Arbor Inn? Had it been wrong to treat them like family?

But she couldn't help herself—despite how broken and strange that word felt to her right now.

10

Because Samuel and Ben were on the same team of installers, it was rare that the two of them got a day off together. The factory wasn't open on Sunday because none of the Amish workmen would be there, and management couldn't build RVs by themselves. But it was open on Saturday, so the men worked four tens and got two days off, plus Sundays.

Yesterday had been payday, so Samuel was feeling flush enough to suggest going out for breakfast.

"I thought you had to put new tires on the heap," Ben said, ambling out of his room and scratching his belly. He tucked in his T-shirt and looked around their bare kitchen for a clean mug.

There wasn't one.

No coffee, either. They were out. They were usually out of something, but in Ben's mind, Sam knew, no coffee was a crisis.

"I do, but I have enough for that and breakfast. We should do a grocery run while we're out, too."

"Coffee."

"*Ja.* Come on."

The Dutch Rest Café in Willow Creek was as cheesy as it got, but the coffee was good and the biscuits and gravy were even better. It was out of their way, and closer to the farm than he'd like, but the odds of his folks being here on a workday were low. Samuel started to salivate as soon as he parked the car.

But when he got out, Ben nudged him. "Hey." He motioned with his chin toward the silver Subaru parked in front of the steps, as though it had been the first one here at seven a.m., when the place opened. A familiar looking Subaru. One he'd last seen tucked up against the barn ramp at home the night before.

"Still game for breakfast?" Ben watched him. "We could go back into Whinburg."

"Why would we do that?" Sam checked his back pocket for his wallet and hoped his face wasn't as pale as it felt. "They make their biscuits and gravy for the tourists there."

They pushed open the glass door and saw the girls immediately, in the last booth by the window, where of course they would have seen them in the parking lot. Good thing they hadn't run away, then. Sam spent enough of his time running. Maybe today was the day he'd stop.

The tall, sarcastic one who'd been out in the orchard last night was in the seat facing the door. She put down her fork with a clink. "Look who's here. Thing One and Thing Two. Or maybe Stalker and Stalkerer."

Sam had no idea what she was talking about, but her tone was clear enough. And it was obvious they knew who he and Ben were.

"*Guder mariye*, Hannah," Ben said with a reasonable attempt at friendliness. "And you must be Leah. Nice to see you again. You remember my friend Sam Riehl?"

"No." the dark-haired one said. She slewed around in her seat. "My name is Ashley Pearson. This is Megan Pearson. Thank you."

And she turned her back once again.

"I guess this means we're not sharing a booth," Sam murmured to Ben as he took the plastic-coated menu card out of the slot by the cash register. No other customers were in here, which was probably good in the event they started throwing plates.

"If my phone had more than a fifty percent charge we wouldn't be sharing a restaurant, either," Ashley said to her sister in exactly the same pitch.

Her sister. My sister. It had been dark in the orchard, and before he'd gotten spooked when he'd heard her say *he* was dead instead of the other way around, he hadn't seen much of Hannah. Megan. Now they stared at one another across the tables and linoleum.

His feet began to move as if he had no control over them whatsoever, and Ben, bless him, followed him over to the booth as though gawking at girls like this was normal.

Since last night, Samuel's rickety construction of *normal* had taken such a hit that it had pretty much fallen down. He hadn't been able to sleep from the shock of seeing this girl, of hearing her voice, of hearing his name on her tongue. Half the night he'd debated whether or not to go back to the farm

122

to talk to her—to find out whether it was really Hannah and Leah or a pair of fakes, like on some episode of *Shunning Amish* where there was a hidden camera waiting to make fools of them all for hoping.

Close up, another shiver of shock ran through him as he looked into eyes so similar to his own it was eerie. Her hair was blond, too. At least, at the roots it was. Kind of a golden caramel color that contrasted with the bleached yellow-white and purple of the rest of it. Her chin and mouth were set in a hard line, but he bet if she smiled he would recognize it in an instant. Hannah had had the best smile, like a cheery triangle of sheer mischief.

She was staring at him, too. "Take a picture. It'll last longer."

Was she serious? "Sorry," he said. "Don't be mad. We're not stalking you. We just came in for breakfast. We didn't know you were here." Which was a lie, since they'd both recognized the car and come in anyway.

"Don't be mad? With you going all Peeping Tom on us out there in the orchard last night? Megan told me you did. Here, *I'll* take a picture." Ashley's phone was still plugged in, but the little white cord was long enough to let her snap a photo of him and Ben. Then she looked at the charge. "Sixty percent. You'd better hope I don't email this to the sheriff."

"Ash," her sister said in a low tone. "Chill."

"Why should I? We don't know these guys."

"They're just guys. Not creepers."

"And you know this how?"

"Rebecca knows them. She told me." Megan nudged her. "This is Samuel. The empty chair?"

Samuel felt as though someone had pushed him in the solar plexus. Mamm and Dat still kept that empty chair at the table. After all this time—even after he'd driven away from her the other day.

"Speaking of, this entire restaurant is empty." Ashley wasn't done yet. "There are a dozen other tables where they can sit."

Amused, Ben looked from one to the other as though he were watching a volleyball game, and Ashley seemed to realize how she sounded when the door opened and an *Englisch* family came in, and then a whole bunch of old folks that took up the other part of the L-shaped restaurant. Waitresses emerged from the back as though a starting bell had rung.

Ashley rolled her eyes. "Fine. Sit. But don't expect me to throw out the welcome mat."

Ben slid in next to her, leaving the only empty seat next to Megan. Slowly, Sam settled into it, careful not to touch her.

"Your mom says to come in for a visit next time," she said to him.

Such casual words. Such a bomb in his gut.

He drew in a breath at the unexpected pain, as fine and sudden as a sliver when you thought the wood was smooth. "I can't," he said before he could stop himself.

"Why not?" she asked. "If we can, there's nothing stopping you. At least you know you're their kid."

He had to turn the topic back on her in self-defense. Never would he have dreamed that they'd just plunge right in like this. Speak the unspeakable in flat *Englisch* tones. "Don't you know?"

124

"No, we don't," Ashley said, studying the menu the way he had studied for the driver's exam. "We have no proof of any of it, except Megan and her weirdness about wood stoves and falling into hay holes."

"My sister *did* fall in the hay hole," Samuel told her. "She wasn't very old. Dat had just got done pitching down the hay."

"Yep, heard that story already." Ashley turned the menu over.

"That wasn't the only time." Why were his jaws flapping when all he wanted to do was eat and drive away? "She fell in the silage bin too."

"Which is a what, now?" Ashley appeared utterly absorbed in the omelette section.

"Silage is chopped-up cornstalks—what's left over after the corn is harvested. It goes in a giant bin in the barn and gets mixed with sprouts in the winter. Lots of nutrients in sprouts." Ben stopped talking and glanced up as the waitress rejoined them.

The girls ordered waffles. Sam and Ben got biscuits and gravy, and a top-up on the coffee. And all the while, Sam struggled with the waves of memory that wouldn't stop. When the waitress left, he could have changed the subject. But he didn't.

"Hannah was running after me when I threw an armload of sprouts down into the mixer. She didn't see the edge coming and overbalanced. It was a six-foot drop in there, probably."

"And it was full of cornstalks and bean sprouts?" Megan asked.

"And the mixing blades. Luckily you fell right between the flanges. Scared Dat half to death, though. It was probably a month before he'd let you back in the barn. And I got a walloping for not taking better care of you."

"Not her," Ashley reminded him. "Your little sister who isn't here. Hannah."

"Right. Hannah."

"Except it *was* me, Ash," Hannah said slowly, gazing across the table at a girl who wouldn't meet her eyes. "I have nightmares about it to this day. A big, dark space that smells, and tall walls I can't climb."

"It's still there," Ben offered.

"Oh, great," Ashley said angrily. "Are you going to push her in and help her get over her phobia? Banish the nightmares?"

"Of course not," Ben replied calmly. "But what if it is the same one?"

"I'm asking the questions."

"And is it helping?"

"It's helping me see this is stupid. Next you're going to say she fell out of a tree picking apples and she'll immediately remember she did. It's called *false memory*, people. And it's as common as repressed memories."

"Says the psych expert who hasn't actually taken a class," Megan said.

"I have a mind," Ashley shot back. "And I read books. Unlike some people."

"Do you two always fight like this?" Ben asked.

"Who's fighting?" Megan said. "We're having a conversation."

"Oh. Sorry. Go on, before someone calls the sheriff."

"Very funny," Ashley said with an eyeroll. "I'm just saying, memory is unreliable. Look at us. Until this week, we thought we had a whole set of memories we didn't actually have. Case in point: pictures that weren't even of us. Or Megan, anyway."

"Pictures?" Samuel managed. Lots of *Englisch* homes had family pictures. No Amish house did—the *Ordnung* forbade graven images.

Megan nodded. "It turns out our folks lost a daughter before I came along. I always thought her baby pictures were of me. It was kind of a shock to find out the other day that they weren't. That it was somebody else." She turned her head to look out the window, her face going pale and a little bleak.

"And there weren't any of me at all," Ashley went on. "Which should have been our first clue. But who looks at pictures on the wall?"

"Before you came along?" Samuel said carefully. That didn't sound right. Most people said that when they meant a baby was coming along. But Megan had chosen those words.

"Mom told us a pretty weird story. That she and Dad found us in the woods, all starving and dressed in rags, and took us home. She named me after the girl who died. Megan."

"Starving? Dressed in rags?" The amusement drained out of Ben's gaze. "But everybody knows you disappeared one afternoon. It's not like you were wandering around for days, lost in the woods, before you ran into these folks."

Megan shrugged. "It doesn't matter. What matters is that our mom had a nervous breakdown and the whole story came out a couple of days ago. So we came here to see if—" Megan choked up.

"To see if we could find anyone who remembered the story," Ashley filled in. "And we did, in the Amish Market." She waved a hand in its direction, and as if she'd been waiting for that signal, the waitress brought their meals over, two plates balanced on each arm.

Samuel's heart was beating so hard he thought it might drub right through his chest. "Who told you?" He was hungry, but now he picked up his fork and wondered if his dry mouth would let him eat.

"Some doctor lady. She was selling herbs and creams and stuff out of a booth."

"Oh, Sarah Byler. The *Dokterfraa*." Sarah was in touch with everyone in the district. No wonder the kid at work had known practically the moment they'd driven in. By now every family in both church districts would know his sisters had come home.

And then what?

"So this lady—the lady who found you in the woods— she knew who you were and told you?"

"No," Ashley said as though he had said something stupid. "She had no idea. She didn't even remember the name of this town, just that it had willows in it. I just said a minute ago that we came asking about the *story*. This Sarah person had heard it and directed us to your parents' farm. But that doesn't mean we're them—those girls. Your sisters. So far the only connection between them and us is what Megan remembers. And who knows if they're real memories? Half the time she lives in an alternate reality anyhow."

"I know when I'm gaming and when it's real life, Ash."

"I'm just saying." Ashley cut her waffles into neat squares, following the griddle lines.

Half of him wanted to believe these were his long-lost sisters, that they would stay *Englisch*, and in some weird way there would be at least part of his family who would accept him and love him even if he was a fence-jumper and unwilling and full of a disobedient, worldly spirit. The other half just wanted them to go away so that he didn't have to think about that afternoon so long ago, and of the way he'd felt growing up, and of the howling pain inside him every time his father's gaze fell on him and both of them remembered what he'd done.

Sometimes you couldn't go back. Did these girls know that? Did they have any idea what they were trying to reconnect with? What would be asked of them? Going to the farm on Red Bridge Road wasn't like checking into a motel. There were expectations.

The urge to run sent a tingle through his calves and feet. He shoveled down his biscuits and gravy and glanced at the clock above the serving window. "I've got to go."

Ben wiped his mouth and slid out of the booth. "We'll pick up the tab, ladies."

"Oh, no," Megan said. "We're splitting it. We don't even know you. Or at least, you know way more about us than we know about you."

"Then maybe we'll see you again." Ben was so smooth. You'd think he talked to girls every day.

"Maybe we will." Megan's gaze finally made it over to Samuel. "If you're our brother, we should, I guess."

If you're our brother. Samuel's knees wobbled, and he straightened his legs to hide it.

"Don't bowl him over with your enthusiasm," Ashley said. "It'll have to be tomorrow, though. We have to go home Sunday—I'm starting school," she told them. "College."

"Tomorrow's good," Samuel said. "Maybe we could take a drive up the mountain. To where it happened. See if you recognize anything."

"Don't humor her," Ashley said. "False memory, hello?"

"It's a good plan." Ben nodded. "The Glicks won't mind if we ramble through the orchard and hike up to the top." He hesitated. "So you're not staying?"

"What for?" Ashley was quick off the mark. "We've got no proof that we're the ones from here. Our mom could have meant some other place with willows in Pennsylvania—or any state around here, as far as that goes. But I just can't think about that. About talking to any other families with missing kids. Or the police. I am done."

"If we're not your sisters, there's no point in upsetting your family any more than they already are," Megan said slowly. "But I think we are. Maybe going up to the orchard—where you said—is a good idea. Maybe it'll jog something loose. Where should we meet?"

They made arrangements for the next morning—with so much emphasis on getting off the Riehl farm early that Ben finally made a joke about it.

"They get up at *four*," Megan told him, "and work and work and eat and work. We were lucky to get out of bread making today. I've never even *seen* bread being made. What would I do to help that Barbie doesn't know how to do with one hand tied behind her back?"

"It's Friday." Sam nodded. "Bread day." And Barbie was so good at housekeeping. Some girls had nice voices or sewed or had a knack for keeping the boys guessing. But Barbie's gift was making a home wherever she happened to be. She loved making bread and looking after chickens and singing songs out of Mamm's songbook while she did the dishes.

His heart squeezed with missing her.

As if Megan had read his mind, she said, "And Friday means volleyball and Sunday means singing. Sounds awful."

"You're going to singing?" Ben's brows disappeared up under his shaggy hair. "For true?"

"No," Ashley told him. "What's that face for?"

"I'd buy a ticket to see that," he said to Sam. "We should go."

"You're crazy." Go to singing? He didn't mean it. That would broadcast to the entire district that they'd both had a change of heart when they certainly hadn't. You didn't just go to singing for the entertainment. It meant something.

Megan looked from him to Ben. "We'll go to volleyball, though, if you go. At least I can do that."

"We will not!" Ashley said.

"I heard there was a hoedown at Young Abe Kurtz's place in Whinburg," Ben said. "We could go to that instead. We'd fit in better, anyhow. I got rid of all my Amish clothes."

"A hoedown," Megan repeated. "What's that? Banjos and knee-slappers and pappy's good moonshine?"

Ben snorted. "More like a boombox in a barn with beer."

"That doesn't sound very Amish."

"It's a *Rumspringe* thing. What kids do when they're running around," Sam explained. "Or some kids, anyway. I'd go. At singing, or even volleyball, it's different. They … expect different things from you."

"I'll say," Ben agreed. "If you go to singing, you might as well take out an ad in *Die Botschaft* saying you're coming back to church."

"Oh." Ashley and Megan exchanged a glance. "The boombox and beer it is, then."

Whether they were his sisters or not, Samuel couldn't help but smile. He hadn't had anything to look forward to on a Friday night for a long, long time.

"We'll pick you up at eight in the parking lot of the Hex Barn in Whinburg." He gave them directions, and hoped they'd understand what he couldn't say—that he couldn't come to the farm to get them. "And keep it quiet, okay? What you're doing?"

"I'm not going to tell anyone I'm going to a hoedown, believe me." Megan checked her phone's charge, wound up the cord, and put it in her pocket. "And plus, sounds like you don't want the family knowing your business."

"You could say that. If I went to the farm, it would just cause a bunch of trouble, and if Dat knew you were coming with us instead of doing what they wanted, well, it wouldn't be good."

"Is he angry with you?" Ashley asked. "For not joining the family business?"

"Maybe some," Sam said slowly. "Disappointment makes folks angry, I guess. And he's been disappointed in me since—"

But that was way too much to confess to two girls who might be his sisters, or who might not. Instead, he turned away and got in the car, leaving Ben to say good-bye.

11

By the time they left the restaurant it felt like half the day had gone, but according to Megan's phone, it was still only nine in the morning. It wasn't until the old red beater that Sam drove pulled out onto the highway that Megan realized they should have gone to see the orchard now, not tomorrow.

Too late. There was nothing left but a cloud of blue exhaust, and in a second even that blew away.

"I'm glad we have somewhere to be tomorrow morning, even if it's a stupid place." Ash climbed into the driver's seat of the Subaru, and held out her hand for the keys. "Rebecca didn't say what Saturday was, and I'm afraid to ask."

"Cow washing day?" Megan wondered. "Hog calling day?"

"Chicken picking day!" Ashley cracked herself up.

Megan smiled too, only because they hardly ever laughed together. Of course, when you saw someone for maybe ten minutes in the course of a week, it was hard to laugh with her. And between her boyfriend and her ambition, there wasn't much room left over for giggling and being goofy like they used to.

"Where to?" Ash asked, gazing across the parking lot. "The Amish Market is probably the only thing open. These people really believe in the early bird, don't they?"

"I'm good with the Amish Market. We can go back to the farm after lunch. Maybe the bread will be done by then. I want to take some pictures in daylight anyway."

"What for?"

"Not to put up in the hallway at home, if that's what you're worried about."

"No. But the Amish are weird about cameras, right?"

"I'm not taking pictures of them. Just the neighborhood. Come on. Let's get going."

They moved the car out of the restaurant's parking space and over to the market's. The Amish Market was just as packed with stuff today as it had been yesterday—jars of jam, jars of fruit, jars of everything under the sun. Pies, cakes, cookies. Yard implements and kitchen stuff made of twisted iron. Leather things, from purses and wallets to reins and harnesses. The only difference was that today they had lots of time to look at it all.

Lots and lots of time.

And there was Sarah Yoder, the doctor-whatever, smiling in her booth as she recognized them. Megan cursed herself for not paying attention and avoiding this aisle.

"Hello again," Sarah greeted them, her gray eyes shining and her smile so open that Megan wondered what she'd done to make her look so happy. "I didn't expect to see you so soon. Did you find the farm?"

Megan nodded. "You give good directions."

"I've lived here a fair while." She reached out and Megan realized a man was standing behind them. He was a tall, thin guy with a studious-looking face and long, sensitive hands, wearing a blue shirt that matched the color of Sarah's dress. "Hannah, Leah, this is my husband, Henry Byler."

"Nice to meet you. Folks around here call me *Englisch* Henry." He shook their hands while Megan got her mouth working again.

"Why did you call us that?" she asked Sarah. "We never said our names before."

"It's all over the settlement that the Riehl girls have come home," Henry said. "Are you all right? Did it go okay?"

He had kind of a Midwestern accent—not Amish. Either he'd been out west a long time, or he'd grown up English. He didn't say his *O*s the same, and the lilting cadence that she supposed came from Pennsylvania Dutch was completely missing.

"Were you English too?" Megan blurted. "Is that why they call you *Englisch* Henry?"

"Gack, Megan," Ashley muttered. "I'll see you around. I can't take it."

The Amish couple watched as Ashley bolted down the aisle and disappeared around a corner stall selling pot holders made to look like chickens.

"Did I say something to offend her?" Henry looked worried, his kindly face wrinkling between his brows and the corners of his mouth pulling down. He still held his wife's hand.

"No, it was me," Megan admitted. "She didn't want to come here in the first place and … your wife called us by those Amish names and she's not ready to accept the possibility that they might be ours."

"Ach, neh," Sarah said in falling tones that clearly meant she blamed herself for upsetting Ash.

"You were serious—everyone knows about it?" Megan asked.

Henry nodded. "When you came in just now, the word flashed through here like wildfire. I expect the Riehls will be inundated with visitors this weekend."

"Is that what they do on Saturdays?" Megan said, only half wanting to know. "Today is bread day, apparently, but Rebecca didn't say what Saturday was."

"Saturday is where you catch up on everything you didn't get done the rest of the week," Sarah said with a smile. "And you get ready for Sunday, when there is no work being done. There are never enough hours in the day."

"I don't see how, when it starts at four a.m." Megan gazed at the bustling market and wondered how early all of these people got up. "I'm ready to go to bed again and it's not even ten o'clock."

Henry chuckled. "You get used to it. But things do take longer without electricity."

"Like laundry," Sarah said. "My boys fitted up the washer so it runs on a generator and propane, but when I had the wringer, washing clothes took all day."

Megan couldn't even imagine. She'd seen a wringer washer in one of those old movies on TCM, but she couldn't see how in the heck they worked. If Rebecca had one, and expected them to help with laundry, they were definitely leaving on Sunday.

Before church.

"Well," she said awkwardly, "I guess I'd better go find my sister. Nice talking to you."

Henry bent closer, as though he wanted to say something private. "I was *Englisch* for twenty years," he said quietly. "I know there's probably a lot that seems confusing right now, but I've been on both sides of the fence. If you or your sister ever want to talk, Sarah and I are sure willing to listen."

He dug in his pocket and pulled out a business card.

HENRY BYLER
NATURAL FORM POTTERY
WILLOW CREEK, PA
(768) 555-0827

"You have a phone?"

He grinned, and Megan suddenly got a clue why Sarah might have fallen in love with a man who clearly had what novels called *a past*. "Out in my studio, because that's where I work. For business use only."

"Right. Thanks." She tucked it in the back pocket of her jeans. The odds of her calling and asking for advice were low, but at the same time, it had been nice of him to offer to help, out of the blue like that.

She said good-bye and wandered off in search of Ashley. In her experience, people didn't just reach out unless they wanted something in return. But it wasn't likely that an Amish potter and an herbalist would want a single thing from her.

Nobody did. Ever, really.

Except Rebecca.

Megan passed a big corner booth that held a kaleidoscope of gorgeous colors and patterns. Quilts hung on all three walls, and were neatly folded and piled high on the counter. She halted as though she'd run into one, staring, her mouth falling open.

She knew the Amish quilted, from some PBS special she'd seen years ago. And there were the quilts on the beds at the Riehl farm. But she didn't know they quilted like *this*, in shimmering, complicated patterns that hung next to plainer ones like the Nine-Patch, the only pattern she knew on sight.

This wasn't quilting. This was art. Amazing, mind-boggling art.

"Are you interested in quilting?"

Megan dragged her gaze off the one on the side wall, whose little tag said *Blooming Nine-Patch*. It didn't look a bit like the Nine-Patch on her bed. It looked like something out of a Moorish palace.

"Sorry?"

The woman behind the counter was one of the most beautiful Megan had ever seen—and without makeup, that was saying something. The ribbons of the prayer covering over her dark hair fell on her chest, tied in a bow at the ends, and her dress was a deep burgundy.

"You looked as though you might be a quilter." The woman nodded at the Blooming Nine-Patch. "My daughter made that one. You'd be surprised how easy it is, and how fast it goes together. The hardest part is choosing the fabrics so that they blend and contrast at the same time."

"How old is your daughter?" Megan asked in amazement. The woman couldn't be forty yet.

"She is sixteen."

Megan shook her head in disbelief, still feeling a little breathless as she took in that quilt's beauty. "Three years younger than me, and she can make something like that?" She couldn't help it—her gaze was sucked back to the pattern again and again.

"She has been sewing since she was old enough to hold a needle and not poke herself with it. I thank God daily that we share a love of sewing. Some, like my friend Sarah Byler, do it not from love, but because otherwise they would have nothing to wear."

"Sarah, the Doctor—" What was the word? "Frah?"

The woman's brows went up in delight. "You know Sarah, our *Dokterfraa*?"

"I was just talking to her. The herbalist, right?"

The woman extended a hand. Unlike her face, which was lovely and unlined, her hand was rough and strong with hard work. "*Ja.* I am Evie Troyer."

"Megan Pearson."

The woman squeezed her hand and let it go. "You are staying at Jonathan and Rebecca's farm?"

Oh, come on. Despite what Henry Byler had said a minute ago, how was it possible that, without cell phones or the Internet, everyone could know so fast?

"Yes," she said reluctantly. "How did you know?"

"Sarah told me," she said simply. "But my husband is the bishop of this district, so it is his business to know of things that may affect his flock."

"You can tell him not to worry. I don't plan on affecting anything." Megan glanced in both directions down the aisle, but Ashley was nowhere in sight. How did she, Megan, get to be the one fielding all the questions from the Amish folks? "I don't even know if we're the ones who got lost years ago. We're just here to see if we can find out anything."

"God will show you the way," Evie said with such quiet conviction that Megan almost believed her. "Are you staying long?"

"Just until Sunday. My sister starts college next week and we have to get back."

"Will you come to church with Jonathan and Rebecca?"

"Probably not—we—um—"

"If you're still here, maybe you might come for a visit on Sunday," Evie went on as though Megan hadn't been standing there stammering like a goof. "The quilting frame is down because we have visitors, but Sallie would be happy to show you the one she's got going in her room upstairs. She's piecing it up there so her little brothers and sisters don't run away with the fabric to make things of their own."

Temptation pulled at Megan. "I don't think we'll be here on Sunday, but I sure would like to know how she does it. It looks so complicated."

"Looks are deceiving, and many things are much simpler than they seem to be," Evie told her, adjusting a pile of folded quilts that looked perfectly straight to Megan. "It's we humans that complicate things, don't we? But God sees the pattern."

Megan didn't quite know what to say to that. "I see my sister," she lied hastily. "Please tell your daughter—"

"Sallie."

"—Sallie that I think she does beautiful work."

"I will. Maybe if you come back for a visit, she could show you, so you could make one of your own."

A quilt like that would take her a month to learn and a year to make, and there was zero chance of that happening.

"Good-bye," Megan said over her shoulder as she escaped down the nearest aisle that led to the door. Out in the sun, she made her way over to the parking lot and saw Ashley leaning on the Subaru, on the phone.

Megan bet herself a whoopie pie that she was talking to Keenan. Then, because Ash was *always* talking to Keenan, she bought the whoopie pie from the Amish woman in a little stand outside in the parking lot and congratulated herself on winning the bet.

She walked slowly toward the car, her mind's eye unable to look away from that quilt. A sixteen-year-old had made a beautiful piece of art. Megan's chest felt muffled, as though there were a weight pressing on it. *It's not fair!* a little voice whined inside her. If she had not been stolen away, she could have been making quilts like that too. She could have had some kind of purpose to her life instead of running to her game console to be someone else, to take up a quest programmed by some geek in Silicon Valley, just to have a reason to exist.

Then again, there was more to being Amish than quilting. There was never getting to put on a pair of jeans again, and covering up your hair with a prayer cap. (Did they sleep in them?) And going to church and driving a horse and buggy and never flipping a light switch and handing over your phone and basically falling off the planet altogether.

Yeah, there was that. Samuel hadn't been able to hack it, and he'd been brought up in it. What chance did a normal person have if they were insane enough to try?

"I don't know," she heard Ashley say to Keenan. "We've committed to one more day, so definitely Sunday. All I know is I can't wait to get out of here. The longer we stay, the more fake memories Megan dredges up. Personally, the *last* thing I want is to find out we *are* the Riehls' kids. Because then what?"

Good question.

If they weren't, they'd just drive away, no harm, no foul, except for a lingering regret that they'd gotten poor Rebecca's hopes up for nothing.

If they were...

"What do you mean, a DNA test? Are you nuts? Test who?" A pause. "Keenan, there is no way an Amish person is going to go to a doctor for that. Are you kidding me? I don't even know if their religion lets them go to doctors at all." Another pause. "Because I'm humoring her. She thinks she's going to see something that brings back all the memories and proves we're the ones. It never occurs to her that I'd have the same memories, right? And so far there's a big old blank there, like there is with any little kid. I mean, what's the earliest thing you remember?"

Megan leaned on the fender of someone's bosso Dodge Ram and tried not to feel hurt that her own sister thought she was making all this up. She'd heard about that silage mixer and nearly fallen through the hay hole. Her memories of those two things were real. Hadn't she been having nightmares about them her whole childhood? They had to have come from somewhere, and what Samuel had said about the silage mixer had been so vivid it was like stepping right back into the dream.

"Okay, so you were three. I don't remember anything from when I was three. Kids don't, Keenan. My first memory is getting lost at Playland in some little town we lived in, and the next one is trying to write my name in kindergarten."

They'd both gone to kindergarten. Hadn't they? Didn't every little kid? But Megan had no memories of it. Aside from the nightmares, being a little kid was a complete blank. Though she did remember Playland. There had been a huge plaster clown at the gate and she'd gone into hysterics at having to walk through its stomach to get into the park. Her dad had had to carry her, screaming the whole way, until she realized it wasn't real and walking through his insides didn't mean he'd eaten her.

She'd been a weird kid. The oddest things scared her to death. Like the talking doll she'd got for Christmas. That was a mistake her parents hadn't made a second time. To this day she didn't like things that had faces, but weren't alive—that just pretended to be human, to be real. Like clowns. She shuddered.

It was odd that she lived for gaming, then, wasn't it? Because none of those people were human, or real. Maybe it was different when she saw something on a screen versus being able to touch it.

Ashley had turned and seen her, lost in thought. "I've got to go, Keenan. See you on Monday. I love you."

She tapped off her phone and Megan straightened. "How's Keenan?"

"He's fine. He misses me."

"He thinks we should get DNA tests? Seriously?"

Ashley looked at her through her bangs. "Eavesdropping is so rude."

Megan only shrugged. "It sucks that he's right. That's the only way we'll know for sure."

Ashley shaded her eyes as Megan joined her, and together they leaned on the hood of the Subaru. "What good will it do?" she asked. "If we are their kids, we're still not going to stay here and live Amish ever after. And if we're not, same result. I don't see the point."

"But we'd know it's true, what Mom and Dad did."

"We already know that, unless you think that Mom's walking out into traffic and trying to kill herself twice was just for our entertainment." She choked, and cleared her throat. "So yes, they took us from our bio parents. What we don't know is whether we're the Riehl kids, or someone else's."

"Ha. Listen to you. The real kids," Megan repeated. "R-E-A-L."

Her sister pushed herself off the fender and opened the driver's door. "Real or not, it's not changing my plans for my life. I'm still going to college next week, still dating Keenan, still having to pay off a student loan co-signed by Mom and Dad after I graduate."

Megan gazed at her. "How come you know what you're doing with your life, and I just feel like I'm acting in mine?"

She expected Ash to blow her off like she always did, with a smart-mouth remark and a roll of her eyes. But maybe there was something in the air here, or in the fields all around them with horses pulling farm equipment and the clip-clop of hooves going by as yet another gray buggy took an Amish family to town. Real things. Earthy things, that simply were. No fakes.

Whatever the case, Ashley paused to give her question actual consideration. "I don't know. I've always known I was going to college. Remember how I wanted to be a vet? And that Hallowe'en I dressed up in one of Dad's lab coats and carried your weird stuffed animal with the long tail? But then in high school, I decided on psychology. To learn why people do the things they do." Her gaze settled on Megan, a little frown between her brows. "I don't know why we're so different when we had the same upbringing. Especially since you graduated, I couldn't figure out why you just hung around, like you were afraid to leave, or you were waiting for something. But I didn't know what, and you didn't seem to, either."

Megan nodded as the truth of it sank into her chest, where the pressure seemed to lift a little. "Maybe I was waiting for this. Coming back. Not acting anymore, but being … real."

Ashley's mouth moved, as though she'd been about to say something and changed her mind. What came out instead was, "And if you find what you were waiting for? What then?"

The question of the day, it seemed. Megan shoved off the fender and walked around to the passenger side, gazing at her sister over the hot metal roof. "I think I need to talk to Sam. Like, really talk. If I can. If he'll let me."

Ash nodded and slid in behind the wheel. "If you must. All we have to do is get through the rest of today, and you'll have your chance tonight. I suppose we'd better go back and see if bread-making is done. And then who knows what joy will be in store?"

They'd probably have to pay for skipping out on the bread. But first, Megan wanted to ask how far away the Troyers lived, and whether Barbie was friends with Sallie the teenage quilter.

12

The athletic bags still upstairs in their room reassured Rebecca that the girls were coming back, but she had no idea where they had gone. The children had come back from Orland's, as Ruthie had taken them all to town to get school supplies for next week, and still no sign of the girls. She did her best to push down the hurt at their abrupt departure—no, at what had come before that. At the unwillingness to be a part of her life for even one day, she who had prayed without ceasing every day that they'd been gone.

But that was pride raising its ugly head, wasn't it—pride thinking that anything she did was worthy of note. God had brought them back again because it was His will, not because of anything she had done. She needed to have faith that the One who had loved them back had a plan for them after that. She needed to be patient until He revealed it to them ... and to be willing even if He did not.

THE LONGEST ROAD

With a glance at the unlit lamp in its place on the sill, she slid the last of the bread out of the oven and set it on the counter. The kitchen smelled of freshly baked bread, and so did the yard, too, probably, for Barbie had opened all the windows. It was so warm that the bread was in no danger of cooling too fast.

Rebecca kept one eye on Katie, outside with the twins in the garden. That little *Maedel* was a budding *Dokterfraa*, endlessly fascinated by what could be eaten and what couldn't, by what had a useful purpose and what didn't. Now that the excitement of new pencils and scribblers was over, she and the boys were examining something in the lawn, no doubt deep in a philosophical discussion about why growing inside the garden made something a weed, while outside it wasn't.

Rebecca would tell her someday that it wasn't where the plant took root that made it a weed, but its nature.

What about her first child, who had left them of his own free will? Would Samuel return to the garden some day, and submit himself to the pruning and discipline of God's loving hand? Or would he be content to live like a weed, always blowing before the wind, the fruit of his spirit wizening and rotting for lack of good fertilizer and care?

And what of Hannah and Leah? Always, her thoughts circled back to them. They did not even know they could bear fruit—that they were the seedlings of a heritage of good harvests that fed the hearts of an entire community.

But allowing her thoughts to travel that familiar path did no good. For all too close to the side of the path was a deep chasm of questions, and once her pride tempted her into questioning God's will, there was no climbing out, and she would not put poor Jonathan's faithful heart through that again.

The crunching of soft tires in the gravel told her that the girls had come back at last. She allowed herself a long breath of relief, but that was all.

The children ran to meet them, and the whole flock of them came in at once, chattering and laughing, even Hannah and Leah. Rebecca's heart yearned over Hannah, who didn't seem to laugh much. Even now, it looked as though she was doing it because little Katie expected her to, not because it was spontaneous.

Her eyes met Rebecca's, and Rebecca's soul flew out to meet hers, aching to wrap itself around her lost lamb. "Would you like some fresh bread and honey?" she asked.

"It smells like heaven in here," Hannah said, nodding. "Thanks."

Rebecca cut slices of her good whole wheat bread, which she was thankful had not come out heavy, and set butter and honey on the table so everyone could take as much as they liked. Though the children had had lunch at their aunt's, you'd think they hadn't had anything since the day before, the way they slathered honey on the bread and stuffed it in their mouths.

"Saul," she said quietly in *Deitsch*. "Not so fast."

"I'm hungry!"

"Be a good example."

"No!" he said thickly, his mouth full. "I'm hungry—I want more."

She gazed at him, her little man who had the spirit of an unbroken horse. But it must be broken, for his own sake. A disobedient child was a miserable child, for how could he know how to manage himself and navigate the world unless she loved him enough to help him learn?

"I do not want to ask you to fetch my hairbrush in front of your sisters," she said. "Is that what you want?"

"*Neh,*" he said in a small voice, and reluctantly put his bread on his plate until he had finished the bite.

"*Gut.*" Her smile held all the warmth of a summer day, and he relaxed back to his normal sweet self, the one who didn't need to show off with defiance in front of company. Discipline gave her no pleasure—in fact, she hated having to do it. But her duty was to guide these little souls into the love of God, and if they did not learn obedience from their parents, how would they ever be able to submit to the God of Heaven?

"Did you enjoy your day?" she asked Leah, who was on her second piece of bread, and who had been behind the wheel of the car just now.

She nodded, and when she could speak around the mouthful, she said, "We had breakfast at the café in Willow Creek with Sam and his friend Ben."

Rebecca's heart gave a great thump, the way it did when someone startled her. "Samuel? You met him again?"

"Yes, by accident. They came in after we did."

"And he's well?"

"Far as I can tell." And Ashley distracted herself licking a runnel of honey off the palm of her hand.

"They've invited us to go for a drive tonight," Hannah said, "so I guess Barbie is off the hook for volleyball."

Barbie looked disappointed at this news, her shoulders drooping. "I thought you might like to come."

Rebecca passed her the raspberry jam, which she preferred to honey. "I did, too, but never mind. If they are with Samuel and Ben, it's all right."

She hardly knew whether it was or it wasn't. Her instinct was to keep them close, so that nothing could be allowed to happen to them ever again. But on the other hand ... for her three eldest children to become acquainted again was *wunderbar*. A miracle. And the fact that they had run into one another by accident, given all the places that Samuel could have been on a Friday morning, was nothing less than the hand of God at work once again, weaving the threads of his plan into something beautiful.

"Where is Samuel taking you?" Barbie asked. "Are you going in his car? Is he coming here to pick you up?"

"The point of a drive is not to know where you're going," Hannah told her with a smile and a glance at Leah. "And no, he's not coming here. He had stuff to do. We're meeting him in town. Which reminds me—Barbie, do you know a girl called Sallie whose dad is the ... bishop?"

She said the word as though it were in *Deitsch*, not English.

"*Ja*, sure," Barbie said a little blankly. "Everybody knows everybody here. Why?"

"Well, um—"

Was she blushing? What could bring the blood to her cheeks like that other than shame ... or a boy?

"I wondered if you were friends. Like, if they wouldn't mind if you took me over there, maybe this afternoon." Hannah looked so uncomfortable that Rebecca wondered what was going on.

"You want to see the bishop?" Barbie's eyebrows had gone so high in astonishment that her *Kapp* moved a little backward on her head.

"No, not the bishop—her. Sallie. The quilter. Her mom invited me to see a quilt she's working on."

Leah put down her bread to gape at her sister as though she'd suggested running naked down the highway. "A quilt? Who are you and what have you done with my sister Megan?"

Hannah's face clouded over as though a storm had rained on her. "Geesh, make a big deal much? Forget I said anything." She pushed away from the table.

But Barbie was faster. She jumped up as though they might go right away. "If you only want to see Sallie, sure, we could go. She's my best friend, and it's only a mile or two away. Can we, Mamm?"

Rebecca was still recovering from the yawning gap between *going for a drive with Samuel* and *going to the bishop's house to see a quilt*. "I—well—"

"Can we take the market wagon?"

"It doesn't fit three very comfortably, and I don't want Leah riding on the step."

"My name is Ashley. And I'm not going," Leah said immediately. "I'm okay with staying here. I brought some reading anyway. Or," she said belatedly and a little reluctantly, "I could help you with something."

"We can take the car," Hannah protested. "We don't need to go to all the trouble of a horse and buggy."

"A car? To the bishop's house?" Barbie looked so scandalized that Rebecca smothered a smile. "It's no trouble. Mamm and I take it to town all the time. I can show you how to drive."

"I'd say I'd return the favor, except you're Amish," Hannah said. "If you're sure…"

Barbie looked at Rebecca with pleading in her eyes, and Rebecca couldn't find it within herself to say no, though the tomatoes waited there on the counter to be blanched, and supper had to be started soon.

Yet … Hannah was interested in quilting. Still, after all this time. Rebecca needed some quietness, to ponder this in her heart. "*Ja*, you may go," she said at last. "If you see the bishop, give him our greetings. And be back in an hour, so that your father does not have to wait for his dinner."

"I will. Come on, Hannah."

The *Englisch* girl didn't correct her on her name.

*

After they had gone, and Melinda and Katie had taken the twins out to the field with a cold drink and some turnovers for their father, Rebecca cleared the table and wiped it down.

Leah lingered, pushing in the chairs and leaning over the bread to breathe in its scent as it cooled. "Can I help you with the dishes?"

"You don't have to, but that would be *gut*." Rebecca felt like bouncing on her toes for joy, but that would probably scare the girl into the next township, so she reined herself in and settled for a smile. "Many hands make light work."

Leah remembered where the drain tray and rack were from the night before, and got them out without direction. Once Rebecca had hot water running into the sink, she began to wash the silverware, her happiness at having this time alone overflowing into music. She began to hum one of the songs from her book.

"Is that ... 'Country Roads'?" Leah asked in astonishment. "How do you know that old clunker?"

"Do you know it?"

"I hear it once in a while on the oldies station my parents listen to. It surprises me that you would."

"When I was a girl," Rebecca said, "I belonged to one of the faster gangs up in Intercourse—"

"Gangs?"

"Not like that. Not like they have in cities. It is what we call groups of friends of a similar age. They have names like the Woodpeckers and the Bluebirds, and some are faster than others."

"Faster how?"

Rebecca struggled to put into words what every Amish teenager knew. "Well, if the boys race their buggies on the roads late at night and the girls don't sew strings on their *Kapps*, or if they go to see movies when they think nobody is watching, they're said to be fast. Just on the far side of complete obedience to the *Ordnung*."

"What's that?"

"It means discipline. The order of life. The tenets we live by."

"Oh. So okay, you ran with a fast crowd. See? We use that word, too. But John Denver? That doesn't seem fast to me."

Rebecca chuckled. "It all depends on what you're used to, I suppose. To us, any song from the radio is worldly, but we liked this one. Because of the country roads leading home, you know. We Amish can appreciate that. Will you sing it with me?"

And without waiting for a reply, Rebecca glanced at the words open on the sill as a refresher, and began to sing. After a moment, Leah joined in, but after the chorus, their two melodies began to diverge when they got to the verses.

"That's not how it goes," Leah protested, and sang the tune much faster, and different from the way Rebecca had learned it years ago.

She'd learned it third-hand, so that wasn't surprising. So she grabbed this opportunity to accept a gift from her daughter who wouldn't admit who she was, and committed the modified tune to memory.

"Thank you," she said, laughing, as she finished the song with the same rhythm and in the same key as Leah. "This has been quite the music lesson. I guess I'll have to climb down off my high horse now, won't I? I was a little too proud of my singing—and for no reason, it seems, since it has been wrong all this time. But that is the way of pride, isn't it?"

Leah had stopped drying the glass, and was staring at her. Then she seemed to recover, and said, "You'll have to listen to the radio so you can hear it for yourself."

Still smiling, Rebecca shook her head. "Not much likelihood of that, unless I am driving somewhere in an *Englisch* taxi. The man we often call keeps it tuned to the news and the stock reports. But I'll remember, and teach Barbie to sing it properly so that when she goes to singing, she can teach the others."

And if Leah left and never came back, at least these few notes of the song would remain, and be passed on to her children and to their friends. Something of her would go on.

Leah put the glass in the cupboard and picked up another one from the drain rack. "Can I ask you something?"

"I hope you will. Anything. And I will tell you anything you want to know."

"What does that mean—get off your high horse?"

Well, that was the last thing she'd expected. "It is something we say when someone is struggling with *hochmut*—being haughty, putting themselves above other people. It comes from long ago, when only the rich and powerful could afford horses, and expected the poor people to look up to them."

Leah polished her glass, put it away, and gazed at the ones that remained.

Rebecca waited.

"Do you really think we're your children?"

Every cell in her body yearned to take this girl in her arms and hug her to her heart. Her arms trembled with the need to do it, but she did not. Instead, she got started on the dirty plates.

"I do, *ja*. You have Mammi Kate's brown eyes, but your sister's eyes and Samuel's are like mine, as blue as speedwell. But there is more to it than that."

"Is there?"

"Your faces have changed, of course, and your voices. You don't remember any of our language, that you used to speak so fluently. But every now and again..."

"What?"

"Your sister," Rebecca said slowly, "being so interested in quilts. Has she always been that way?"

"Not that I ever saw. She doesn't even have a bedspread on her bed, just a blanket. The only thing she cares about is computer games."

"And yet, the little girl I taught to sew loved them. The patterns, the colors … she would lay out the little scrap patches on the floor until the pattern pleased her, and then sew them all together with used basting thread that I would save for her. It wasn't any pattern I ever saw, just her own. I kept one of them in my hope chest. I didn't have the heart to throw it away."

"What about your second daughter?"

It broke Rebecca's heart that she did not say, *What about me?*

"My Leah," she said with a smile, remembering. "She loved the poultry. She would follow me out to the barn every morning to let the birds out into the yard, and collected the eggs so carefully in her apron. Little ones, you know, have a hard time holding onto eggs, so you have to give them a basket. But she treated each one as if it were something precious, and never dropped one. I would find her out in the yard time after time, just sitting in the grass with the birds pecking all around her, as though she were one of them."

The young woman frowned. "Lots of people like chickens."

"That is true. I do, myself. But I never had the heart to tell her where her chicken and dumplings came from for supper, or the chicken noodle soup she loved so much."

Leah actually took a step away from her. "You mean you're going to eat those chickens I saw out there?"

"Of course, eventually." Why did she look so shocked, so appalled? "Everything on this farm has a job to do, and once the hens stop laying regularly, their job is to provide food for our family."

"Oh, no." Gripping the last drinking glass, Leah turned in a circle, for all the world like a hen trying to escape the fate she sensed was coming. "You're not going to kill one while I'm here, are you?"

"No," Rebecca said slowly. "Not if you don't want me to. There is plenty to eat at this time of year without it."

Leah drew a deep breath and seemed to be telling herself to calm down.

"This is a farm," Rebecca said gently. "We raise as much food as we can right here. I am sorry you didn't realize that." How far from the land she had gone, to a place where food came in neat plastic packages that had no real connection to plants and animals she had fed and raised?

"I wish you wouldn't kill them at all," Leah whispered. "It's horrible." Tears actually swam in her eyes—the soft brown eyes of a gentle girl whose tiny hands had been so careful with the eggs.

"I won't. Not while you're here. But you see what this means, my dear one?"

"What?" Leah gulped, as if trying to hold back a sob.

"This is exactly how my little Leah, my sweet, loving girl, would feel about her hens. I knew I would have to tell her one day. Perhaps I just did."

Abruptly, Leah put down the dishtowel, and with a single glance at Rebecca that felt more like a glare of betrayal, she pushed out of the kitchen door and ran down the back steps.

Rebecca didn't need to ask where she was going.

She could see her through the window, running for the enclosed hen yard as if she thought Jonathan might already be out there, the metal cone and the knife in his hands.

13

The horse's harness was probably the most complicated thing Megan had ever seen. None of it made sense, and yet when Barbie had backed the horse between the buggy's rails, her clever fingers reached right in, straightening straps and buckling them and before you knew it, the rig was ready to go.

"How do you remember all this?" she asked her. "I can't make heads or tails of it."

"You get used to it," Barbie said with a modest smile. "Can you roll the door closed behind me?"

That much she could do. For such a big door, it rolled surprisingly easily, and she jogged around to the left side of the buggy, put her foot on the step, and climbed in.

Barbie clicked her tongue to the horse, and they lurched and took off. Megan wriggled farther back in the seat in case that happened a lot. No point in getting whiplash. They went pretty slowly up the gravel drive, but when they turned left on Red Bridge Road, the horse picked up speed without Barbie even telling it to. The wind came in through both doors and beat gently on Megan's cheeks, pushing her hair back a little.

But under her *Kapp*, not a hair dared blow out of place on Barbie's head. No surprise there. So much competence in a sixteen-year-old was kind of hard to imagine.

"Do you want to try?" The girl lifted the reins to indicate what she meant, but Megan shook her head.

"Maybe on the way back." She'd ridden a horse a time or two, but never driven one. And how did you manage traffic lights and turns and other cars?

She soon had her answer. The buggy came with side mirrors, and she could see a couple of cars piling up behind them, waiting to pull out and pass. "Aren't you going to pull over?"

"They will pass when it's safe. I can't go over any farther or we'll be overturned in the ditch, and I don't want to be the one explaining to Dat how that happened."

Good point.

The driver gunned his engine with a roar and passed them, laying on the horn, and Megan couldn't help herself. "Idiot!" she hollered into the open passenger window as he went by.

"Feel better?" Barbie said mildly.

"No. But that was rude. Obviously you're doing the best you can."

"You get used to that, too. Most people are pretty polite, except sometimes the tourists will pace the buggy so they can take pictures."

No sooner had the words left her mouth than a van cruised up next to them, driving in the oncoming lane with all the windows lowered as someone with a giant telephoto lens aimed it at them. Over the sound of the engine and the rattle of the buggy wheels and the clip-clop of the horse's hooves, Megan could hear the shutter going, *click-click-click*, on automatic.

"Barbie? Is this all right with you?"

"*Neh*. We don't like it, but that won't stop them. Tourists take pictures of us all the time."

"But it's not safe. Look, he's pacing us. Hey!" she said loudly, over all the noise. "Get by before you cause an accident."

"Can you lean back? You're in my shot," the guy said.

Exactly the wrong thing to say. Megan leaned forward even more, waving her arms and making herself as big as she could. "I said, pass us before someone hits you!"

The driver hollered and punched the gas, and the camera guy nearly dropped his expensive equipment out the window as the van goosed ahead and swung in front of them. A farm truck roared by on the other side, its horn blaring. The van driver beat the camera guy on the shoulder as he accelerated away up the road.

"So much for peace and quiet," she said. "Does this happen all the time?"

"Not all the time." Barbie looked as though she was trying not to laugh. "Midnight and I just ignore them and I find something to look at that way—" She pointed to her right, where corn waved tall and green. "—so they get a nice picture of my *Kapp*."

"Next time, we give Midnight a break and take the car."

163

"All right. Meanwhile, don't get worked up about it. You can't control what other people do. Only what you do."

Megan said nothing, just sat back and attempted to enjoy the sunny afternoon. In about twenty minutes, Barbie pulled on the right-hand rein and they turned into a long drive. A mailbox with the name TROYER on it in black paint stood at the end, and a few feet away was a shack about the size of a phone booth. After a second Megan realized that was exactly what it was. A phone shanty, Rebecca had called it.

As they drew up in the yard, the front door opened and a girl came down the steps. Like Barbie, she wore a black kitchen apron, but unlike Barbie's dress, which was the yellow-green of new spring leaves, hers was a dark Lincoln green, like Robin Hood's doublet. Her *Kapp* was crisp white, its strings tied neatly at the ends.

She greeted them in English, which Megan hadn't expected. "Hallo! What brings you over this way?" She offered a hand to help Megan down.

Barbie jumped out the other side and tied the horse to the top rail of a white fence that ran between the yard and the biggest vegetable garden Megan had ever seen. It had to be twice the size of Rebecca's, and that was saying something.

Megan stuck out her hand. "I'm Megan," she said. "You must be Sallie. I met your mom in the Amish Market this morning."

The girl was beautiful, with the same dark brown hair and heart-shaped face as her mother. The only things that marred the perfection were a couple of zits on her chin. In a weird way, the zits made Megan feel better.

"Did you? Was she in the booth?"

Megan nodded, and Barbie joined them. "Hann—Megan saw your Blooming Nine-Patch and wanted to come over to see the one you have going."

Sallie's face lit up. "You're a quilter?"

If only! "Are you kidding? I've never sewn anything in my life. But I saw the one your mom has hung up in the booth and I just wondered … how hard it was. It looks hard. But she said it wasn't as complicated as it looked."

The girl shook her head, and motioned them toward the house. "It's just a lot of straight seams. If you can sew those, you can sew that quilt. *Kumm mit.* I'll show you."

"Where are the little ones?" Barbie asked as they climbed the stairs. "It's too quiet in here."

"Aendi Lovina took them for the day—one of their dogs just had puppies. It won't be quiet long. We're expecting Aendi Mariah and her family back from town any minute."

She showed them into a bedroom that had a set of bunk beds, pushed against the wall so that the floor was left open for a quilt top spread on a big sheet.

"Wow." Megan stared at the beginning of the quilt, which might have covered a twin bed. It looked like it was missing some of the outer rows. "Is this the middle of it?"

"*Ja.* I'm kind of stalled—I can't decide between two fabrics for the next two rows. Maybe you can help me."

She separated a couple of the rows, and suddenly Megan saw that it was constructed on the diagonal, not the horizontal. Sallie's mom hadn't been kidding—it wasn't nearly as complicated as it looked.

Sallie laid out the next rows around the pattern in the middle, and Megan nodded. "You're right. The two blues should be reversed with the pale green, so that the color fades toward the edges."

"But does it?" Barbie asked. She reversed the ones on her side. "Or does she want the final border to be darker, so it has a definite end—so that it looks closed?"

Sallie tilted her head to gaze at both sides, and squinted through her lashes. "I like Megan's way better. The eye will be drawn to the middle of the bed, where the darker colors begin, and as it fades toward the border, those lighter colors will be on the drops anyway."

"What if someone buys it to hang on the wall?" Barbie objected. "You know how some of the *Englisch* do."

"Then they'll have bought it because they like the fade," Megan told her. "No matter if the wall is light or dark, the pattern will still show really well."

"*Gut*, then," Sallie said, and a few minutes later she had laid out the rest of the rows on the top left corner. Megan even stepped out on a limb and helped on her end, nearest the door, while Sallie did the right side.

It looked amazing. Deceptively exotic, and so simple that Megan wondered how she hadn't figured it out before.

"How long will it take you to sew all these rows?" Megan asked. "Weeks? Months?"

The girl laughed, and even Barbara grinned. "Maybe until next weekend," she said. "Once you get going on these long rows, even with the old treadle it goes quickly."

"You use a *treadle* sewing machine?" Hadn't those gone out in like 1904? But wait—no power. As old-fashioned as a treadle machine seemed, sewing these long seams by hand surely couldn't be the alternative.

"Mamm's machine runs on compressed air. If you wanted, maybe you could come over some time and we could work on it together," Sallie said a little shyly. "You could use her machine and I'll use the treadle. I bet we could get the top pieced in a day."

"And I could run the rows back and forth to you," Barbie said. "One and one, then two and two, four and four ... you know. We could get it done in a day that way, for sure."

She must be nuts, about to reveal her complete ignorance to both these girls. But Megan plunged in regardless. "What about Sunday?" she said. "I could come over in the car."

"Oh no, not Sunday. We have church."

"It's an all-day thing," Barbie said. "We don't work on Sunday."

"Is this work?"

"*Ja*, it is. See how clean the house is?" Sallie said. "We had church here two weeks ago, and we spent weeks working to deep clean it. The men only finished painting the barn and the yard a couple of days before. Aendi Mariah and my cousins and I did the windows and the dusting, and my other auntie managed the children."

"How many little brothers and sisters do you have?" Megan asked. "It sounds like an army."

Sallie laughed. "It feels like an invasion sometimes. There are six. I'm the oldest—" She stopped as a flicker of pain crossed her pretty face. "Except for my brother Ben. He's the oldest, really."

"Ben?" Megan glanced at Barbie. "Not the Ben who was with Samuel last night?"

She nodded, the smile fading from her face, too. "Samuel jumped the fence first, and then Ben a few months later.

167

They got work in the same place, and now I think they're roommates."

"So you don't see your brother, either?" Megan asked Sallie.

She shook her head. "I wish I could. I miss him. But he and Dat always fight, and Mamm gets upset, and it hurts Dat when Mamm is hurt, and so ... he doesn't come."

"Ashley—my sister—we're going to a hoedown with them tonight. If you came with us, you could see him, couldn't you?"

Sallie's eyes widened. "Is that true?"

"Yes, of course it is. We met them by accident at breakfast and I told them we were going to volleyball, but they said that would mean expectations, and so then they invited us to this hoedown. I mean, it doesn't sound like much, but you should come."

"Where is it?" Barbie's voice dropped, as though she thought someone might be listening in the stairwell.

Megan had to think for a second. "Abe somebody. No, Young Abe somebody."

"There are a lot of Young Abes," Barbie pointed out. "A lot of old ones, too."

"Young Abe Kurtz, I bet," Sallie said. "He owns that farm over east of Whinburg and has no wife to settle him down."

"That was it," Megan told her. "Young Abe Kurtz. So will you come?"

"I don't know ..." The rekindled light went out of Sallie's face again. "Not a hoedown. Mamm would never let me go. Dat is the bishop, and it wouldn't look good."

"But you'd go to singing."

"That's totally different. And a lot closer. It's just at Millers, and I can walk there and back."

"Or just there ... and drive home with Simon Yoder," said Barbie to no one in particular, looking with great interest at something out the window.

"Simon Yoder is a flirt and nobody in her right mind would go anywhere with him," Sallie said crisply. "Besides, I'm way too young for him. He's twenty-one and Dat would never allow it even if I was interested. Which I'm not."

"Who's Simon Yoder?" Megan asked, smiling. Twenty-one and a flirt, huh? Maybe he'd be at the hoedown instead of volleyball, too.

"He is the stepson of *Englisch* Henry's Sarah," Barbie told her. "He is very good-looking, and he knows it."

"The *Dokterfraa*? Her son?"

"*Ja*, from her first husband's first marriage."

Okay, that was a little too complicated. "I met her. She and Henry seemed nice."

"She is nice," Sallie agreed. "When they fell in love, Henry repented of his ways and joined church. He was a fence-jumper, too, years ago."

"I didn't think he sounded Amish. He offered to talk to us, if we wanted to. Maybe Samuel might like to, as well."

Barbie glanced at her. "You could drop a hint."

But that was getting a little too involved—more even than sewing seams on a quilt would be. "Maybe. Um, we should be getting back. I'll wait for you by the buggy."

And before they could say any more, Megan clattered downstairs and went outside. These people were so tight and so up in one another's lives. In one way it was lovely and safe. And in another way it made everything incredibly complicated, and a person could get sucked in before they knew it.

Did she want to be sucked in?

Why was she even asking herself that question? She couldn't be Amish. What was she thinking?

Barbie and Sallie seemed perfectly happy living the way they did, but their older brothers sure didn't. She really needed to find Samuel and have a talk about the pros and cons before she got any rash ideas. No one was forcing her or even thinking about her making any giant lifestyle changes. And they'd be gone on Sunday anyway. What difference did it make?

Your leaving will make a big difference to Rebecca.

But she wasn't *leaving* leaving. No one was stopping her from coming back whenever she wanted to. She wasn't in Samuel's situation. She could ... well, not email. But she could send letters. They could be pen pals, and stay in touch.

Pen pals with your real mother? You could have a life here.

Right, like she didn't have a life in Pitt Corner. A normal life.

You don't. You have an existence. Not the same thing.

But her family was in Pitt Corner. Her second family. Their feelings had to be taken into account.

Do you think Janet is praying for you right now, and lighting lamps in kitchen windows to show you the way home?

Maybe. Well, maybe not the lamp, but she'd bet Janet was thinking about her. She'd promised to call that morning, and she hadn't. Megan dug in her pocket for her freshly charged phone, and pressed auto-dial.

After four rings, she thought it might go to voice mail, but when someone picked up, it wasn't the canned message. "Hello?"

"Hey Mom, it's Megan."

Silence.

"Mom?"

"Am I still your mom?" came a wobbly voice that clearly was on the edge of tears.

"Of course." Oh help, what was wrong now? "Mom, are you okay? You sound awful. Is Dad home?"

"It's Friday. He's at school. I've been sitting here looking at your pictures and wishing you'd call."

"It's been kind of busy." She should have called this morning. "You would not believe how early the day starts around here. You could have called me, though."

"I didn't want to interrupt. Maybe you wouldn't want to talk to me. Maybe you'd even hang up on me."

"Mom, calm down. Why would I hang up on you?"

"Because of what I did. Do they hate me?"

"I don't think Jonathan and Rebecca know how to hate anybody."

"Are those their names?"

"Yes. Jonathan and Rebecca Riehl. And our names—the names of the little girls—were—"

"Hannah and Leah."

If Janet had been standing there and had hauled off and slugged her, the shock couldn't be any greater. "Mom!" She struggled for breath, and was glad she'd climbed into the buggy so that she was sitting down. "You mean you knew all this time? Why didn't you say?"

"I guess I forgot. But it doesn't matter. Your name is Megan. You were always meant to be Megan. Hannah is an ugly name, and Ashley is nice. Elegant. The two of you would call each other by those other names and it took me months to train it out of you."

Are you crazy? Who does that? Makes a little kid who has her own name go by the name of a dead girl?

But of course she didn't say that. Not with Janet two breaths from a breakdown.

"How did you find them? The parents?"

"I told you last night. Everybody in Willow Creek and for miles around knows the story. I get the impression the whole district was looking for us back then. So when I asked at the market if there was a family who had lost two girls, they pointed us right to the Riehl farm. Ashley still doesn't believe it's us, but when I tell her about this—about you knowing our original names—she will."

"Why doesn't Ashley believe it now?" Her voice perked up a little, as though she was happy about that.

"I don't think she wants to. She has her own life now, all planned out, and she's not about to make changes in it just because of this."

Just because she'd returned to her real family. Who had never forgotten her, not for one moment ... not for one meal.

"And what about you? Are you ready to come home?"

"We just got here—and we committed to stay until Sunday. Stuff is happening. We're going out with a guy— Samuel, my older brother, who isn't Amish anymore. He's offered to take us to where he last saw us tomorrow morning."

"Be careful, Megan."

"What of? Mom, they're not strangers. They're not bad people. There's nothing here to hurt me, except for the hay hole. Can you believe it? I've been dreaming about falling through the hay hole my whole life, and wouldn't you know that practically the first thing I did was nearly fall through it? If it hadn't been for one of the kids hollering, I would have for sure."

"What's a hay hole?"

"Where they fork hay down for the cows. No cover or anything. Crazy—with little kids running all over the barn, too. And that wasn't the only thing. I figured out why I'm so scared of ovens. Apparently I burned myself on one when I was really little. So much for learning to bake. Not happening."

But Janet didn't laugh. "I wasn't talking about holes or ovens. Be careful about … getting involved."

Megan's face tingled with a chill. "What do you mean?"

"Just what I say. Yes, we made mistakes. Yes, your life might have been different. Not better, just different, especially if they ever got around to feeding you."

"Mom." She couldn't help it if her tone sounded like a warning. Mistakes? Is that what she thought she'd done thirteen years ago—made a mistake? That was as crazy as thinking that Rebecca wouldn't have fed her kids. Even if they'd been dirt poor, Rebecca was the kind who would give her own share to her child if there wasn't enough to go around.

She couldn't say that to her mom, either. In fact, there was a whole other conversation that she should be having going on behind this one, but she couldn't say any of it. Couldn't tell the woman she thought of as her mother the truth. It would hurt her. And worse, it would send her off the rails again, and if Dad wasn't home, that wouldn't be good.

So Megan had no choice but to tell her mom what she wanted to hear.

"I'm not getting involved," she said slowly. "I'm finding out as much information as I can. It's hard, because Ash thinks I'm dredging up false memories and doesn't believe me about the hay hole and stuff."

"Do they? These Amish people?"

"Oh, yeah. They remember some of the same things. But it's like there was a missing link—yes, the Riehls lost their kids, and yes, you found us out in the woods. But the connection between the Riehls and the woods wasn't there."

"Wasn't? You mean these might not be your—" Janet hesitated. "They might not be the people you went looking for?"

"It didn't fit together until what you just said. Your knowing our Amish names. That's the connection." Had her mom let it slip accidentally, or on purpose? Why hadn't she told them she'd known their names? How could she just forget something like that?

Silence crackled down the line, and somewhere in the maple above Megan's head, a pair of wrens sang, their little feet scratching on the bark as they chased each other around the trunk.

"Mom?"

"Guess I should have kept my mouth shut."

"It's okay." *Don't cry again. I can't stand it when I know there's no one with you.*

"Is it? What do you think they'll do?"

"Who, Jonathan and Rebecca?" *My mother and father. For sure—wait. What did you say?* "What do you mean, what will they do?"

"Do you think they'll sue? Press charges? Take me to court for kidnapping their kids?"

You should have thought of that before you loaded us in the Volvo, Mom. And no way was she getting involved in anything like that, anyhow. No one was talking about it, and that was just fine with her. "I have no idea. Do Amish people sue?"

"Everybody sues. If it comes up, can you try to talk them out of it?"

This is surreal. I am not having this conversation. "Of course. But I'm sure it won't. We're back now, and—"

"Remember what I said, Megan. Don't get too involved. Promise me."

Now, wait a minute. That wasn't fair. "How involved is too involved?"

"When they don't want you to leave is too involved, honey."

"Of course they don't want us to leave. But we are. On Sunday, as planned. If we don't, Ashley will probably catch a bus, or call Keenan to drive out here and get her. She runs her battery down talking to him, and both of them have college on the brain."

"That's good." Her mother actually sighed with relief. "I'm so glad you called to let me know everything was all right."

Was it? Was it really? How could it be when Janet had stolen Rebecca's kids—stolen their lives? Suddenly Megan couldn't wait to get off the phone. To talk to someone about things that were real and truthful.

"I'll call again when we hit the road on Sunday. It took us nearly all day to get here, so we probably won't be back in time for supper Sunday night. We'll just catch a hamburger on the turnpike."

"All right, honey. Take care."

"Bye, Mom."

"I love you."

"I love you, too."

As she thumbed off the phone, she saw Barbie and Sallie come down the front steps of the house, talking a mile a minute in Pennsylvania Dutch. She was kind of glad they hadn't come out any earlier.

She was pretty sure they wouldn't approve of her telling her mother a lie.

14

Samuel didn't really think the *Englisch* girls would come to the hoedown with them; in fact, he came within a hair's breadth of telling Ben he wanted to just call the whole thing off and have a beer on the back porch instead. But curiosity got the best of him, and now here they were, pulling into the lot at the Hex Barn to see that the Subaru was already parked there. But no one was in it.

"Girls," Ben grunted. "They're inside shopping."

The Hex Barn was a laugh—it advertised AMISH MADE and AMISH ARTISANS—MADE BY HAND but ninety percent of the stuff they sold had a *Made in China* sticker on the back. Even the handwoven wool place mats came from South America. How nobody noticed this was a puzzle he'd never figured out.

Megan was standing next to a cold case of whoopie pies, and she turned when he came up next to her.

"If you're looking for the real thing, don't buy those," he said in a low tone. "They get them from an *Englisch* bakery in Lancaster."

"Aw, man." She put the pumpkin one with the salted toffee filling back on the pyramid of its fellows. "What about the one I got at the Amish Market?"

"It's real," he told her. "I mean, at least it was made by an Amish person—Gracie Lapp, I think, if you mean that stand she has out front."

"Ready to go?" Ben ambled up. "We're getting the stink-eye. They close at nine."

Megan collected her sister and they climbed into the backseat of Samuel's old red Valiant. "So we're going to Young Abe Kurtz's place east of Whinburg?"

Ben glanced at her over his shoulder. "Good memory."

"Your sister Sallie told me earlier today. She says to tell you that she wants to see you sometime. That—"

But Ben turned away and gazed out the passenger window, his face freezing over like it did when a subject was *verboten*.

"Okay, then," Megan said, flouncing back in the seat and tossing back her multicolored hair. "I did what I said—passed on the message—and you can just go ahead and ignore me."

"It's not easy, talking about our families." Samuel didn't have much of a gift for smoothing things over—just look what happened every time he bumped into his folks—but she didn't deserve the cold shoulder just for saying something nice.

"I don't suppose it is," Ashley said. "I'm about done with the whole subject."

"It's probably worse when you're the bishop's kid—and the oldest son," Megan said thoughtfully. "Right?"

Ben was biting his lips now. Sam hoped he wasn't about to lose his temper and ruin the whole night.

"Right," Ben ground out. "So how did you meet my sister?"

"Barbie drove me over in the buggy this afternoon. It was an adventure—guys pacing us on the highway with a big camera and me waving at them and screaming. Barbie was so calm. She's used to it. Anyhow, I went over to look at a quilt Sallie's making."

"Which is about the weirdest thing *ever*," Ashley remarked, her thumbs busy on her phone. "I saw you posted a shot on Facebook."

"I wanted to remember the pattern."

"Why? What are you going to do—make one?"

"Maybe."

"Really. Right after you get a better job and go to college."

Megan's face crumpled up and she sat back again, her arms crossed over her chest and her lips pressed together as though *maybe* was the last word she planned to say tonight.

"Sallie's a nice girl," Samuel offered. "She's sixteen now, ain't she?"

Ben nodded. "Almost seventeen. Old enough to go to singing and start on *Rumspringe* if she wants. Hard for me to believe."

"Maybe she's going, maybe not," Megan said, unfolding to lean forward to talk to Ben. "She knows you're going to be at the hoedown, but your Aendi Mariah and her kids are visiting, so she figured she wouldn't be able to get away. But you never know."

"You sound so freaking *faux* Amish," Ashley said to her phone. "Cut it out."

"At least I'm experiencing it. Unlike some people, who'd rather live in their plastic bubble in case they actually learn something."

"Do you girls ever spend five minutes not fighting?" Samuel almost didn't want to ask—they both might turn on him. It was so strange to see this, and remember the little girls who had held hands and done almost everything together.

Ashley looked at him in surprise. "We're not fighting. If we were, there'd be ripped pieces of clothing going out the windows. We're just discussing."

"Okay. Good thing we're almost there, then. Here's our turn."

He could see the lights from a quarter mile off. Young Abe had left the gate open on a field that was fallow this year. They bumped across the field, with Sam hoping every minute that a rock wouldn't take out the Valiant's decades-old exhaust system. A bunch of cars and a couple of souped-up pickups were parked in a circle, the lights shining into the center. Sam eased into a space between a pickup and the car of another ex he knew from Oakfield, shoved it into Park, and got out.

"Can I get you a beer?" he asked the girls. "I brought a six-pack, but it's probably warm."

"Coolers are over there, by Jebbie Zook," someone said as they passed, heading out into the field probably to take a leak.

That was a shocker. "What's Jebbie doing here?" They'd been such good friends when they were little, but it had been years since he'd seen him. "I'd have thought he'd have joined church and got married by now."

"Guess not." That was Ben. Mr. Helpful.

But then, he could hardly expect Ben to know anything about Jebbie when he saw as much of their old gang as he did. Probably less. No one wanted to admit to the bishop that they were hanging around with his son and not exhorting him to return to the fold. Sometimes a guy just wanted to have fun without a whole bunch of strings attached. To be accepted just the way he was. Hoedowns were kind of lame, but at least no one was pretending to be anything they weren't.

"Those girls are wearing *Kapps* and dresses." Megan gripped his elbow as they walked over to the coolers. "What's up with that?"

"They can wear whatever they want. They probably don't have *Englisch* clothes, or if they do, they've got nowhere to hide them that their parents won't find."

Megan bent and grabbed a soda, then passed a root beer to Ashley. "Looks weird, Amish girls drinking."

"But you're not." He'd have bet money that someone who looked like Megan, with her purple hair and skinny jeans, would have been popping the cap on her second one by now.

"I'm underage, and so is Ash."

He dropped his beer into the communal cooler and picked a Coors for himself. "So? No cops out here asking for ID."

"Yet. I'm not willing to take the chance."

"Ain't that law-abiding of you," Ben said, knocking back a slug of Corona.

"It's not about being law-abiding. It's about—about not giving *your* folks any trouble."

"Say what?" Samuel stared at her, his beer halfway to his mouth.

"Well … say we get hauled in to the station and they call our folks. Then we have to say what we're doing here, and the story comes out about who we are. The Amish all know, but nobody else does."

Ben snorted into his beer. But to Samuel, this wasn't so far-fetched. "There's a file at the station in Whinburg with your names on it. Probably a cop there who'd like to see it closed, too. They spent a lot of years looking for you."

"Right." Megan's grateful gaze made him feel useful and smart for once. "So then they get our other parents' information, and then maybe somebody starts asking questions, and before you know it, they're calling the FBI and arresting our other parents for taking us away all those years ago."

"Other parents? You are so full of it." Ashley hopped down from the tailgate and stalked off around the outside perimeter of the circle. Maybe she was going to find the outhouse. Or take a sightseeing tour of Amish kids dancing to the hip-hop blasting from the boom box in the middle. But one thing Samuel could pretty much guarantee was that she wasn't walking home. It was too dark and too far.

"You sound pretty convinced about who your real parents are," Samuel ventured, when Megan sighed and returned her attention to him, leaning on the front of the Valiant.

"I am. I know who we are. I called our other mother this afternoon and she told me something I never knew before."

"What's that?"

"She knew our names. Our Amish names. She told me without my prompting her or hinting or anything. She said it took her months to train us out of using our real names and calling each other Megan and Ashley instead."

"Did you tell Ashley—Leah?"

"Can't you tell? I did, and she's been a complete bear all afternoon. You totally have my permission to drive away and leave her if you want."

"Truth hurts," Ben said, his gaze on the kids in the middle, the headlight beams flickering off their legs and making the shadows slide in the girls' dresses. "Want to dance?"

It took Megan a second to jump to the new train of thought. "Who, me?"

"Well, I'm not planning on asking Sam."

Samuel's stunned brain took even longer to get on the train. Ben had no business asking any such thing. Since when did he know how to dance?

"Well ... sure. I guess."

Ben didn't seem to care that she sounded more confused than excited at the prospect. They didn't hold hands, either, on the short walk into the middle of the circle. The music changed to a slow country number, and Ben held her around the waist a little awkwardly until Megan, who obviously had picked up a clue or two in her life, showed him how to hold her left hand properly, with the other staying at her waist.

Samuel had no intention of dancing, now or ever. Making a fool of himself in full view of everyone while still completely sober was not a happy prospect. But Ben didn't seem to mind. They swayed back and forth, and Ben even twirled Megan out and back in as though he knew what he was doing—or at least remembered what the stars had done on an episode or two of *Dancing with Celebrities.*

His sister. Sisters, he amended as he caught sight of Leah still stalking around the perimeter. She'd made it to about three o'clock on the circle, and by the time the next song started and Megan and Ben decided to dance it, too, Leah had rejoined him.

He had no idea what to say to her. Here they were, leaning on the hood and coming to grips with what they meant to each other—and not a word struggling into the silence between them.

"So," he began a little diffidently. "Your sister told you what your mom said. About her knowing your Amish names."

Leah glared at the tussocks of grass. "I wish I could say she was making it all up. But I called Mom and she told me the same thing. I'm so freaking mad I could spit."

"Mad at who?"

"At you—at my mom—at Megan—your mom. Everybody. I hate this. Why did this have to happen now?"

"I don't know. But why are you mad at my mom?"

She made a sound of frustration. "For existing, I guess. For standing there in the kitchen with that *please love me* face. For being the choice I refuse to make."

"I don't think she'd force you into making a choice. That's not how she is. And she'll love you no matter what."

"That's a little weird, coming from you. Seems to me both your parents are waiting for you to make a choice. Or rather, the *other* choice. Like you're making the one they don't like right now and if they cut you a little slack, hold the carrot out a little farther, you'll come around eventually."

She noticed a lot for a girl who would rather be anywhere but here.

"You're right," he admitted. "They are, I guess, when you put it that way."

"And it doesn't make you crazy?"

"I don't see them much," he said mildly. "I know what they want—Ben knows what his folks want—but neither of us want the same."

"What is it you don't want?" The edge of anger seemed to be softening into curiosity. "What's it like, being Amish?"

He huffed a one-breath laugh. "If I asked you what it was like being *Englisch*, could you answer?"

She thought about it for a second. "Probably not. Because I never think about it."

"Right. That's why they have *Rumspringe*—that means 'running around.' So that kids will think about it. So they know what life is like on both sides of the fence and they can make a choice without always wondering what it would be like on the other side."

"Does it work?"

He shrugged. "It does. Most people choose to join church. So you don't have to leave your family, *ja?* And you can't get married to another Amish person if you don't."

"So if you and say, that girl over there—" She pointed to a slender brunette in a dress and *Kapp* by the cooler. "—wanted to get married, you both have to join church and commit to your religion first? You can't just go to a justice of the peace and do the church thing later, when you're ready?"

"Nope. You don't get married by an *Englisch* authority. The bishop marries you. In church. For good. No divorce."

"Wow. Hardcore." Leah was silent for a moment. "So I guess you can't be in church and date an English girl either, then."

"You could, but what's the point? You can't marry outside, so why look outside?"

"And what if you are outside? Like you guys are now?"

"Then you can ask as many *Englisch* girls to dance as you want, I guess." He gazed at Ben and Hannah, who seemed to be talking more than dancing, but were still swaying back and forth almost in place. The song was almost over.

And then it ended, and something fast came on that was evidently too much for Ben, because he led Hannah back to the car.

Holding her hand.

Samuel pushed himself off the hood. "I'm going to go say hi to Jebbie."

And he walked off, the music loud and harsh in his ears. It wasn't until he was halfway across the grass that he realized he'd crumpled his beer can into a little wad of metal in his fist.

15

Lost in a daze and with a brain that wouldn't quit spinning stories about impossible stuff, Megan tried to tiptoe up the stairs, but Ashley's foot caught on her heel and she nearly fell flat on her face on the landing. And she hadn't even had a single beer.

Then again, right now she didn't need a beer to feel light-headed and not quite in her own body.

"Shh!" Ashley whispered. "You'll wake the whole house."

It was one in the morning and people would wake up in three hours to do whatever was on the agenda for Saturday. Oh yeah, finishing up what hadn't got done during the rest of the week. Luckily for her and Ashley, the boys were still on for a trip out to the walnut orchard on the hill. She had a feeling that Rebecca wouldn't be as upset with their missing out on the chores as she might be if Samuel hadn't been part of the group.

Megan wasn't quite sure how she felt about seeing Ben again so soon. Happy, yes. Scared, a little. Bowled over, mostly.

Light glimmered behind Barbie's door before Megan could get her feet under her, and the next thing she knew, there was enough light from the lantern the girl carried that Megan could shut off the flashlight app on her phone. Which was good, because it sucked up the battery life like crazy.

"What are you doing up?" Ashley whispered to her. "Go back to bed."

"I don't want you to fall down the stairs." The girl lighted them into their bedroom, where she put the lamp on the dresser. "Did you have a good time?"

Ashley shrugged. "It was all right. Chalk one up for the *life experience* file."

"Did you see Samuel? And Ben?"

"We rode with them. And Megan danced with Ben."

Barbie's eyes rounded.

"TMI, Ash." Megan finally got a word in edgewise. She should have thought to warn her sister about zipping her lips about private things.

"But he's much older than you!" Barbie whispered.

"It was a couple of dances, not a diamond ring," Megan said. Why did she have to look so shocked? "What does it matter how old he is?"

"But … if he took you to the hoedown, and you danced together, are you going to be special friends now?"

The girl was so serious that Megan choked back her urge to laugh. "Special friends? Is that like boyfriend and girlfriend?"

"That's what we call it. If a boy comes calling, and has meals with your family, and you're of the right age, we say he's your special friend. And then in time you might get married."

Do not laugh. "Well, that's not happening," Megan said quickly, before Ash could hoot hysterically and wake everybody upstairs. "Nothing's happening. He asked me to dance. He's not very good at it. End of story."

"He might not be able to dance, but you certainly had plenty to talk about," Ashley said.

Which had been only one of the surprises of the evening.

"Did you talk with Samuel?" Clearly Barbie had her reasons for waiting up five hours past her bedtime to ambush them on the stairs.

"A little. Ashley talked more with him than I did."

Barbie turned those eyes on Ashley. "How is he? Do you think he is happy away from us?"

"No, I don't," Ash said bluntly. "You guys are a very sensitive subject with him ... but you've all brought it on yourselves, haven't you? With this shunning stuff."

"He is not shunned. He never joined church, so he cannot be under *die Meinding*."

"I get that. But why can't he come back and sit in his chair at the table like it's clear your parents want him to?"

Barbie's face fell as she seemed to struggle for words. "They do want him back. We all do. But he must come willingly—accepting the Lord's will. Not his own."

"You want him back if he joins church, in other words," Megan said. "And if he's not willing? Then being separate from his family is the price he pays?"

Barbie nodded miserably.

"Who makes these rules?" Ashley asked nobody in particular.

Which would practically guarantee hurt feelings in Barbie, who clearly didn't make them, and had no answer. Ash should know better.

"Barbie," Megan said, "in the morning we're going up to the orchard where Samuel last saw us thirteen years ago. Do you want to come? Maybe you'll get a chance to see your brother and talk to him."

For a moment she looked as a little kid might when someone offers a present when it isn't her birthday. Then she clearly thought better of it. "Dat has said that Samuel is welcome to come back if he lives in obedience to the *Ordnung*. I don't think he would like it if I snuck off the farm to see him instead."

"You don't have to sneak," Ashley pointed out, pulling off her sweatshirt and T-shirt together over her head. "Just hop in the car with us and come."

"In the car? Why? You can walk up to the orchard from here, down Jed Zook's harvest track and through the fields."

"They're meeting us on the far side of the hill," Megan explained. "Apparently Samuel has a theory about where my—where they parked and started their hike. The Pearsons."

"Mom and Dad, Megan. Sheesh." Ashley picked up the lamp and stalked into the bathroom with it, leaving Megan and Barbie in the dark until their eyes adjusted to the silvery shaft of moonlight coming through the curtainless window.

Curtains, she had learned, were fancy. If a house had to have them, there was only one, not two that could be drawn together.

Never mind. "Come with us, Barbie," she urged, though she sat on her bed and Barbie was invisible against the wall with its row of dress pegs. "He's your brother. Your dad can't keep you from him, can he?"

"He doesn't," the girl said almost inaudibly. "It's hard to explain. It would hurt them—that I broke Dat's expectation, made it of no account by going around it. Samuel knows he has separated himself from us. The price of being a family again is his willingness—and it's the same price to be one with God's family. The one is an illustration of the other. Can you see that?"

The problem was that she could. See the illustration, that is. Megan just wasn't so sure that the carrot-and-stick method was going to work.

"He's pretty determined to live on his own terms," she said softly. "Is it worth being separated from him your whole life?"

In the dark, she couldn't see Barbie's face, but the soft little hitch in her breath told the whole story.

Megan's heart felt as though it was swelling against her breastbone. Something unfamiliar, something she'd never experienced before outside of the urge to save the baby birds that fell out of their nests, propelled her up off the bed and over to the girl.

"Don't cry," she whispered. Soft cotton met her hand—a nightie. Then a warm, slender form, trembling but silent. "Come here."

And for the first time, she held her little sister and let her cry into her shoulder.

And something broke in Megan's heart.

Hannah's heart.

Now she knew for sure who she was. Now she knew that this was her sister—this was her family, for once and for all. She was Hannah.

The waiting was over … but now what was she going to do?

*

Samuel waited until he saw the glow of the lamp up in the girls' room before he ducked under the orchard fence and jogged down the wagon track to where Ben sat in the Valiant with the engine idling.

He slid into the passenger seat and they rolled quietly down the road. "Someone waited up for them," he said. "I hope it wasn't Mamm." Or worse, Dat. He had pretty strong views about late nights when there was work to be done the next day, and cut nobody any slack.

"What does it matter?" Ben turned onto the highway and pressed the gas. "Your folks don't have any authority over those girls. They could stay out all night if they wanted to."

"Maybe not, but if they're under Dat's roof he's going to expect obedience."

Ben shook his head. "They're *Englisch*. Guests. He won't want to chase them away anyhow. Not now that they've come back."

This was true, so there was no point in arguing. But there was one thing worth bringing up, and he meant to do it, even with Ben Troyer, who typically didn't talk much about himself. "Got any plans to keep Megan out all night?"

"Talking about authority—you don't have any, either."

Whoa. Samuel was a little taken aback. Not even a second's hesitation, and out came the answer. Or a form of one. "The two of you sure looked like something was going on."

He wasn't sure how he felt about that. Protective? Maybe. Confused? Probably. Helpless, because he didn't have any right to feel both of the above? Definitely.

"I never would have thought I'd say this about a girl with purple hair and a black *Star Wars* T-shirt, but she's interesting. She's just as confused by all this as the rest of us. And Ashley's attitude doesn't help."

Which didn't answer his question at all, but at least Ben was talking. Samuel decided to go with it. "She's going to have to accept that she's my sister, with what their other mother said today," he said glumly.

"Megan says that it's not going to stop her from going off to college next week."

Samuel was silent, watching the mist curling across the road in the headlights. "So Mamm will lose her again."

So would he. But how could you lose someone you hadn't had in more than a decade? Could the ties that bind be broken just from the unrelenting pressure of time?

"Maybe something will shake loose in the orchard tomorrow," Ben suggested. "Maybe if she remembers something for herself, she'll think different."

"Maybe." It was a big maybe. "What about Megan? Did she say anything about her plans?"

"I don't know if she knows how to make plans," Ben said slowly. He turned into the mobile home park, then brought the car to a stop beside their trailer. "All she does is play video games, and work in a coffee shop once in a while. She's sure different from Ashley."

Samuel let them into the trailer, though he didn't know why they bothered to lock it. They had nothing anyone would value. "All we do is work, and play video games once in a while. We have the same life, only flipped."

A life on hold. A life that didn't go anywhere, because he couldn't leave and even if he did, he didn't know which road to take. Was that how Megan felt? That her old life had been taken away from her, and she couldn't get her new one going until she put the pieces back together?

Maybe he should ask her tomorrow. Maybe they were more similar than he'd thought.

"Are we bringing them here after they see the orchard?" Samuel tried to look at their place with the eyes of *Englisch* girls. "Maybe we should pick up a little." As the eldest, he'd been the first to learn the rudiments of housekeeping, even before he'd gone to the schoolhouse to learn reading and writing. Mamm had taught him to sweep and do the dishes when both broom handle and kitchen counter were still above his head.

"We're not meeting them until nine. I'm going to bed." Ben walked off down the hall, and in a minute Samuel heard the water running in the bathroom.

They couldn't bring guests in here. They'd think he and Ben were a couple of slobs. Samuel cleared the empty pizza boxes and soda cans off the secondhand table in the kitchen, and dumped them in the trashcan outside. Then he hunted up the pillows that were supposed to sit on the couch from where someone had chucked them behind it, and plumped them the way he'd seen Barbie do. A couple of minutes of picking up shirts and dirty socks off the floor made a big difference, and he stuffed them in the canvas bag they used to take the laundry down to the Fluff 'N' Fold in Whinburg once a week.

There. That looked better.

Their mismatched dishes from Goodwill were still piled up in the sink with crusty food left on them, but they could do them in the morning. He wiped down the table, now that it was clean, and swept the linoleum. They weren't much on housekeeping, but it was funny how different the place felt when it was picked up. Bigger, with more air in it.

If they'd still been Amish, he and Ben would have been looking around and taking notice—his mother's expression for getting interested in marriage—because they would have been feeling the need of a wife.

Lots of guys went for the pretty girls without thinking too much about living with them afterward. But Mamm used to tell Barbie when she thought Samuel wasn't around, "A boy should look more than skin deep when he's taking notice. A good man looks for a woman who can keep a tidy house, who knows how to work, and who glorifies God with every service and sacrifice she makes for her family. I want you to be that kind of girl, *Liewi*. In turn, you look for a boy who works hard and saves his money, whose family respects him and who respects you. You don't just marry a man, remember. You marry a family. A way of life. If his family is fancier than ours, then you can show him a better way to live. Don't go down that slippery slope and wind up wearing no *Kapp* and purple satin at your wedding."

Barbie had laughed at the outlandish idea, but Samuel knew now that there were churches much more liberal than their Old Order Amish *Gmee*, where a purple satin dress was just that and not an indication of how sinful and vain you were.

Maybe he should look into one. As he brushed his teeth and climbed into the sleeping bag that lay on top of his mattress, he wondered what Dat would say to *that*. For him, being baptized into a liberal church was just another road to hell. But if he wouldn't let Samuel come to visit, there was no way he'd ever know, was there?

16

For once, Rebecca woke before Jonathan, who was usually up at four even without an alarm. She'd asked him once how he did it, day after day, but he'd only smiled and said God shook him awake when it was time to tend His creation. Perhaps He did. She only needed the alarm on the rare occasions when Jonathan was away, though when the twins were small it hadn't been necessary either. God must have shaken them awake, too, at regular intervals—for feeding, and then drinks of water, and then cuddles in the night.

Jonathan drew a sudden breath and shifted, rolling over to kiss her. "Wake up, *Liewi*."

"I'm awake. I was lying here thinking."

"About the girls?"

Of course she knew which girls he meant. "*Ja*. They came in so late. They'll never wake up in time for chores, or even breakfast."

"That is the price they pay for worldly behavior, and if you were awake listening for them, you will have to pay it, too. I'll wake them if you want."

They *were* worldly, to her everlasting sorrow. Did their other mother let them stay out until the small hours? Did she and Jonathan have the right, now, to override that upbringing? Did they have the right to do anything at all? Or was she to treat her daughters as guests for the rest of her life?

She tried to breathe calmly, to settle the burning in her stomach at just how wrong this was.

"We can't discipline them for worldly behavior, Jon. That would be like disciplining a horse for galloping. They've been in the world and of it, and much as it grieves both of us, we have to remember that they know nothing about our life except for a few distant memories."

He sighed deeply, the sigh of an honest man who acknowledges the truth, much as he doesn't want to. "I know it. But it is hard—once I accepted that they really are our girls, how can I not treat them as such? How can I make a difference between them and our other children, and not treat them as though they are part of the family once again?"

"I don't know," she whispered. "Breakfast and prayers are one thing—they do join in, willing or not. But the deeper things? I don't see how we can even speak of those things to them, much less expect them to change."

"So waking them for breakfast is the closest we can come to sharing our lives with them?"

"I only have two more opportunities before they go away. If that is all I can have, I don't want to miss one."

Jonathan didn't answer for a moment. Then, in a voice so low it was almost a whisper, he said, "I believe we must face that they ought to go away, Becca. They are not our children now. And ... I fear for the others. Barbara is much too interested in their lives, and even the twins can't take their eyes off them. What if they draw our other children after them into the world? What if they become a temptation?"

The breaths she was struggling to take went out of her altogether and laid her flat, as still as an effigy she'd once seen on top of a tomb in the encyclopedia. This had never occurred to her, not in all this time. The shock of such a thought rendered her immobile. And speechless.

It was a full minute before she could find her voice. Jonathan was a patient man in many ways. He did not rush her answer, but at the same time, she sensed he was waiting for it, even as the cows and the farm waited for him.

"Surely *der Herr* would not put that burden on us?" she finally managed. "Not when He has asked so much of us already."

"He asks only what we can bear."

She had reached her limit, then. "The world has already taken three of my children. Surely the *gut Gott* wants the other four for Himself."

"We cannot know the mind of our *Gott*, Becca. But I hope so, too. I surely do. We must protect Barbie, Melinda, Katie, and the boys as best we can."

She knew how he wanted to protect them, and she hastened to forestall it. "But I cannot show Hannah and Leah to the door and tell them they are no longer welcome." *I cannot treat them as I must treat Samuel. I cannot do it.*

"I did not say you had to," he said softly. The light was strengthening in the sky now. She could see the outline of his nose and lips as he lay beside her, like a mountain range.

Strong, dependable. And immovable. "But if you were tempted to ask them to stay? What then?"

"Even if I were, they won't. Didn't you hear Leah talking about going to college? Chattering about her young man? She has her life's plans already made."

"She doesn't know God's plans. Maybe His are different."

"Maybe they are, but it's not likely He'll reveal them to us before Sunday."

A breath of a chuckle came from her husband. "What of Hannah? She's a strange one. Rootless. Settling for worldly entertainment instead of satisfying work."

"Could she put a few roots down in Whinburg Township?" She hardly dared say it aloud, for fear of what his reply might be.

The light strengthened almost imperceptibly, and as it did, almost without her realizing it, she understood what she hadn't before. "If she asks to stay, Jonathan, I won't tell her no. I won't speak the words that send my daughter away. She will have to say them herself."

"Becca—"

"I know. But what if this rootless life means she is waiting for God? For a reason to return to our family, to our way of life? If her soul is lost and seeking, how can we be so presumptuous as to turn her away? Jesus never did such a thing."

"Yes, He did. He turned away the Canaanite whose daughter was vexed with a devil. He told her it wasn't fitting to take the children's bread and give it to dogs."

Becca took a long breath as the pain skewered her heart, to hear him draw such a parallel between that woman and the girl sleeping across the hall. "And she came back again and again, telling Him that even dogs ate the crumbs that fell from the table." She fought to keep the triumph from her tone—to advise, not argue. "And then He accepted her. If Hannah is looking for even a single crumb, we can do no less."

"And if the cost is the soul of one of our other children?"

"I do not believe that if we do as Jesus did, we will be asked to pay that price," she told him desperately. "I cannot believe He would allow it."

They had come full circle.

"Then I pray you are right," he said at last. "Come. The sun will be up soon. This of all mornings I feel the need to seek God's face."

Together, they slid out from under the warm quilts and knelt on the braided rug next to the bed. Her elbow touching his, her skin pebbled with the chill, Rebecca prayed in silent desperation. For wisdom. For courage. And above all, for the strength to do what was right for all her children, Amish or not.

*

At the big kitchen table, Megan palmed the sleep out of her eyes and buried her nose in the coffee cup as though it alone would keep her from falling off the hard chair. After only a couple of hours of sleep, coffee was a miracle that mustn't be wasted. Only after she'd swallowed a whole mug was she able to contemplate with some interest the massive breakfast that was an everyday occurrence on the Riehl farm.

Then again, Jonathan and the kids had been working for two hours already, doing cow and milk things out in the barn. They'd washed and scrubbed, but she could still detect the smell of manure coming from somewhere.

"What are your plans for today, Megan?" Rebecca asked gently, offering her the plate of bacon.

She would never have thought she could eat before noon, but there was something about the food here that made you want to stuff yourself even before the sun was up. She took two pieces.

Then she glanced at Jonathan, two places away at the head of the table. "We're going up to the walnut orchard," she said in a tone that she hoped was simply passing on information, not being defiant or kicking up an argument. "The boys thought that maybe if we saw it—the place—you know, that we might remember something."

"That *I* might remember something, you mean," Ashley managed to say from the depths of her own mug. "I don't know what good it will do."

"You never know," Hannah said mildly. "Memory is weird."

"You would know."

"Ash."

"Megan," she shot back in the same tone.

Something flared and then firmed up under Hannah's breastbone. "Can you not call me that anymore? It was never my name—it was hers. That little blond girl in the pictures. My name is Hannah, so I'm going to go with that from now on."

Ashley stared at her. "What?"

202

Hannah didn't dare look at Rebecca, or Barbie. Or even Jonathan. The younger kids were chowing down like little garbage disposals, but everyone else at the table seemed to be frozen in place.

"Is that so weird? To want a name that's my own, and not secondhand? Guess I'll have to get it changed on my driver's license, won't I?"

Rebecca made a little sound, and swallowed her food with a gulp that sounded like a sob.

Jonathan put down his knife and fork and pushed his empty plate away. "We will return thanks."

And Ash was forced to keep whatever else she had to say to herself for the duration of the silent prayers.

When Jonathan got up, he laid his hand on Rebecca's shoulder in a gesture of comfort, then told the kids he would be waiting in the living room with the Bible.

"Are you going in?" Ashley whispered. "Is that step two to turning Amish?"

"Don't be such a butthead."

Rebecca glanced back at the two of them from the doorway, and herded the children into the living room, but Hannah didn't move. "Don't you see how upset they are? Your attitude doesn't help."

"*My* attitude!" Ashley's whisper practically disappeared into the upper registers. "Do you think you can just erase the last decade and a half? Change your name to protect the innocent? What are you doing?"

"Can we talk about this later?" Hannah whispered back. "After we're done in there?"

"Sure. Whatever you want. It's all about you anyway." Ashley stalked over to the door. "I'll be outside."

203

Hannah had no memory of what verses they read, only that the sound of them was comforting, especially when Barbie helped the younger ones with the difficult words. That was how sisters were supposed to be. Helpful. Kind. Not angry and sarcastic and—

—and exactly how she and Ashley had always been with one another. The days where she'd been helpful and kind to Ash were few and far between. There were a lot of days when she'd tamped down a secret wish that Ashley would take her brilliant self and just go away, leaving her to her basement room and her mediocrity.

Hannah let out a long breath of disappointment in herself. Well, she was getting her wish. On Tuesday, Ashley would leave for college with Keenan and who knew when they'd see one another again? Maybe she should shape up and be the one doing the right thing, instead of expecting people to do right by her all the time. What right did she have to ask anyone to do that?

None.

By the time the dishes were done and everyone was off doing their Saturday catch-up tasks, it was close to eight a.m. Back in the day, eight a.m. would have been an excruciatingly early morning. Had she really slept half her life away?

She told Rebecca she was going to find Ashley, and headed down the steps and into the yard. In the distance, across the fields, she could see Jonathan driving out the six-mule hitch, the twins hanging onto his waistband so they wouldn't fall off. He'd said he was cutting hay. Was that wagon thing they were riding on the cutter? She had no idea how hay was cut. It just turned up in bales in front of stores at Hallowe'en. A smaller figure in pants and suspenders rode behind them—the hired boy, she guessed.

Hired because his eldest son was no longer able to come back.

Meanwhile, where was Ash?

A stroll through the chicken yard and the barn left her none the wiser, so she rambled around the garden, where a slender girl could disappear among the massive tomato plants, the pea teepees, and bean bushes.

Not here.

Maybe she'd gone to get the mail. Hannah walked up the long gravel drive, scored by the narrow tracks of buggy wheels, and listened to the chirruping of birds and the whisper of the wind through the tall grass on the other side of the white painted fence. In the distance, out on the road, horses' hooves clip-clopped by, sounding like a metronome set to double time. They used retired racehorses here. And the boys in fast gangs sometimes got in trouble for racing them. Wouldn't that be a sight to see? Did the horses remember the cheering from the people in the stands?

A distant crunching in the gravel turned out to be Ashley, walking back with letters and periodicals in her hands.

"I'm sorry if I upset you," Hannah said when she came within earshot.

Ashley looked up from reading the return addresses on the letters. "Why would I be upset that you want to erase yourself? You can do what you want."

"I'm not erasing myself. I'm finding myself."

"And while you're doing that, what about me? I hope you don't expect me to answer to Leah when somebody calls, because I won't."

"No one's asking you to. Look, Ash, this is weird and new for all of us. Just give it a chance, okay?"

Ashley tried for a glare, but not before Hannah saw her lower lip tremble. "I am giving it a chance. I'm giving it three whole days of chances, and then I'm out of here. I can't take it, Megan. Hannah. Whatever."

"I know. It's hard for me, too. The worst part is wondering who I'm going to hurt more, Janet or Rebecca."

"Why would you hurt them? What are you planning to do?"

Hannah looked away to try to gather words into sense. The grass was so neat. If it hadn't still been wet with dew, she'd be tempted to sit on it, like a thick green quilt. But Ashley wouldn't let her off the hook.

"Hannah?"

That was a concession. Hannah hadn't expected her to actually use the name, so she smiled in appreciation. "Who do I call *Mom*, for starters, I guess."

"Point taken," Ash said, tapping the mail into a pile graded by envelope size. "Who are you going to keep a relationship going with?"

"Another good question."

"Why do we have to choose?"

"Best question of all," Hannah said. "And I don't have an answer. Come on. We still have an hour to kill. I guess we'd better suck it up and offer to help with chores."

"That's one good thing that's come out of this adventure."

"What? Me doing chores?"

"Right? Next thing you know, you'll be cooking that breakfast singlehanded, and as God is your witness, you'll never be hungry again."

Hannah swatted her on the butt, and she actually found herself wanting to laugh as she jogged down the drive after her sister.

The kitchen was spotless when they came in, though how Rebecca and Barbie had done it kind of amazed her, considering all the dishes and pots and frying pans that had been heaped all over the counter. She made her offer of help, half hoping Rebecca wouldn't take her up on it, but that was like throwing corn to chickens and hoping they wouldn't eat it.

Which was how Hannah and Ashley found themselves out in the garden, picking tomatoes the size of baseballs off the giant mutant plants and breathing in the spicy scent.

"I love that smell." Ashley breathed deeply. "Do you know that in the Middle Ages, tomatoes were called love apples, and the church forbade people to eat them because they thought they were an aphrodisiac?"

"Good thing they couldn't see these ones, then." Megan cradled a particularly big one in her hand; her fingers could barely contain the thing. Plus, it was warm from the sun. "Entire villages would be excommunicated."

"More crazy reasons to toss people out of church," Ashley muttered.

But Hannah wasn't about to get into that again. "I want to cut one up and salt it and stuff it in my face, even though I'm still full from breakfast. Everything tastes so good here. Maybe there's something in this farm-to-table movement."

They filled their two big plastic mixing bowls in about ten minutes, and then learned about blanching the tomatoes to make the skins come off, then cooking them down a little to make chunky sauce, then filling canning jars and boiling them to seal the lids.

"Do you do this every day?" Hannah asked Barbie as she lifted out jar after steaming jar with a pair of grabbers and set them on a towel on the counter. Just like she had been doing when they'd arrived.

"Not every day. But you have to keep up with tomatoes or they'll rot—or the birds will get them."

"They're meant to feed the family," Rebecca told her, filling jars with a precision and speed that had clearly been developed over years of practice. "Not birds or rodents. So if that means we can a few every day, then that's what we do. *Denki* for your help." She smiled at all three of them, though Hannah had to admit that wiping the tops of jars free of spills before the lids went on wasn't much in the way of help.

But still. If she had the equipment, she could probably can tomato sauce now. Between that and frying bacon and eggs, she could live on breakfast fixings and spaghetti. At least those didn't require the use of an oven.

Rebecca glanced at the clock over the door. "You were meeting the boys at nine? It's past that now."

"Oops. Come on, Ash. Better hustle."

The boys were leaning on the fender of the beat-up Valiant when they pulled up behind them into what Ben had called the parking lot, but what Hannah would call a wide spot in the road. At least it had been easy to find.

"Guder mariye," she said, trying the words on for size.

"Hey," Ben tossed back.

Alrighty then. No *Deitsch*—a word that didn't look a bit the way it sounded, after Barbie had written it out for Hannah. Like *die*, with a *ch* after it. It was where the Dutch in Pennsylvania Dutch had come from, because it was German, not Dutch. And why was she thinking about that when Ben's gaze lay on her still, as if he was expecting something other than a sad attempt at a language he didn't want to speak anymore?

"Ready to take a walk?" he asked.

She nodded, while Ashley said, "If I'd known we were going to be hiking and gardening and playing with farm animals, I'd have brought my boots."

Hannah didn't see anything wrong with her sneakers, but that was Ashley. Miss Precision's shoes had *applications*. They didn't just get thrown on because they were the closest things to hand.

The walk up the hill was pretty, at least. Tall firs mixed with maples and elms let the sun through in a speckly, wavering way, a bit like light under water. The path cut through tall grass in places, and granite started pushing up in big outcroppings the higher they got. At the top, she could see the countryside for a long way around.

"Is that the farm?" Hannah pointed. "That's Jonathan on the cutter, isn't it?"

Samuel gazed down at his father. When was the last time he'd seen him?

"Do you come up here much?" she ventured.

He shook his head, turning away. "The last time was about ten years ago, when the new sheriff's deputy came up here. He had the whole story in a file, but he wanted me to tell him again."

File. Sheriff. Right. Who knew a crime had been committed, but not who had done it. Was it only a matter of time before he started asking questions? Before someone in Willow Creek told him the news? Because no way was she going to be the one to tip him off. No matter what the Pearsons had done, she wouldn't turn them in. How could she, when they were the only parents she'd ever really known?

Her dad used to watch old episodes of *Law & Order* whenever they could afford cable, she remembered for some random reason. Why? Was he hoping to learn something about staying one step ahead of the cops? There was probably an FBI agent out there somewhere, too. What were the odds he would go paging through his cold cases one day and decide to find out if there was anything new going on in Whinburg Township?

A cold feeling needled its way into her stomach, and she gazed around to give herself something else to think about. "So. It's a nice view, but I can't say it rings any bells. Ashley?"

Her sister shook her head. "What's this, a fire ring?"

With the toe of her sneaker, she pushed at some blackened stones that had been set in a circle, but it was empty now. No fire had been lit there in months.

"When it happened, the original deputy thought they— the people—the Pearsons—had camped here. There were fresh ashes," Samuel said awkwardly. "I don't know. I wasn't looking at stuff like that at the time. Come on. The orchard is down this way."

A trail wound down the other side of the hill, which had a much gentler slope. The trees were different, too. Younger and thinner, which meant there were more of them. Maybe a fire had burned through here decades ago, and had gotten stopped at the top, leaving the older growth on the other side.

Soon the path took them alongside an old-fashioned split rail fence, silvery with age and splotched with gray lichen. Beyond it lay the orchard, with tall grass growing between its rows of walnut trees. Here and there, the leaves of the maples were just beginning to turn, but not the walnuts.

"It's colder up here at night," Ben said, following her gaze. "The trees turn a little sooner, but the walnuts wait. Come on. I'll give you a hand if you need help climbing over."

Ashley was already over the fence, heading down the slope in the direction of another section of fence and a field beyond it. That section was covered in a climbing vine bearing puffs of feathery seed.

"Ashley," Hannah called when she'd got both her legs over the fence and jumped down without assistance. She'd be a regular country girl soon, at this rate. "Where are you going?"

At the second row of trees, third one from the end, Ashley stopped and looked up into the branches. "Nowhere," she said when Hannah walked up. "This looks like a good one. Are they ripe yet? Can we pick some?"

Neither of the boys answered. Hannah looked at Samuel curiously. "Sam? Is that okay?"

But he was staring at Ashley. "Do you remember it?" he finally said.

"What? Can we pick some of these or not?"

"This tree. Second row, third one in. It's the tree Dat always said was the best one. You walked right to it. Just like we all did on the day those people took you."

17

Most people, Samuel supposed, took memory for granted. You remembered to go to work in the morning, to put gas in the car, to go to the dentist for your checkup. Over the last couple of days, he'd thought back to his earliest memories, wondering just how many of them Hannah and Leah shared. But before starting school at the age of six, it was all kind of a blur, except for things like the dog they'd had back then. Samuel could remember him real well, but not doing anything with him. Just hugging him. And the horses. He remembered their legs, and how tall they were ... and how enormous their hooves seemed to him.

Now, watching Leah standing with one hand on the trunk of Dat's favorite walnut tree, a blank look in her eyes, he couldn't help wondering what was going on in her mind. Because it didn't seem like she was looking at anybody right now. She seemed to be looking at the past.

He was, too. Reliving those moments when he'd realized his little sisters were gone, and no matter how much he begged and pleaded with God, there was no going back in time to change what he'd done. Now, standing here in the soft air of the orchard, just warming up as the sun rose in the midmorning sky, he felt a similar tingle run over his skin.

And then she turned and walked slowly back up the slope, over the fence, to the trail through the trees. "You were playing with those boys," she said. "I got tired of waiting for you, so Hannah and I decided we'd go to the top and see if we could see the farm." She stopped on the trail. "I lost my other mitten and I knew Mamm would be angry at having to knit me a new pair when I'd already lost one before."

Samuel's skin pebbled. It wasn't dread. Not anymore. It was relief. "We found it. After."

The relief was breaking over him in a wave—the way the ocean did to a drowning man the moment before a hand reached down and pulled him out of the water.

It was over. The girls were home. They knew they were home, and now maybe things would be different.

"I can't believe this." Megan panted along behind Ashley as the four of them retraced their steps up to the top. "Now? Just like that, you remember?"

"Not everything. Just bits. The tree. The mitten." Ashley sprang up the last slope of the hill like a deer—she was clearly in better shape than Hannah—and walked right past the fire ring. "And then two people, a man and a woman. The woman looked at us and fell down on her knees. She was crying."

"How can you remember that when I don't?" Hannah demanded, as though it wasn't fair. "You were only five."

"I don't know," Leah said honestly. "It's like a picture on a wall. I opened the closet door in my mind and there it was. But that's it. The tree. The mitten. The lady—Mom—falling down and crying. After that, there's nothing. Until Playland."

"And then school started."

"Yeah. And they wanted to take pictures. I remember thinking it was wrong, but I didn't have a meltdown like you did."

"They take pictures of kids in *Englisch* schools?" Samuel asked. "What for?" A dumb question, maybe, of all the questions he wanted to ask. But it made him part of their discovery.

"Keepsakes, I guess," Hannah said. "To send to relatives. Mom always ordered one eight by ten, put it in a frame, and hung them in the hall in every house we lived in. Except neither of us noticed there was a gap between three and six, when the original Megan died and the replacement Megan started school and brought her picture home."

"That's just weird," Ben muttered. "Replacement."

"Yeah, we know," Ashley shot back, as if he'd been critical of her *Englisch* mother somehow, instead of the idea of a replacement child.

Privately, Samuel thought the woman had to be crazy as a bedbug, to steal a child to replace the one she'd lost. Most people just went through their time of mourning, then had another baby and got on with their lives, didn't they?

Like he was going to get on with his. They stood at the top, gazing down at Mamm and Dat's farm in the distance. "So now what?" Samuel said.

Leah shrugged. "So I remembered some stuff. So now I have no choice but to believe that I'm your sister—and I prefer you call me Ashley, thanks, not Leah. It doesn't change a thing. I'm still going back to Pitt Corner tomorrow, and still going to college on Tuesday."

"How can it not change a thing?" Hannah demanded. "Ash, this changes everything."

"How?"

"Well ... well, now we know our real family is here. Not in Pitt Corner."

"Uh-huh, and if you think I'm going to put on a bonnet and learn to drive a horse, you've got another think coming."

"Maybe not that, but don't you want to give them a chance? To get to know them?"

"I am getting to know them. Right, Sam? We're getting to know each other, aren't we?"

Samuel hardly knew how to answer. The questions seemed huge to him. "Sure," he said at last, sounding lame even to himself. "But seems to me you ought to start getting to know yourself, now that you know what happened."

"I know myself perfectly well," Ashley said crisply. "I can't see that remembering what happened when I was five is going to make a difference. It's a couple of pieces put back in the puzzle, is all. It doesn't change who I am."

"Yeah, the queen of denial. It changes who *I* am," Hannah said. "I can't believe you don't feel the same way. I feel like I have to rebuild myself from scratch, like Anakin Skywalker after he fell in the lava."

"Hopefully you'll manage without the mask."

"I've been living behind a mask for thirteen years," Hannah retorted. "Being somebody else. So have you. I want to

215

know what's real. Not what's been fabricated for me out of lies and dodging around the state staying one step ahead of the cops—you've got to believe that's what they were doing, Ash, with all those moves—and trying to overwrite my childhood."

"What about Mamm and Dat?" Samuel asked when it didn't seem like Ben was going to help him out at all, or add to this strange conversation. He just stood there, gazing at whoever was talking and letting none of his thoughts show on his face. Which was just like Ben. It drove Samuel nutty sometimes. But until he was ready to talk, he wouldn't, and that was that.

"What about them?" Ashley asked. She turned and headed slowly down the hill, back in the direction of the cars.

"They'll be happy you remembered the tree. And everything. That you believe you're their daughter."

"I don't see how that will make anybody feel better. It'll probably just make it worse when she leaves," Hannah said.

Ashley stopped in the middle of the trail and stared at her. "Wait, what? When *she* leaves? Don't you mean when *we* leave?"

Hannah brushed past her and took the lead. "I don't know what I mean." Then she slowed down. "Or maybe I do. Maybe I can't face going back to Pitt Corner right now. I'm too upset. Too angry. Maybe I want to stay here for a while and get to know our family."

"You're an adult. There's nothing stopping you."

Samuel practically had to jog to keep up with them.

"You do what you need to do," Ashley went on. "But what I need to do is call Keenan and get on with my life. In fact, if you're going to stay, there's nothing stopping me from leaving this morning." She checked her watch. "It's only ten thirty—though it feels like three in the afternoon."

To Samuel, it felt as though he'd lived an entire lifetime in an hour.

"Don't, Ash," Hannah begged. "Just one more night. Give Rebecca and Jonathan that, at least."

"What difference will it make?"

"And I thought *I* was the selfish one," Hannah said to the sky. "Don't you see? Now that you remember who you are, they'll want to know. Maybe talk about when we were little. Fill in that big fuzzy blank that we probably made ourselves because it hurt too much to think about home."

They'd made it down to the road, and Ashley gazed at her. "That's the first intelligent thing you've said all trip."

"Um. Thanks?"

"But I don't want to."

"Don't run, Ash." Hannah reached out and touched her sister on the shoulder, awkwardly, as though she hadn't had much practice at it. "Please? Just one more night, and then leave tomorrow, like you planned. I've never asked you for anything, have I? But this is important."

Ashley's eyebrows crinkled together. "Don't you see how hard this is for me? Don't you get that I need some time to accept all this, and process it, and figure out what it means?"

"I have to, too."

"Right, but you want to stay here and process, and I need to go back. I'm so freaked I don't even know what I'm going to say to Mom and Dad Part Two. I have to figure out how to be with them, never mind trying to figure out how to be with Jonathan and Rebecca. It's too much."

"Mamm would be glad if you stayed." Samuel wasn't sure how wise it was to butt in, but somebody had to tell the truth. "Just a few hours of you knowing you're her daughter would be a gift to her."

"It doesn't seem like much of a gift," Ashley muttered.

"Not to you, maybe, but she hasn't had anything for thirteen years. Being able to talk about you girls being little—bringing out her memories for a happy reason instead of being something that makes her cry—I call that a gift."

"Please, Ash?"

Ashley took a long breath and let it out again. "All right. I'll stay overnight. But let's not make a big deal out of it, okay? I don't know how much—" But she stopped and didn't finish.

How much what? How much she could take? Or how much she'd be able to give? Samuel wasn't about to ask.

He must have moved or something, because Ashley fixed her gaze on him. "What about you, Sam? When do you get to go home and give your mom that gift?"

Ben turned away and swung open the car door. Either he was saying *hurry up* or *this is none of my business*. Neither of which was going to give Samuel any help.

"I told you before—if I go home, it's going to mean something, especially to Dat. The price for me to go home is that I repent and join church." His voice rasped a little. "Not the same thing as you."

After a moment, Ashley said, "I guess. I wonder why they haven't said the same thing to us? How come we get to come home to hugs all around and you don't, when the three of us are in the same boat?"

"It's not the same," Hannah said slowly. "We haven't been brought up Amish. Samuel was. We didn't get the choice. He did."

Samuel nodded. For someone with purple hair, she picked up on the essentials pretty fast. "I made my choice to jump the fence, but you two got dragged over it against your will. Mamm and Dat understand that. And nobody's asking you to join church. Nobody's probably even thinking it. The opposite, I'd expect."

"What does that mean?" Ashley leaned on the Valiant's fender. Not that it would make much difference if her weight dented it. It had a bunch of dents and rust holes in it already.

"They're probably thinking that you'll make Barbie or Melinda want to jump the fence too, and go and see the *Englisch* world for themselves."

"That's crazy," Hannah said, her forehead wrinkling in alarm. "We'd never do that."

"Those girls wouldn't survive two seconds out there," Ashley agreed. "Well, if it comes up, Rebecca and Jonathan have nothing to worry about. I've got enough trouble managing my own life without dragging somebody else into it along with me." She spun and yanked on the Subaru's door. "Unlock the door, Hannah. See you guys later, okay?"

"Meet you for breakfast in the morning?" Ben asked. "A farewell party?"

"Maybe." Ashley climbed in and Hannah settled behind the wheel. "We'll call you."

As Samuel swung open the driver's door on the Valiant, he saw Hannah nod at Ben, as though she meant to have that breakfast no matter what her sister thought. Good for her.

Ashley was a bossy little thing. But she had a lot on her plate.

It was time for them all to think about what they meant to do with themselves. Samuel, for one, was sick to death of idling in place and not going anywhere. Ashley might have problems accepting her past, but he envied her certainty about her future.

Even if it would take her away again.

*

Not surprisingly, Ashley and Hannah found Rebecca, Barbie, and Melinda in the kitchen, scrubbing potatoes and vegetables for lunch. It never ceased to amaze Hannah how much work went into the simple act of feeding people. Of course, it wasn't very simple when you had to plant the food, pull it out of the ground, wash it, peel it, cook it, and serve it. Rebecca probably wouldn't know what to do with a microwave dinner if someone handed it to her. And come to think of it, the thought of eating one now was kind of disgusting, after all this fresh food.

"Did you have a good hike?" Rebecca smiled at them. "You must be hungry. There are whoopie pies in the cooling cupboard."

"I'll get them." Melinda hurried into the pantry, where there was a cupboard that had a sliding door to the outside to let cold air in. It was like a second fridge, only less predictable.

"Yes." Hannah raised an eyebrow at Ashley.

"I remembered some things when we got there," Ashley said slowly, after a pause. "The walnut tree that Jonathan always said was the best kind of started a landslide."

"Second row, third tree in?" Barbara dried her hands on a towel. "You remembered that?"

Ash nodded. "And I remembered I lost my mitten, which apparently you found when you were looking for us."

Rebecca made a gasping sound and Hannah finally dared to look at her. "You know now that you're our children," she whispered. "Ach, Leah. *Ach, mein Gott, denkes. Denkes.*"

Before Ash could insist on her other name, Rebecca crossed the room and took her into her arms, her chest heaving as she wept. *"Mei Dochder,"* she whispered brokenly. *"Mei Dochder."*

My daughter, Hannah translated with no effort at all.

But what was the matter with Ashley? Instead of melting into her real mother's arms, she just stood there, patting her back in an awkward way that was totally unlike her.

When Rebecca reached out blindly to pull Hannah in, and then the younger girls leaned in for the group hug, too, Hannah felt something crack in her chest. Under her hand, Ashley's shoulders were rigid, as though her body still had not accepted the truth her mind was grappling with. But Hannah's body was making up for it. Because she was crying for the first time in years. The little girl she had been had given up crying, given up grieving for what had been taken away from her.

But now, she could try to take back what had been taken away from her.

Now, she could cry for happiness, for relief, and grieve only for what had been lost in the past, not what might be lost in the future. Real tears, that came up out of some tight, wrenching place inside herself that hurt.

But it was a good hurt. The kind that you knew would heal some day, and heal clean.

18

The house felt almost full again. Rebecca settled into her chair in the sitting room after supper and evening prayers. She pulled little Katie into her lap while Mammi Kate got the twins interested in the coloring books she'd picked up at the Gordonville bookstore earlier in the week. Coloring all the animals in Noah's ark ought to keep them busy for a few evenings, and they'd learn their English names at the same time.

The only beloved face missing was Samuel's. If he had been here tonight, the lamplight glinting on his blond hair, her happiness and gratitude to the *gut Gott* would truly have been complete. But wasn't that just like human nature? To look up from the gifts she had and wish for more?

Forgive me, Lord. My heart is overflowing tonight, and I know you have Samuel in the hollow of Your hand. Help me be patient and meanwhile, to pray without ceasing that his heart will change, so that the happy picture I see in my head will become real some day.

"What do you remember of the time before, Leah?" Barbie asked eagerly. "I wasn't born then."

A flicker that might have been confusion, or maybe loss, crossed her face before she caught herself and took a breath. "Can you still call me Ashley?" she asked gently. "Not that I'm discounting the name or trying to distance myself from you all, but it's still a lot to take in. I feel more myself when you use *Ashley*."

Barbie glanced at her father, who nodded. "All right. Ashley. Can you remember anything?"

"Just bits and pieces. It's weird that this house doesn't make me remember anything—unless it's those animals upstairs on the dresser."

"Gediere," little Timothy muttered as he turned a page in the coloring book. He hadn't started school yet, so he knew only a few English words, but even so, he was right. Animals. Rebecca smiled as he pointed at the giraffe on the page of his coloring book. *"Was ischt, Mamm?"*

"That's a giraffe," Ashley said, clearly figuring out what the words meant. Would more words come back if she stayed? Would they finally be able to speak the language of home and worship together some day?

But that was a question far too large to answer, and maybe a little presumptuous, too. The Lord would bring all things about in His own good time, and her impatience to have things her way wouldn't affect His timing one bit.

"I do remember playing with him, because of his long neck. I couldn't figure out what kind of cow he was."

When Melinda translated, Timothy laughed in delight. "It's not a cow!" he told her with all the wisdom of his six years, and Melinda translated it back.

"I know that now," Ashley said with a smile. "Meg— Hannah remembers about the barn and the hay hole, but I don't. It's weird, isn't it, that I'd remember something as random as a giraffe and a walnut tree? And not even anything specific. Just that there was something special about that tree."

"Now there's something even more special about it," Jonathan said quietly. "I'm glad Byron Glick has no plans to cut the old orchard down, once he finally got his hands on it after all its legal troubles. It will stand for many years— maybe even long enough for Mamm to make her Christmas nut cake again."

Rebecca thought her heart would overflow. "This year, I promise I'll make it." And maybe there would be some way to make one for Samuel, and take it to wherever it was he lived near Linden.

"You do Christmas?" Hannah asked. "Isn't that kind of … worldly?"

Rebecca laughed at the outrageousness of such a question. "The birth of our Savior is the farthest thing from worldly. We don't celebrate it on December twenty-fifth, as the *Englisch* do, but a few days later, on Old Christmas. All your uncles and aunties and cousins come here to the home place, and it's a wonderful family time for us. We set up three tables that reach from the kitchen there all the way in here—" She indicated the line the tables usually took, twenty feet or more. "—and they practically groan with food that everyone provides."

"Do you give presents?" Hannah persisted.

"We do, to the little ones," Barbie said. "Or my sisters and I might make something for Mamm and Dat. And we send pretty Christmas cards. But mostly it's the family time and the worship that make Christmas."

"What a concept," Hannah murmured.

"Don't you do the same?" Rebecca asked her. Surely, with all the fuss that the world made of Christmas, these girls at least knew about the birth of the Christ child?

"We used to give presents when we were little," Ashley said. "But after we got to be teenagers, the sparkle kind of went out of it, you know? And we moved around so much that we were always too far away from family."

"Our—Janet—well, a few years ago she had kind of a breakdown around Christmas, and after that the holidays kind of lost their spirit," Hannah said a little awkwardly.

Rebecca dropped her gaze to the handwork waiting for her in the basket next to the chair, to hide her expression. Janet had had a breakdown just before the girls had got in their car and come here, too. Was she a nervous person, or was there a deeper cause?

Guilt could do harmful things to one's body—just look at Oran Yost. He'd cast out his only son for something the boy hadn't done, and spent decades afterward being eaten up inside for it. If it hadn't been for Sarah Byler and her ability to see past the body's complaint to that of the spirit—some people called it sheer nosiness, but Rebecca knew it wasn't that at all—poor Oran might be in a hospital by now. As it was, Sarah had brought about a reunion between father and son, and though the latter had married a Mennonite girl and attended a more liberal Mennonite church, the relationship was well along its way to being restored.

"Maybe we could come for Christmas, too," Hannah said shyly, almost as though she thought they'd refuse.

"You are our family," Jonathan said, his voice rough in the way it had when he was holding back his emotions. "You would be very welcome."

"That's good to know." And Ashley looked pointedly at Hannah, who swallowed and smiled.

"I wondered—Ash and I were talking earlier—and she plans to leave in the morning, but—" Her throat closed up.

"But?" Rebecca repeated. "Have you changed your plans?" *Oh, please let them have changed their plans. Let them stay for more than three days. Jesus stayed after his resurrection, didn't He? And haven't my daughters been resurrected and restored to us?*

"Kind of. I wondered if—if it would be all right for me to stick around for a little longer. I'd help around the house," she added, as if this would make a difference. "Ash has to go to school next week, but I don't have anything on the schedule."

It was all Rebecca could do not to leap to her feet and sing. Instead, she clutched Katie until her youngest daughter wriggled and slid out of her grip to join the twins on the floor with the crayons.

"I would like that very much," she managed with heroic understatement. "But your job? And will your—your other parents agree?"

Megan lifted a shoulder as if neither of those things held much weight with her. "I'll just call the coffee bar and tell them I'm out of town. Izzy will probably fire me, but that's the least of my issues right now."

"And the Pearsons?"

"They'll have to understand, won't they? It's only for a few more days. I mean, after that I'll run out of clothes and have to go back."

Rebecca wasn't so sure it could be as simple as that, but all she said was, "I hope you are right. Here, of course, it's for Jonathan to say, as head of the household."

"I have been thinking about this all day, out in the hay field. If you think it's a good idea, *Liewi*," he said in rapid *Deitsch*, "then I have no objection. But we must both remember what we talked about this morning."

There was that. And then there was teaching this poor worldly, purple-haired flower that had been so cruelly uprooted how to grow again.

Rebecca stuffed down the intractable pebble of rage and unforgiveness against their other mother. She couldn't seem to dissolve it—this desire to see her and her husband punished somehow for taking her precious flower, though it went against every principle of peace and *Uffgeva* she'd ever been taught. It was only the thought of peace that finally allowed the love in her heart to flow around the pebble and come uppermost before she spoke again.

"Your father says that if I think it's a good idea, then he does, too. And I do. I would love for you to stay as long as you like. I can't think of anything I would like more, unless it's that Ashley might stay, too."

But Ashley shook her head. "Thank you, but I can't. It's good to know that I could, though. So thank you for that as well."

"You are family, as Dat says," Rebecca said softly. "Your bedroom has been waiting for you for thirteen years, and it will wait for you for as long as you want it."

For the first time, Ashley smiled. "That's kind of hard on Barbie and Melinda, isn't it? I bet they'd like rooms of their own."

But Barbie was already shaking her head. "Not me. I like having Melinda to whisper secrets to at night."

"And to tickle," Melinda said, sticking out the very tip of her tongue at her sister.

"None of that," Rebecca said, laughing. Then she switched to *Deitsch* once more. "Come, boys, it's seven thirty. Time for you to be in bed."

They only whined because they had an audience, but one look from their father silenced that, and Barbie took them upstairs, along with Katie, to get them ready for bed and to hear their prayers.

"I never saw such well-behaved kids," Ashley said in a wondering tone.

"It's never too early for a child to learn to obey," Jonathan said.

"Babies don't know how to, do they?" Ashley objected.

"*Neh*, but toddlers do." Rebecca picked up her piecing and found the place where she'd left off. Handwork was soothing, so sometimes instead of sewing a quilt's seams by machine, she did it by hand at night before sleep.

Hannah moved closer to watch.

"I've never seen a toddler that did," Ashley said. "I've seen them having meltdowns in the toy aisle in Target, and hitting their moms in the mall, not obeying them."

"I feel sorry for those children, then," Rebecca said, setting a fresh line of stitches. "They are frightened because they have no fence around them to trust. They're trying to get their parents' attention, their love. We feel that to discipline a child, to teach it to obey, is the greatest gift we can give it. No one wants to be around one of those screaming children. They drive people from them instead of inspiring love in others. Did your other mother not discipline you?"

After a second of silence, Hannah said, "I don't remember her ever spanking us."

"That's probably because that work was already done," Jonathan said. "Long before—when you were two and three years old."

"You might be right," Ashley admitted. "I remember being sent to my room once or twice, and I think I even went without supper one time."

"I remember that. We were moving, and there was nothing to eat," Hannah said. "Mo—Janet never sent us to bed hungry. Only that once. Sometimes it was only a chicken nugget, but at least we ate."

Rebecca's heart was wrung like a dishcloth between two hands at the thought of her children going without even one meal, when she would have been feeding them properly and watching them grow with such joy if she'd had the care of them.

"Janet said we were skin and bones when she found us, and that was part of the reason she felt she had to take us in," Ashley said. "But I've seen nothing but food around here. I don't know how she can be right, unless you were way poorer then than you seem to be now."

"We were getting established on this farm during those years," Jonathan said, after Rebecca's mouth had opened and closed fruitlessly a time or two. "But I can't ever say that anybody was skin and bones. You were going to gather nuts for Mamm's Christmas walnut cake. Those weren't the actions of hungry children, only the happy task of *Kinner* who wanted to help their mother make their favorite treat."

"Good point," Hannah said. "Maybe she had some wishful thinking going on there."

"We shouldn't talk about her when she isn't here to defend herself." Ashley knelt and began to put the crayons back in their box, sorted by color. "It makes me uncomfortable, especially when ..."

"When what, dear one?" Rebecca asked.

"When you could—when you're in the driver's seat. You know, legally."

Mystified, Rebecca gazed at her. "I don't know what that means."

"Well ..."

"Ash. Don't." Hannah lost her focus on Rebecca's piecing and moved restlessly. "We know what they believe. There's no point."

"No point to what?" Jonathan gazed at them, as confused as Rebecca was.

"You could ... make things hard for them, that's all," Ashley said reluctantly.

Rebecca had a feeling that Janet Pearson had made her own life as hard as it could possibly be, to the point that maybe even Sarah Yoder's herbs couldn't help her. And deep down, she was glad of it.

"Hard how?" Jonathan persisted.

"I mean, she and Dad took ... your kids. Us. You could—I don't know—call the police on them or something."

Rebecca stared at her, then looked up to meet her husband's astonished gaze. "The police?" she repeated. "We talked to the sheriff when you first went missing, because our bishop thought it was wise, but why would we call them when you've returned?"

"Because they took your kids?" Ashley said slowly. "That's illegal in Pennsylvania, isn't it?"

"You could call the sheriff," Hannah said, as though she were telling the truth when she'd much rather tell a lie. "If you wanted to. To get justice."

"Justice?" The corners of Jonathan's mouth turned down. "This is not a matter for the sheriff. It's a matter for our family. God has brought you back to us, and He will help us become a family again."

"So you wouldn't have them arrested?" Hannah didn't sound convinced. "Seriously?"

"I don't like the sound of such words in your mouth, Hannah." Rebecca reached out and touched the girl's hair. She didn't miss the stiffening in her back that told her she'd barely restrained herself from jerking away. As though she wasn't used to being touched. Hugged. Loved.

Oh, they had so much to make up for. And that woman had so much to atone for.

Justice.

Rebecca's very soul shuddered away from the word, not because she didn't believe in it, but because only God was capable of true justice. Humans only created a shadow of it, and sometimes didn't achieve it at all. Their family didn't need worldly justice. They needed forgiveness. And love.

She struggled for it daily. Seventy times seven.

And if only Hannah were willing to accept it, well, that was the place where they would begin.

Forgiveness and love. And after that, joy and thanksgiving.

*

Once they were upstairs getting ready for bed, Hannah shot off a quick text to Ben before her phone lost the last few electrons of its battery.

Megan: See you at Dutch Rest for coffee 7am.
         Ashley is going. I'm staying a few days more.

He could make of that what he wanted. Meanwhile, she had a thing or two to clear up with her sister before they parted ways tomorrow.

"Why'd you have to bring that up, Ash?" Hannah whispered, conscious that there were kids in the rooms around them who might not be asleep yet. "Are you trying to put ideas in their heads?"

"Bring what up?"

Honestly, sometimes Ashley's habit of playing dumb was really annoying. "You know what. Telling Jonathan and Rebecca all that about justice and calling the police. Do you want to make life harder for Janet than it already is?"

"No, of course not. But I needed to know. And you saw how they reacted. Like it was the last thing they'd ever do in the world. Which was all I wanted. I feel better about it now."

Hannah slid under the heavy quilt and pummeled the pillow into the shape she liked. "You could have found out another way."

"I already did." Ashley slid into the other bed and laid her phone on the little dresser between them, next to Noah's animals. She woke sometimes in the night, and had to know what time it was. Why, Hannah didn't know. Night was night, right? "I did some research while you guys were making dinner, and found out how the Amish feel about the police and the justice system."

"And how do they feel?"

"They avoid contact as much as possible. They're nonviolent and pacifist. Even if somebody assaults an Amish person, they'll turn the other cheek. Like in *Witness*, remember?"

"We're not talking about ice cream on Harrison Ford's face. It's pretty hard to turn the other cheek when somebody kidnaps your kids," Hannah pointed out. "I mean, not that it matters now, but if I were them, I'd be giving serious thought to going after the Pearsons with an army of lawyers."

"Not very Amish of you."

Hannah let out a long breath and settled into the pillow. "No. Not very Amish." But if the Riehls did something like that, wouldn't it at least show that they cared?

It's obvious that they care. Every time Rebecca looks at you, you can see how much she cares. How is calling the cops and hiring a lawyer going to show that any more?

"I'm not staying for the religion anyhow. I'm staying for them—for the people who were our parents. *Are* our parents."

"Can you separate the two? Religion and parents?"

"I don't know." Then honesty compelled her to say, "I suppose not. But I don't have to separate them, do I? Why can't I have one and not the other?"

"I guess we'll find out." And Ashley blew out the lamp and rolled over onto her side.

Hannah stared at the dark patterns of the trees wavering on the walls in the light of the moon. No, there was definitely no separating Jonathan and Rebecca and their kids from their religion. And who would want to?

But what if they wanted her to make a choice, the way Samuel had to? In order to have family, did she also have to have religion? Could she do that?

Because being Amish wasn't just a religion. Not like being an Episcopalian or something, that you did on Sunday and kept in the back of your mind the rest of the time. Being Amish was a way of life that was deeper and far more complicated than simply going without electricity and wearing dresses that were all alike.

It was three or four hundred years of history and culture and tradition that it took a lifetime to learn. It had its own language, for Pete's sake. Joining church would be like moving to China or Brazil, and never being able to come back. Total immersion, permanently.

Hannah couldn't imagine herself ever making that choice. Would Jonathan ever ask them to make it? She had no idea. She was pretty sure that he would let her stay for more than a week—a month, or longer than that. But could a person be happy being a tourist in the strange country when they had the opportunity to be a citizen, a native? Would she and Ashley be happy with an annual visit at Christmas instead of a real family?

An empty space seemed to hollow itself out in her stomach. If she abandoned the Pearsons and didn't go all in with the Riehls, then where would that leave her? Ash had her own life and was heading off to it, full speed ahead. But what did she have? No college acceptances, no boyfriend, no plan, no life.

How in the heck had she allowed herself to come to this?

Hannah stared at the shadows, but they didn't have an answer. So much for the writing on the wall. The only thing there was a stitched sampler that said, *It takes the effort of every blade of grass to keep the meadow green.*

Which was so cliché and obvious it was no help at all.

19

In the morning, Hannah didn't have the heart to tell Rebecca that she and Ashley had made plans to go somewhere else for breakfast. So there she was at six a.m. when Jonathan and the younger children came in from the barn, turning bacon and helping Barbie dish up the eggs and something she called *scrapple*. Hannah didn't want to ask too many questions about what was in it, but at least it tasted good.

"Are you sure you won't stay for church?" Jonathan asked as he mopped up his plate with a piece of bread. "We leave here at seven thirty because it's close—over at the Isaac Masts'."

"Their Priscilla is in my buddy bunch," Barbie informed them. "I was thinking—if you wanted, Hannah, you two are a similar size. You might borrow some clothes for while you're here."

Hannah stopped chewing. "What, Amish clothes?"

"Take a selfie," Ashley murmured behind her coffee mug. "Send it to me."

Hannah looked down at her black T-shirt and jeans, which were pretty much all she ever wore. "Isn't this good enough?"

"Of course it is," Rebecca said. "No one would ever hint that anything you wore wasn't good enough, and put themselves above you in their own minds. That would be prideful."

"Pride is a sin," little Katie informed her solemnly.

"I see," Hannah replied, though she didn't, not really. Pride was a good thing, wasn't it? Pride was self-respect and self-esteem. But she didn't really have either of those things, so maybe she fit in around here better than she thought.

Except for the jeans and the T-shirt.

"Please come with us?" Melinda begged.

"I need to get on the road," Ashley said. "We're going to have coffee with Sam and Ben before I go."

"We said we'd meet them at seven," Hannah put in. It wouldn't be so bad if she missed church, would it? Three hours of sitting on a hard bench would be totally miserable.

Three hours of separating yourself from your family, of learning about them and what they believe. You're not staying to separate yourself. You're staying to be part of them.

"Ash needs to head out—it's an all-day drive," she agreed slowly. "But maybe you can pick me up at the Dutch Rest in Willow Creek on your way. It doesn't take long to drink a cup of coffee." *Or to say good-bye.*

If Ashley took the Subaru back to New York, she'd be stranded here. Maybe she should have thought of an exit strategy a little sooner. Did the buses even run through here? Or a train?

You're thinking about this now? After you made such a point of wanting to stay and get to know your family? Suck it up, girlfriend, and stick by your decisions for once.

After another one of those glances between Rebecca and Jonathan, Rebecca said, "We will do that. Your clothes will be just fine for this morning. Everyone knows you've grown up in an *Englisch* home. They'll just be glad you're with us again."

"And after the fellowship meal, if you want to, we can find a dress for you," Barbie said. "I know Pris won't mind."

Hannah glanced at the clock. "We've got to go."

"I'll just brush my teeth and I'll be ready." Ashley jumped up.

In the flurry of hugs and farewells at the door, it was easy to slip out before anybody realized they hadn't helped clean up. *I'll do it tomorrow,* Hannah promised herself as she climbed into the passenger seat.

"I can't believe I'm doing this," Ashley muttered as she made the turn out of the long gravel lane.

"Doing what? Skipping out on church?"

"No, you goof. Leaving you here without a way home."

They were having a mind meld, which didn't happen very often. "I'm not six anymore, Ash. I'll be fine. I want to stay—I wouldn't have asked if I didn't."

Even though some part of her was still tempted to stay in the car and urge her sister to put the pedal to the metal, the truth was that she really did have nothing to go back to. Could she go back to Pitt Corner, back to the people she'd called parents, and take up her old life again? She didn't think so. Not now that she knew what they'd done—and what she was leaving behind here. Something had changed inside her and now she wanted more than what she'd been satisfied with before, even if *more* meant a whole lot of things she'd never done.

Well, that was probably the case for anybody, right? When someone said, "I want more out of life," by definition that meant things they hadn't done or said or had before, didn't it?

"But what if reality hits and you decide you can't stand it?"

"For a week, I can probably stand just about anything. But if it makes you feel any better, if worse comes to worst, I'll just hop on a bus and head for New York. If you get a text from Schenectady, that'll be me." She still had her credit card, and the balance wasn't too big. A little plastic escape hatch if she needed one.

"If you're sure."

"I am. You have more to think about next week than me hanging out on a farm eating whoopie pies and canning tomatoes."

The village would be coming up soon, and Ashley glanced at her as though she realized as well that their time for talking was running out. "But you've never been the kind of person to take a risk. It just seems so out of character."

Out of character in real life, maybe. She took plenty of risks when she was playing Qu'riel ... but there weren't many consequences in a game that couldn't be solved by a gold coin or a health crystal.

How weird. Gaming used to be her whole life ... and here she went hours at a stretch without even thinking about it.

"Whose character?" Hannah said out loud. "Maybe it's time to find some. Or at least learn whether or not I actually have one."

Ash wheeled the Subaru into the little lot in front of the Dutch Rest Café's flowerbeds. "The boys are here."

Hannah had already spotted the old red beater, stashed off to the side of the building by the Dumpster as though Samuel didn't want a passing buggy to see it on its way to church. "Ready for more good-byes?"

"Not good-bye," Ashley said with a hint of a smile. "Just 'bye for now."

Which, Hannah reflected as they walked into the place, was progress. The girl who'd arrived here on Thursday hadn't wanted anything to do with anybody. And now it sounded like she wanted to stay in touch.

Feeling happier than she could remember being in a long time, Hannah led the way over to the booth. Part of it was the change in Ashley's attitude. And part of it was knowing that Ben was waiting there at the back. The boys were sitting across from each other, as though great minds were again thinking alike.

She slid in next to Ben with a smile for both of them. After the coffee came, she could tell Samuel had something on his mind.

"So," he said at last. "How did the folks take it? About Ashley remembering?"

"Your mom cried," Hannah told him. "They were happy that both of us remembered, not just one."

"It was weird and nice all at the same time," Ashley told him. "Playing with the kids, talking, you know." She glanced at Hannah. "Until I opened my big mouth about the police. That kind of put a chill on things and we went to bed."

"The police?" Ben repeated, as though that was the last thing he'd expected to hear.

Hannah sighed and toyed with the sugar packet. "Ash wanted to know if they were going to call the local sheriff and press charges against our other parents."

Samuel's brows lifted so high they got lost under his bangs. "I could have told you the answer to that. No, of course not."

"Well, how was I supposed to know?" Ashley sipped her coffee—her fourth cup of the morning, but who was counting? She'd be looking for gas station restrooms all the way down the turnpike at this rate. "It was a reasonable question. But you're right. That's the last thing they'd ever consider. Your—our parents seem willing to let the past stay in the past, so I'm good with that. I'm still coming to terms with what our other parents did—I'm just not ready to handle the police on top of it. Not when I have a life to get on with."

"You're going, then?" Ben asked. "And Hannah's still staying for a while."

Hannah nodded, and while his expression didn't change much, she could swear she saw warmth in his brown eyes and they crinkled a little at the corners. Like he was happy she was staying. For a second, she wondered how Jonathan would feel about Ben coming to pick her up in the evening. Maybe she ought to lay some groundwork before it came up, just in case.

"The family is going to pick me up on the way to church," she said. "About seven forty-five, I guess. Church is at the Isaac Masts', wherever that is."

Samuel pointed toward the kitchen and presumably to what lay beyond it. "About ten minutes that way. Are you going to change first?"

"I have nothing to change into, and before you say anything, your sister Barbie has already offered me her friend Priscilla's clothes. I haven't figured out yet how I feel about that."

"You're going to dress Amish?" Now Ben's eyebrows shot up, and he laughed. It changed his whole face, and she was struck with how good-looking he was. "Better pick a purple dress, then, to go with your hair."

Even Ashley laughed, and it felt good to be silly for once, after all the drama and heartache of the last couple of weeks.

"Maybe I will. Or maybe I'll just stick it all up under a *Kapp* and pass for a real Amish girl."

"You don't walk like an Amish girl, or talk *Deitsch*," Ben told her, leaning over to bump her with his shoulder. "Besides, everybody in the district knows who you are. The only people you might be able to fool are the tourists."

"Rats." Hannah pretended disappointment. How did an Amish girl walk, anyway? "Like Harrison Ford, pretending to be Amish and everybody trying not to laugh."

"So they're coming here to the cafe?" Samuel said, the laughter fading from his face. "The folks?"

"Mm-hm," Ashley said. "So if you want to be gone before they show up, you should order breakfast. We already had ours."

"I don't need to be gone." He picked up his menu, though Hannah wondered if he even saw what was on it. "This is a public place. And it's Sunday, so even Dat won't feel right kicking up a fuss. I can say good-bye to my sister like any other person."

One thing about this diner, they didn't waste time. By seven forty-five, they'd eaten and paid the bill, and were back out in the parking lot.

"'Bye, Samuel." Ashley was a hugger, and more open and direct than Hannah ever could be, whether it was speaking her mind or doing physical things like gymnastics or track. She hugged him and even gave him a smack on the cheek. "You take care of yourself. You have my number?"

His arms fell away as though he wasn't quite sure what to do with them, and he patted his back pocket. "Right here."

"Stay in touch. I mean it. Both Meg—Hannah and I want you to, okay?"

The crack in Hannah's heart widened a little more at the gratitude on his face, and the blush that suffused his cheeks. Poor guy wasn't used to affection, or even acceptance. Was this what it would be like for her, too, if she told Jonathan once and for all she didn't plan on becoming Amish? Always outside looking in, hoping someone in the nice warm room would look up and notice her?

"Okay," he said gruffly.

Ashley gave Ben a hug, too, and then turned to Hannah. "I'll talk to you soon. And I want that selfie in the purple dress."

"You'll wait a long time," Hannah said with a smile. "Drive safe. Give my—" She was going to say *love to Mom and Dad*. But was that being honest? "Give Mom and Dad a hug for me. Tell them I'm okay, and I'll be back in a week." She pushed the words out even though it took some effort. But Ashley only nodded, as if she understood.

The clip-clopping of approaching horses' hooves slowed, and Ashley turned to see the big, gray-sided family buggy pulled by a familiar glossy black horse. She waved and slid into the driver's seat of the Subaru. A moment later, she pulled out, still waving, and the sound of the engine faded into the morning.

The buggy crunched to a halt about ten feet away, and Ben walked over to hold the horse's head.

"Benjamin Troyer," Jonathan said through the open door, with a nod of greeting.

"Jonathan Riehl. Rebecca. *Wie geht's?*"

"*Gut. Und dich?*"

"*Auch gut.*"

Rebecca's hungry gaze seemed to consume her son. "Samuel."

"Mamm. Dat." He grinned at Barbie and the younger ones, who crowded the windows to see him. "It's good to see you."

"Have you had a good breakfast?" Rebecca looked as though only the thought of what Jonathan might do was keeping her in the buggy. Her body seemed to yearn toward Samuel, standing there next to Hannah with his hands stuffed in his pockets.

"*Ja.* We wanted to see Ashley off."

"Hannah, are you ready?" Jonathan said.

She nodded. "Is there room in there for me?"

"There is always room." Rebecca looked up at her son. "For you, too, Samuel, if you wanted to come with us."

"Mamm—"

"Please, my dearest one."

"We, uh … Ben and me, we have plans this morning. But Hannah's ready. Come on around, Hannah. I'll show you how the back door works."

He walked around to the back of the buggy where his parents couldn't see him. Little faces bobbed behind the plastic covering on the square rear window, and you could hear everything both inside and out, so Hannah simply gripped his upper arm in sympathy. His blue gaze, swimming with tears, flashed up to meet hers in acknowledgement, and the reddening in his face told her he was on the edge of breaking down.

Moments later he had the snaps undone and she found herself being boosted up into the back of the buggy with the kids.

"'Bye, Hannah. See you around."

She hadn't even had a chance to say good-bye to Ben. By the time she got herself settled on the rearmost bench with little Katie, Samuel had fastened the back and Jonathan had flapped the reins over Midnight's back. Her last sight of Ben was his rear view as he and Samuel loped to the car.

Well, nothing she could do about that now. Hannah braced herself with both hands on the bench, as though that would help her face the next adventure the morning held.

Man, was this buggy loud. Between the rattle of the wheels on the road and the sound of Midnight's hooves going at speed, a person could hardly hear to speak. And it was warm back here, with kids squished in and the sun beating down on the buggy top. The doors in front had been slid back into their slots, but it didn't help much.

THE LONGEST ROAD

Thank goodness she only had to hang on for ten minutes before they were turning into another long gravel drive, with buggies ahead of them and behind in a long line.

Time to go to church.

20

How was it that the three hours between five and eight had passed in a flash, while the three hours between eight and eleven crawled past like the eons before the dinosaurs came? Hannah didn't know whether to laugh or cry as she shifted on the backless bench and cracked her spine for about the two hundredth time.

Two women glanced over their shoulders at her, their capes and aprons rustling. For Sunday, these were made of stuff similar to the organdy *Kapps*, white, and their dresses were black. All the women wore either blue or black today—no cheery yellow or raspberry-pink here, no sir. Barbie and the little girls wore blue, while Rebecca and the ladies who had now settled to face the preacher wore black. It must have something to do with whether they were married or not.

The men and boys, who all sat on benches on the other side of this giant basement room, wore black pants and vests without exception, and white shirts. Samuel and Ben, if they'd come in their plaid shirts and jeans, would have stood out as crazily as she did—the only woman in a congregation of sixty or seventy who was wearing pants and had her hair not only uncovered, but down.

And purple.

She didn't care. Of course she looked different. She wasn't Amish and had known about her background for a total of a week, if that. But some niggly feeling deep inside wanted not to stand out so much. Or maybe it was less that than just wanting to be like Barbie and Melinda and Katie, who sat shoulder to shoulder next to her, in order of age, as comfortable here as if they were in their own living room.

They were big on that around here—order. Everyone had come into this room in order of age, the teen boys last. The men and women were separated by an aisle down the middle of the benches. Jonathan sat with Daadi Riehl, the twins between them to keep them out of trouble.

With a last long—seriously long—eternally long—hymn that she did her best to follow in the fat little hymnbook called the *Ausbund*, it seemed the service was over. Then one of the men at the front who had led the service got up.

"We have a few announcements to make," he said in English, which made Hannah blink in surprise. "We give thanks to our merciful God and extend our welcome to Hannah Riehl, whom God has returned to her family, with her sister Leah, after many years."

Shocked, Hannah blushed, which made twice that had happened here when it hadn't happened in a decade before that. Barbie took her hand and squeezed it, while the ladies in the row ahead turned again to look at her. Their faces were kind, Hannah realized belatedly. Not critical. Maybe they had wanted to include her before, or were sympathetic about the hard benches. One of them smiled, and Hannah managed to smile back while the man up front went on.

"The parents of Linda Glick and Thomas Stolzfus have told us that their wedding will be on October fifteenth." He listed off a number of other couples who would be getting married in a month or so. How come all the weddings were bunched together like that?

"Wedding season," Barbie leaned over to whisper in her ear. "Our young folks get married during the winter, when families can travel because the work in the fields is done for the year."

That made sense, she supposed. If you had to take a train or a van or a horse and buggy to get to a wedding, it wouldn't be a matter of a couple of hours, would it? It would be a couple of days. What was an Amish wedding like? Did the Riehls know any of these folks well enough to take her along?

Then she caught herself. This was all happening a month and more away. Who knew where she would be in a month. This was why she didn't like planning things, why looking into the future to say, "I'm going to do this on this date," had always made her feel anxious, and a little sick. It was why she had never quite gotten serious about going to New York Comic Con, even though it meant only a couple of hours on the train.

Planning a future was hard when your folks moved all the time and life was unpredictable. The longest they'd ever stayed anywhere was the house in Pitt Corner, and that was probably only because she and Ashley were out of the school system now, and—dared she even think this?—possibly harder to track.

No, that was stupid and paranoid and not the truth at all.

The preacher wound up with something about a volunteer fire company benefit supper and all of the elders paced down the aisle. This seemed to be the signal for people to get up and go out, again in order of age, to stand in groups on the lawn talking and greeting one another as though they hadn't seen their neighbors in forever.

Hannah would have been perfectly happy to climb back into the buggy and head for home, but the buggy sat with its rails down in a row of others exactly like it in a field, and the horses roamed behind a fence. She wasn't exactly sure if she could even pick the Riehls' buggy out of the lineup. If she wanted to hide and have a few moments where people weren't trying not to look at her, she'd probably get in the wrong one and embarrass herself to bits.

A few brave souls came up to shake her hand and even to hug her—women who were clearly Rebecca's closest friends. They had been in the same buddy bunch, she learned eventually, after several introductions. A buddy bunch was a group of girls who were all around the same age, like Barbie and her friends over there under the tree.

Were there nineteen-year-olds somewhere in this crowd who would have been in her buddy bunch if she hadn't been taken? She was such a loner that the thought of having friends for life felt weird and impossible. Something that you read about in books. Sure, she had friends, but they were all online, and except for one—Raheem in Calgary, who had come to New York with his brother last year for a holiday— she'd never met any of them in person.

There was being a loner, and then there was being Megan Pearson—friendless, directionless, lifeless.

As though she'd heard her thinking, Barbie separated herself from her bunch and came over. "Come and eat the fellowship meal with us."

When Hannah looked to Rebecca, she found a smile already waiting for her. "You go and enjoy yourself. The girls are a little younger, but I think you'll like them. There will be time enough to meet the *Youngie* of your own age later."

Would there? But there was no time to wonder how that was going to come about, because Barbie was dragging her over to the group of girls in blue dresses and white aprons—*Alice in Wonderland: The Amish Edition*. Some were tall and slender, and others were shorter and rounder—about half a dozen in all. She tried to keep their names straight: Priscilla, Rosanna, Marjorie, Lovina, Amy, Ruthann. At least she could tell who Priscilla was—she was the only one with glasses. She was pretty, though, with ripply blond hair drawn back under the *Kapp* and a dimple beside her mouth.

"Come with us," she said. "We'll eat together, and then we'll go upstairs and see if we can find something you like to wear."

"I don't really need to take your clothes," Hannah said awkwardly. "This is all Barbie's idea."

But she only laughed. "I can sew another dress, don't worry. I can lend you a kitchen apron, too, but you can use a cape and belt apron of Barbie's if you need it. They're pretty much one size fits all."

"Sure. That'd be great." At least she knew what those were. She was learning.

She felt as though she were standing outside herself, though, agreeing to clothes that she'd probably feel too embarrassed to put on. But she'd take them. If she was still around for church next week, she could wear them then, just so she didn't feel like such a sore thumb sticking out. Conspicuous was worse than weird.

The fellowship meal turned out to include something called *Bohnesuppe*—bean soup—with enough loaves of bread to feed an army a lot bigger than this one. There were all kinds of other things, too—jam and pickles and red-beet eggs and coleslaw and cake and whoopie pies and some amazing thing that went on the bread that Hannah couldn't get enough of.

"It's peanut butter spread," Lovina said, laughing. "It's the best thing ever."

"There's more to this than peanut butter," Hannah said with her mouth full, like a total pig.

Lovina nodded. "Marshmallow crème from a jar, and brown sugar, and syrup."

"I'll write the recipe out for you on a card, if you want," Barbie offered.

Hannah's eyes were nearly rolling up in her head with ecstasy. If she took nothing else away with her from Whinburg Township, the recipe for how to make this amazing stuff would be it. The first recipe she'd ever had of her very own.

After lunch, a few people hitched up their buggies and went home, but the Riehls showed no signs of doing the same. Priscilla wandered off with a dark-haired, substantial boy who looked as though he could pick her up with one hand.

"That's Joe Byler," Barbie confided, watching them walking slowly near the flower borders, talking. "They've been special friends since he came back from Colorado last autumn."

Special friends again. Another thing she didn't have to ask the meaning of.

"Did he live there?"

Barbie shook her head. "No, he was working on a ranch, taking care of the horses for the summer. So was Simon Yoder, over there." She nodded in the direction of a tall guy in a circle of other boys and a few girls, who was way better looking than she expected an Amish guy to be. So that was the rakish Simon Yoder, whom a girl wouldn't want to ride home with. "Sarah, the *Dokterfraa*, is Simon's mother. She was married to Simon's father before he got cancer. Now she's married to *Englisch* Henry Byler, who is Joe's uncle."

"Good grief. I need a flow chart to figure all this out. They call him *Englisch* Henry because he was English for a long time, right?"

"*Ja*. And because his uncle is also called Henry, and one of his nephews."

Hannah looked without looking like she was looking. "Simon's hot, isn't he?"

Barbie primmed up her mouth. "And he knows it, too. Priscilla was sweet on him for a while, but he never wanted to be more than just friends—until Joe started paying attention to her. She sure had to set him straight then."

"Good for her. Joe looks nice."

"He is." Barbie gazed at the pair with affection. "He's a hard worker. His father is letting him and his twin, Jake, work a couple of their fields. They'll get the money from the harvest."

"Do you think Joe and Pris will get married?"

Barbie laughed. "It's too soon to think about that. But it doesn't hurt a boy to start saving for a place of his own."

Priscilla joined them about twenty minutes later. "Come on, let's find you a dress or two. Joe is taking me for a drive a little later. He has to take his parents home, and then he'll be back."

Priscilla's room was so tiny that the three of them crowded it. Tucked into a gable over the porch, it held a bed and a sewing machine; everything that might have gone into a dresser lay on shelves in a closet the size of a bookcase. Several dresses hung from hangers on pegs on a rail about eye height.

"Don't you hang these in the closet, too?" Hannah asked.

"No room." Pris shrugged. "But I like the colors all around me. Take your pick, if you like, except for the green one. Joe likes it." She blushed, as if this were something indecent.

Hannah didn't know much about color, but she figured someone with skin and hair like Pris's would probably look her best in clear, fresh colors. So she chose a purple one for Ashley's benefit, and one of three blue ones.

"In case I do make it to church next week," she said to Barbie.

But she shook her head. "It's our off week. Bishop Troyer has the responsibility for two congregations—ours and Oakfield. Most bishops do. So we meet every other week."

"Oh." She hung up the blue dress and eyeballed an ugly taupe one that Priscilla shouldn't be caught dead in. She'd be doing her a favor to take it off her wall. "How about this?" She laid it against her chest and for the first time realized that there was no mirror in the room.

"It doesn't matter—that's a work dress," Pris said. "I use it in the garden and in the barn."

"Perfect." It had snaps up the front. Hannah tried it on over her clothes, where it hung like a flour sack even after the snaps were done up.

Barbie nodded with satisfaction. "I thought you two would be about the same size."

"It seems a bit big." She held out the sides of it an inch on either side of her hips. Under it she could feel her skinny jeans and her clingy T-shirt.

"You don't want to show off your figure. We wear them roomy for modesty, and so we can work comfortably." Pris handed her a kitchen apron. "This goes over it."

"Thanks. I mean, *denki*." She hesitated. "I still don't feel right taking your clothes."

"Honestly, it's nothing. But … I guess I am a little curious about why you'd want to dress Amish." Pris glanced at Barbie. "Usually it's Amish girls all on fire to dress *Englisch*."

"I don't know … Barbie suggested it, and I … well, I felt weird this morning. I really stood out."

"That you did." Priscilla grinned. "But we were still glad you were there. I notice you picked the purple. It's a good match. Does the hair dye come out?"

"No. It's permanent. I'd have to grow my hair some and then cut it all off if I wanted to get rid of it."

"Do you?"

There had been a time when making the statement, asserting her personality as a warrior—Qu'riel had purple hair—had meant everything to her. She'd met Raheem and he'd been so impressed at how cool she was, even if she was a gamer geek who spent most of her time in the dark. But now?

"Not really," she said. "I don't think about it most of the time."

"I wish I could say that," Barbie sighed. "My hair is the cross I bear. It never does what I want, and no matter how much I wet the comb, these still come sticking out when it dries." She tugged on the tendrils that curled near her forehead and ears. "I wish God had given me Mamm's hair, like you, instead of Dat's."

Hannah thought her sister's curls were adorable, but clearly they were not plain enough. "I used to be really blond, but it's gotten darker."

"How would you know?" Priscilla wasn't being sarcastic, she was sincere.

"Before I colored it, I mean. It's been purple for a year and a bit."

A child hollered up the stairwell and Priscilla smiled. "Joe's here. Can we give you a ride home?"

"*Neh*, Mamm and Dat are still here." Barbie elbowed Pris in the ribs. "We don't want to butt in where we're not wanted. I'm sure you two have all kinds of things to talk about."

The way she said *talk* gave Hannah the impression she was teasing her about kissing on the side of the road. But Pris only laughed and they all trooped downstairs, the dresses and apron folded in a bundle that Pris's mom tucked into a brown paper bag.

On the way across the yard to the big field where the buggies were parked, Rebecca stopped a blond girl who was walking alone toward a gate that opened on a different field. "Amanda Yoder," she said. "This is Hannah, our eldest daughter."

When the girl smiled, it changed her whole face, which had been somber and thoughtful, as though she had something on her mind. Her hair was golden under her crisp white *Kapp*, but her skin was reddened in spots, as though she was struggling with acne. She too wore a blue dress under her white cape and apron, and wore black Oxfords like everyone else.

"Hello," she said, extending a hand to shake Hannah's. "I'm just on my way home. I live across there." She pointed over the fields to a white house with a grain elevator behind it, similar to the one looming up on this property.

"Any relation to Simon Yoder?"

The smile grew wider, and the big dimple in her cheek deepened. Hannah had no dimples whatsoever, and they kind of fascinated her. "All the Yoders around here are related. The answer is yes. I'm—well, technically I'm his aunt, since my older brother was his father, but I'm only a couple of years older than he is. I'm very happy to meet you. And—and that you've been restored to us."

"Thanks," Hannah said. They'd pretty much restored themselves, she and Ashley, as soon as they'd decided to come and find their birth family. But if everyone wanted to give the credit to God, that was fine, too. It prevented a lot of awkward explanations she'd just as soon not make anyway.

Rebecca said, "I wanted Hannah to know you, Amanda, since there aren't a lot of older girls in the district for her to be friends with."

"There aren't?" Hannah blurted. "I thought I saw some who might be my age."

Rebecca shook her head. "You're in a bit of a gap. There weren't nearly so many babies born that year. Lots before, and lots after, but you and Samuel were two of the few born in that gap."

"And Ben," Hannah said. "Him, too."

"Ben?" Amanda asked, focusing suddenly on Hannah's face. "Ben Troyer? The bishop's son?"

Hannah nodded. "He's friends with my brother. We had breakfast with them this morning, before my sister left to go back to New York."

"You had breakfast with Ben and Samuel." Like a bird swooping, her gaze swung from Hannah to Rebecca and back.

"There was no reason she shouldn't have," Rebecca said mildly, her voice a little hoarse. "We picked her up at the café. It was nice to get a glimpse of Samuel."

Hannah had to get this conversation onto another track, before Rebecca choked up. The poor woman had been through enough for one morning. So she asked Amanda to point out some of her friends, only to find out she really didn't have that many. Maybe she was a loner, like Hannah.

"Maybe you'd like to come over one day this week," the girl said shyly. "I hear you like to quilt."

"I love to look at them," Hannah said. "I have no idea how to actually do it. Where did you hear that?"

"The bishop's wife. And Sallie. She said you'd been over."

The quilt materialized in Hannah's head. "She's making this gorgeous quilt that I just love. It's called a Blooming Nine-Patch."

"I'm making one, too. They go really fast once you get them started, so a lot of us girls are working on one. We could organize a quilting frolic, maybe, if you were free on Wednesday?"

"I think she'll be free," Rebecca said, that smile breaking again on her face like a sunrise.

"I'll talk to Sallie and see who's ready for stitching. I can let you know by Tuesday night."

"Wow. Thanks. That's really nice of you."

Amanda really was pretty when she smiled—she should do it more often. "I'm glad you're here. It will encourage me to get the last border on mine so that everyone comes to our place."

With a laugh, Hannah and Rebecca walked on.

Just like that, she had things to do. People to see. She had the tiny beginnings of a life.

For a week, she could definitely live with that.

21

On Monday morning Hannah woke to the tap on her door, and then heard similar taps on Barbie's and the little ones' doors right after. It hadn't been any picnic getting up only a little later than she'd once gone to bed—but Hannah was glad that she'd gritted her teeth and done it, despite the fact that she wasn't a morning person. Because now she felt included. Funny how something as simple as a knock could make you feel that way. It still wasn't easy getting up, but she did it, pulling on her undies and jeans and sweatshirt in the cool darkness mostly by feel, so she wouldn't have to mess around with the lamp.

Ashley had lit it in the morning, and now Ashley was gone. She was in Pitt Corner now, probably still asleep, surrounded by packing boxes already labeled and taped up, ready to go in Keenan's car for tomorrow's drive down to the college.

Hannah felt her way downstairs, to be joined a few minutes later by Barbie, dressed in burgundy and tying a blue paisley scarf over her hair.

"No *Kapp*?" Hannah asked.

"Laundry day," Barbie said by way of explanation. "No one is going out, and since most of the women will be doing the same, Mamm isn't expecting too many visitors. This is called a *Duchly*, and we wear them for outside work."

She looked more boho now than Amish, and Hannah couldn't help but smile.

Melinda turned up a moment later, and then it was all hands on deck to make breakfast, to milk cows, to get Melinda and Katie and the twins off for their first day of school. Then they had to get the laundry going in the washing machine that ran on some kind of motor with a pulley on the side of it. Hannah had never before considered that you had to plug a washing machine in to make it work. Without electricity, Barbie explained, you either used the ancient wringer washer like Mammi Kate used to, or you converted a modern washing machine. Jonathan did it for people in his spare time in the evenings, and it brought in some extra income.

By nine a.m., Hannah had finished pegging out what had to be five tons of laundry. Her biceps were going to feel this by tomorrow, with all the stretching up and bending over. Rebecca had two lines running from the back porch and over the garden to a tall pole in the corner of the yard that looked like it had been a telephone pole in a previous life. Maybe it still was, since there was a phone in the garden shed.

There was something kind of satisfying about seeing the lines of clean laundry flying like a bunch of flags in the breeze—dresses in green, yellow, and burgundy, shirts in blue and green, and a dozen pairs of black pants graded in size from Jonathan to Daadi Riehl to the twins. They'd done a bunch of underwear, too, but Barbie was laying it out on racks upstairs. "The tourists like to take pictures of our wash lines. I have no idea why—but the last thing Mamm wants is people having photographs of our underwear."

Barbie was showing Hannah where to put away the last basket in the laundry room when they both heard the sound of gravel crunching in the yard.

"What did you say about visitors, Barbie? Famous last words," Rebecca said from the kitchen. Then, "Oh!"

Barbie dropped the basket on its shelf and hustled back to the kitchen with an urgency that told Hannah that *Oh!* didn't mean ordinary company. A glance out the living room window showed her a black and white car with a sheriff's deputy just climbing out, saying something into the radio unit on his shoulder.

"Oh!" she echoed in exactly the same tone.

Unless Jonathan had exceeded a speed limit out there in the field with the mule hitch, there was only one reason the sheriff would have come.

To talk to her.

"Barbara, go fetch your father."

Barbie took off at a run, the kitchen door slamming behind her. Rebecca began to whisper in *Deitsch*, almost as if she were praying. Then, with a shock, Hannah realized she *was* praying, her eyes closed as she stood with her hand on the doorknob. When boots came clumping up the steps, Hannah caught the name *Samuel* and realized with a tingle of shock that there were actually *two* reasons that might have brought the sheriff out to the farm.

Not Samuel. Oh no. Don't let anything have happened to Samuel, not now when I've just begun to know him.

The deputy knocked and Rebecca swung open the door. "Deputy Prinz. We have not seen you in a while."

He took off his hat, which made him look younger all of a sudden, though he had to be forty at least. "Mrs. Riehl. I hope I'm not intruding." His gaze went past her and settled on Hannah. "I just got some information I wanted to check out."

"There is—is there a problem?" she managed. "Samuel—"

"I've seen your son around town and he seems okay. He's not in any trouble, if that's what you're worried about."

Rebecca exhaled on a long sigh of relief.

"May I come in?"

She seemed to recover herself. "Yes, of course. Would you like some coffee? My daughter has gone to get my husband."

"I understand. And coffee would be great, if it's not too much trouble."

Hannah pulled several whoopie pies from the cooling cupboard and stacked them on a plate, then cut some slices off a loaf of bread. Then she got down two kinds of homemade jam and a jar of honey, and set out plates. By the time Rebecca put the coffee mug in front of him, they'd practically conjured a feast out of thin air.

Jonathan came in right afterward, breathing heavily and looking disheveled, and the deputy stood to shake his hand. "Nice to see you, Mr. Riehl. I'm sorry to have disturbed your

work this morning. Please, folks, sit down. This looks great."
He said it to Jonathan, but he looked at Hannah.

She sat in her normal chair. The deputy had taken Rebecca's usual one, so she settled into Samuel's, on Hannah's
left. With Barbie on her right, she felt ... safe, especially
with Jonathan in his usual place at the head of the table.
Hannah had been hungry a minute ago, eyeballing Rebecca's
ginger peach jam and thinking that the jam would be recipe
card number two in her collection. Now she just felt uneasy,
even though this visit should be open and shut.

"I heard a rumor in town that you had company," the
deputy began. "Now I see it's true. Is this your daughter?"

Before Jonathan could speak, Hannah transferred her
slice of bread and jam to her other hand and reached across
the table to shake his. Might as well jump right in. Open and
shut. "I'm Hannah Riehl. I was Megan Pearson for thirteen
years, but I decided to go back to my real name. My sister
Ashley—Leah—and I came on Wednesday."

His grip was firm and warm. "And what brought you
here, Hannah?"

"The um, unexpected news that the people we'd thought
were our parents all that time actually weren't."

"Wow. That must have been really hard."

How much should she tell him? Running under her
brave-but-casual exterior was a hum of anxiety that, despite
what Ashley had said about the Amish being pacifist and
nonviolent, Rebecca and Jonathan might actually change
their minds and decide they wanted to pursue something legal. Better to downplay things. Make them sound as normal
as possible.

"It was. Super hard." She took another bite, and then noticed that nobody else was eating. She set the bread down.

He nodded. "Hannah, I get that talking to me has got to be pretty difficult. Like you say, for all these years, you thought they were your parents. While I can't say I know what you're going through right now, especially with me wanting to ask a bunch of questions, I can say that I do know it's not easy for you. So I appreciate your strength and your helping me understand what happened. We'll take it slow, okay?"

Strength? She felt like a quivering blob of jam herself, inside. That's what you got for role-playing other people ... it didn't give you much practice in role-playing yourself.

When she nodded in answer to taking it slow, he went on, "Can you tell me a little more about that unexpected news? Was it your mom who told you?"

"Yes. She mostly told us about that day in the woods. When they found us. She thought we were lost. Malnourished."

Rebecca shifted on her chair, but said nothing.

"She thought we'd been abandoned, so she said she and my dad took us to McDonald's and fed us." What had Janet said when she'd finally told the truth? "They tried to find our parents, but they couldn't, so eventually it just seemed easier to take us home. It was autumn. Cold. They couldn't leave us outside with no one to look after us, and school had already started."

Rebecca was biting her lips now, clearly trying not to speak.

Hannah took her hand and squeezed it. "It's what they told us, whether that part was true or not. I don't remember

266

much about that day, and Ashley doesn't either. Just losing her mitten and being afraid she'd get in trouble."

"A little black mitten?" the deputy asked. "I read the file. It was so tiny—did you knit it, Mrs. Riehl?"

Rebecca nodded. "We got it back. Only the one. Years later. I made a mate for it and Melinda wore them when she got big enough." Her eyes glistened with unshed tears.

The deputy smiled at Hannah. "I never thought I'd get the chance to see you safe and sound, Hannah. I just want you to know I'm really glad for you. There's no doubt, right? You and your Amish parents know that for sure?"

Jonathan spoke up. "They have their memories, Hannah more than Leah. But we have no doubt. Look at Hannah's eyes and her mother's—and Ashley's hair and eyes are like those of our youngest daughter, Katie."

The deputy's gaze traveled between Rebecca's face and Hannah's before he said, "Where did you say your sister was?"

"She went home yesterday," Hannah said, relieved to be getting away from the subject of Janet and Carl Pearson and their lackadaisical logic on the subject of lost kids. "She starts college on Thursday, so she'll be driving down tomorrow."

"She's where, now?"

"Pitt Corner, New York. That's where we live."

"And your parents' names? Your English parents?"

Hannah hesitated.

"Hannah," he said gently, "It's just for the record. And later on."

Later on. What would happen later on? "I know—I get it," she said quickly. "But we're here now. It's all right. Neither of us turned out bad, and we've come back safe and sound. You don't need to—" She stopped. She wasn't really sure what he would do, but it couldn't be good.

"I'd still like to have their names," he said.

Still she couldn't say anything. Rebecca was giving her an odd look that plainly asked, *Why aren't you telling the truth?*

"Let's talk about something else for a minute, then, okay?" He got more comfortable in his chair. "You and your sister went to school, right?"

"Ashley wouldn't be going off to college with a four-point-oh GPA if we hadn't," she said a little too quickly. Better back off. "We moved around a lot, but she never seemed to get behind like I did."

"You have your high school diploma as well?"

"Yeah, but only just. I think I had a three-point-two in my best year. Probably because of geometry. I liked it." Why were they talking about school? Never mind—it was better than talking about arresting the Pearsons. But if she made a big deal out of not telling him their names, he might think she was hiding that they'd really done bad things. She needed to play her weird life as though it had been normal.

"What name did they register you for school under?"

She wasn't going to be able to dodge this. He'd just keep coming back from a different direction, and she'd wind up looking like she was hiding something. "As Megan and Ashley Pearson. Our other parents' names are Janet and Carl Pearson, and our address is 1152 Lincoln Lane, Pitt Corner," she said, the words feeling as though they had been peeled off her dry tongue. "Dad is an admin assistant for the school district, and Mom works in retail."

He nodded, writing in a little pad he'd taken out of his shirt pocket. "So you both have high school diplomas. I bet your mom and dad were proud, huh?"

"They were. More of Ashley than of me, though."

"I bet they were proud of both of you. My boy is only six, but I practically bust my buttons when he reads Dr. Seuss out loud to me. I think it's just a thing with parents. Listen, Hannah. I don't know your other parents. They may be the best parents in the world, or the worst?"

Was she supposed to answer that? What could she say? "They were okay. Better than okay, even, sometimes." When her dad wasn't away, and her mom wasn't trying to shoot herself. There *had* been good times along with the bad and the weird.

"They may be the best, but you know what? From my experience in dealing with people who have not made the best choices or may not have used the best judgment, what I often find is that they can suffer from … problems. You know, emotional or psychological ones. Many have been diagnosed or institutionalized. I imagine it was like that in your house growing up?"

She stared at him. How did he know that when a minute ago, he hadn't even known their names?

He gazed at her. "Maybe one or the other of your parents had some coping issues, relationship problems, work problems. I bet that wasn't easy for you?"

"How do you know that?" she blurted. His eyes were brown and had long lashes, and they were filled with compassion. How much weirdness had he seen in people, living out here in the land of farms and fields?

"I've talked to a lot of people, seen a lot of stuff that maybe I wish I hadn't seen," he admitted. "I'm sorry you had to go through some of that, Hannah. Can you tell me what it was like growing up in your house?"

She hesitated again. "Like anybody's house, I guess. Nobody knows what normal is, do they? But we live in a normal house, as far as that goes. Dad's been trying to grow rhododendrons in the backyard ever since we moved there. He works long hours, goes to conferences and stuff. Mom ... well, she hasn't been very well lately, but she cooks and goes shopping. Pretty much like everybody else I know."

"How long have you lived there? On Lincoln Lane?"

Hannah thought back. "Three years?"

"And before that?"

Before that, and before that, and before she knew it, she'd given him all the places she could remember. When they'd been little, they'd moved a couple of times, too, but she didn't remember much about it. It was foggy, with only brief scenes poking out of her memory.

He gazed at his little note pad. "Nine homes in thirteen years? That you can remember?"

"We used to joke we were like army brats, only without the possibility of going to Germany or Guam."

He smiled. "I was an army brat. And I never got to go to Germany, either. How did they seem, your mom and dad? Emotionally—personality wise?"

"I don't know. Like everybody else, I guess? Mom is kind of nervous."

"Nervous?"

This felt like a betrayal. On either side of her, Rebecca and Barbie were utterly silent, self-effacing to the point of almost not being there. Jonathan sat like a mountain at the head of the table, watchful and ready—for what, she couldn't imagine. But she was glad he was there. For her.

"Anxious?" he went on. "Moody? Maybe they got kind of stressed in times when things were relatively calm?"

She sort of half nodded, half shook her head. "Everybody gets stressed once in a while. Probably even the Amish."

Rebecca's gaze hadn't left her face, but she didn't smile. Then again, how could she be feeling now, as Hannah tried to make her life sound normal and happy when hers had been miserable from having her children taken away?

Get real, Hannah. They stole you from your mother. Rebecca doesn't want to hear that everything was rosy. She wants to hear the truth. Why are you trying to protect them?

The Pearsons had done their best. Yes, it had been wrong. Yes, it had been weird and sometimes life wasn't much fun. But it had all turned out right in the end, hadn't it? She was here, wasn't she?

"Did your other mom ever have a breakdown or anything like that, that you can remember?"

Hannah stared at him. "What kind of question is that? I just told you we lived in a normal house and had a mostly normal life, just like anybody." Which did not seem to convince him one bit. Probably because he could tell she was lying.

"Hannah, I'm not going to treat you like a little kid. You're over eighteen and have probably seen some things I wouldn't want my kid to see."

The rifle—the glass everywhere—you've got that right.

"It's a pretty safe bet that a woman or a couple who would take someone else's kids has more going on emotionally and mentally than the average person. Which is why I have to ask you about it. Not to hurt your feelings or make you mad, but so I can understand and help you."

"What will you do if I say yes?" she whispered.

She could tell him about the suicide attempts and the stints in seventy-two-hour hold. She could mention the reason for two of their moves, which had been because of breakdowns—less serious than this last one, but still. Life had been rough enough on Janet. When she was well, it had been happy sometimes. A lot of times. Hannah just couldn't bring herself to condemn the woman she'd thought of as her mother—had loved, even, most of the time—up until this week.

"She had her problems," she finally added when he didn't say anything, tears welling up and stinging in her eyes. She dropped her gaze to her half-eaten slice of bread and jam, and her cooling coffee. "Sometimes things got weird. But I can't say bad things about her. She was the only mom I knew for thirteen years. She cared about us. I know she did. I don't want anything bad to happen to her."

When he spoke, his voice was soft. "Hannah, I don't know what's going to happen to your parents. I don't make that decision. My job is simply to find out what happened to *you*. Everything that happened. The good and the bad. And present it to the people that do make that decision. That's all."

She looked up and palmed a tear away before it could run down her face and upset Rebecca more than she was already. Crying again. Second time in three days. What was it about this place? Or maybe it was Hannah herself. Changing. Getting softer. Becoming someone else? Or becoming more herself?

She dragged her attention back to Deputy Prinz, who was obviously struggling to arrange his words so they wouldn't wind up creating a room full of crying women.

"I appreciate your loyalty to the folks you believed were your parents. I really do. But you understand that they can't just go on with their lives, now, right? Even if you're well and unharmed and have come back to your birth family of your own volition."

"What do you mean, can't just go on with their lives?" That didn't sound good.

Rebecca tried to speak, but no words came out of her mouth. As though he had heard them, Jonathan said, "We will not press charges. As you say, the girls are well and God has brought them back to us. We will leave the matter there."

The deputy gazed at him with compassion. "I appreciate your making that clear, Mr. Riehl. But this one is out of our hands, I'm afraid. The Pearsons took your daughters over a state line into New York. We have to proceed when there's a kidnapping, even though I know your people would prefer to let things lie."

"What?" Hannah said, the full horror of what he meant sinking in. "You mean you really are going to charge them with kidnapping us, even though they didn't hurt us? Even though they brought us up as well as they could?"

"That part isn't up to me, like I said. I don't know if there will be charges. I just have to go ahead and do my job, and other people will make those decisions."

"But this was so long ago," Jonathan said, his brows crinkled together in a frown of distress. "Surely it's not necessary when it has all been resolved now. It's not our way to be vengeful or seek punishment, Deputy. That is in God's hands, not ours. We can't be a party to such a thing, and you see already how Hannah feels about it. We must forgive, and move on."

Rebecca looked down at her tighly clasped hands, her mouth working.

"I'm glad you feel that way, Mr. Riehl. Forgiveness is a healthy thing, and you have your daughters back, so you can begin to build a relationship with them even though they've been brought up so differently. It was a long time ago, but regardless of what you or I feel, there's no statute of limitations on a kidnapping. And think about this for a second." He leaned forward, his elbows on either side of his plate. "Think about what would happen if we did nothing. How many people would decide that kidnapping Amish kids is an okay thing to do, because there's no punishment for it?"

Jonathan and Rebecca stared at him in horror, and Hannah pushed her plate away as her stomach turned over.

"I don't want to think about it, either, Mr. and Mrs. Riehl. But my job is to protect the folks in Whinburg Township, both Amish and English. What happens if bad people hear about this? The Amish children walk by themselves to school. They operate fruit and vegetable stands at the ends of long driveways. They play in big yards close to the road. Anyone could come along and snatch one of them, figuring that they wouldn't be prosecuted because those other people weren't. I don't think you want to be the family that sets that precedent, am I right? I sure wouldn't want that."

Oh, this was horrible. "Don't say things like that," Hannah croaked. "Can't you see you're upsetting them?"

274

He gazed at her while Jonathan's face reddened with the effort to stay in his chair. Hannah could hardly blame him. She'd rather be out with the mules right now herself.

To her surprise, the deputy closed his book and held it loosely between his hands. "I'm sure you're scared, and I'm sorry if I upset you. It's an upsetting thing to talk about. So how about we do this. I'll keep you informed of what's going on and you can ask me questions anytime you want. Just call me." He pulled a card out of an elastic wrapped around the back cover of the notebook and handed it to her. "My cell number is on there, too. And when the time comes, if there is a discussion about your other parents having to answer for what they did, I will let you talk to the people who make that decision, okay?"

She gazed at him. "Like the FBI, right?"

"Them, and the people who decide whether or not to go ahead with charges. But you don't have to worry. I'll be right there with you throughout this."

She didn't know how he did it, but the kindness in his eyes calmed her down a little. His boy was a lucky kid. "Okay," she said slowly, trying to breathe calming breaths. "I don't have to testify, do I? I don't think I can do that."

"We don't know yet. Anything like that is a long ways away." He gazed at her with compassion in the lines around his mouth, too. "Are you planning to stick around for a little while?"

"I—I don't know." She glanced from Rebecca to Jonathan. "A week for sure. Maybe two."

He nodded. "Nothing is going to move that fast. But when you leave town, maybe you can drop by the office in

Whinburg and let us know, and confirm that you'll be at the Lincoln Lane address after that."

"Sure. Okay."

He flattened his palms on the table and rose, pushing back his chair. "Now I have to ask you one more thing."

She didn't think she could take one last thing, but she nodded anyway.

"Like I said, I need some time to research this a little before I go any further. So I'm asking that you don't tell your other parents that you spoke to me, okay?"

Because of course the one thing she wanted to do once he drove away was to call Ashley and tell her. And Ashley would tell their mother, and there would be another breakdown—and hours of weeping—and maybe even another suicide attempt. And her sister was supposed to be leaving for school tomorrow.

She couldn't do that to her.

"No," she said at last. "I won't call."

He smiled and fitted his hat on his head at the door. "And that goes the same for you, too, Mr. and Mrs. Riehl. If this gets out and we don't have control of it, people may start making decisions without Hannah, and I don't want to see that happen. Also, the media might get wind of it and that will make it very difficult for all of you—and your other parents as well. So give me a little time to sort all this out, okay? Can we agree to that?"

"Ja," Jonathan said gruffly. Rebecca nodded.

He let himself out, and they stood there motionless around the door until the sound of the car faded away up the drive.

"I'm going back to my bean field," Jonathan said tightly.

"I'm going out in the garden."

"Do you want help, Mamm?" They were the first words Barbie had spoken since she'd left the laundry room on the run.

"*Neh,* dear one. I would like to be alone with God for a time."

Hannah went upstairs and sat on the bed, feeling a little like someone must when there has been an earthquake or a bomb explosion. Shell-shocked, that was the word. Not quite sure if it was safe to come out yet.

When she got up some time later—she had no idea how long it had been—she wandered over to the window and looked out.

Movement caught her eye. There was Rebecca, in the garden with a hoe. But she wasn't praying. Or hoeing—at least, it didn't look like it. It looked like chopping. Hacking. Rebecca was beating the living blazes out of the dirt, with soil being flung every which way, and plants flying through the air in chunks.

It looked for all the world like she was trying to kill something that was attacking her.

22

Panting, Rebecca leaned on the hoe and surveyed the destruction around her.

Forgive me, Father. Forgive me. But it was this or speak, and my words would have done far more damage than my hoe.

The lettuce was over for the year anyway, and this section of the vegetable garden was to be turned over soon before they put the winter radishes in. But if she hadn't been driven by despair and agony, she might have gone at it in a more orderly way. Calmer now, and still a little breathless, she began to hoe out the spent plants, tossing them in a pile at the end of each row.

Malnourished! She still hadn't recovered from the sting of that word.

Her children would never be malnourished, not if she had to sacrifice every one of her own meals to make sure they were fed. Clearly Janet Pearson had been telling herself stories to justify taking another woman's children. Oh, she had been wicked.

But wasn't Rebecca just as wicked for that secret flush of happiness, deep down in her heart, at the news that the police were not going to do as Jonathan had asked, and let bygones be bygones? Happiness that the hand of the Lord would move through the *Englisch* government to deal punishment to the people who had taken her children from their family, their faith, their community? Wasn't she wicked to feel this raw satisfaction that maybe, at the end of it, their freedom would be taken from them even as they'd taken her children's freedom?

Oh, dear me, yes. *The heart is deceitful above all things, and desperately wicked: who can know it?* Even she, who had concealed so many tears over the last thirteen years, had had no idea of the depth of the vengeance that lay in her heart, that had boiled over there in the kitchen as she realized what Deputy Prinz meant by *statute of limitations* and *answer for what they did.*

The Amish had nothing to do with worldly statutes and answering to authority. The only statutes that meant anything were the ones in the Bible, and the only authority they answered to was God, with the exception of obeying those who had rule over them, like the police and the tax man, as the Bible said. In eternity, nothing else would matter, so it was important that nothing else should matter here on earth, either.

But oh, she was glad! And equally ashamed for feeling so!

Slow footsteps swished in the grass and she looked up to see her mother-in-law coming across the lawn. Rebecca had a moment to be grateful that she hadn't appeared ten minutes ago, to see her son's wife behaving like a madwoman in the lettuces.

"Jonathan has just told us about the deputy's visit, and what he said." Mammi Kate bent to gather the dead plants into a heap on the grass. When she straightened, she gazed at Rebecca with eyes that probably saw right into her sinful soul. "Are you all right?"

"I am now," she said honestly. "It was a shock."

"It wasn't very kind of him to make poor Hannah answer all those questions."

"Who better to give the answers?" Rebecca chunked the hoe into the bare dirt, leveling it with even strokes. "She told him their names, their address, a little of what her childhood had been like. Nine homes in thirteen years, Mammi. When they could have grown up right here and been knit into our church—why, Leah might have been taking baptism classes all summer instead of going off to a worldly college in such a hurry."

"Thinking about what could have been won't do any of us any good, *Dochder*," Kate said quietly. "Though I've fallen into that temptation many a time, believe me. What's happened is God's will, and we must submit to it, not say that we are wiser than He is by wanting to change it."

"I know." Rebecca sighed. The pendulum swing of the hoe faltered to a stop. "Did Jonathan tell you that the law was going to go ahead whether we want it to or not?"

"He did. I don't see how it can be possible, but there are a lot of things in the world I think must be impossible, and yet they exist. I wish it were not so."

Somehow Rebecca knew she meant the prosecution of the Pearsons, and not the impossibilities of a fallen world in general.

Confession cleansed the soul. That was what the bishop said, and she knew it to be true. At Council Meeting, two weeks before Communion, everyone in the church searched their hearts to be sure there was no root of bitterness against their neighbors to prevent their taking the Body and Blood of Jesus during the service. If there was, you went to your neighbor and confessed it, and you were forgiven.

Forgiveness was the important part—the part where their old human nature most closely approached that of Jesus. Council Meeting was a few weeks away yet, in October, but maybe God had given her this opportunity to begin the process of cleansing, here in the privacy of her own garden with a woman she had regarded as a mother since her own had passed away.

Oh, but it was hard!

"I am glad," she said fiercely, ramming the hoe into the soil and staring at it as tears sprang to her eyes. "I'm glad that this burden is out of my hands, now. The law will roll forward like a loaded wagon, and once it gets going, nothing will stop it until it reaches its destination ... wherever God wants that to be." She had no control over its direction or its weight, and for that she could be thankful.

"What burden do you mean, child?"

"The burden of vengeance, Mammi." Was this what real cleansing was like? She could hardly breathe. A weight sat on her chest despite all her puffing and panting. "The reins of that wagon have been put in someone else's hands. I'm certainly not capable of holding them. Nor is Jonathan. But I'm glad—glad!—that someone does—the *Englisch* police, the judge. Not me."

"It's wrong to wish punishment on someone else, *Liewi*," Kate said. "It means you have already judged them and condemned them, too. But I don't have to tell you that."

"I've never wished punishment on that woman and her husband, despite their destruction of our family and the eternal danger my daughters' souls are in because of them."

"Haven't you? Then what is this I'm hearing?"

"I thought it was over." Her lips trembling, Rebecca gazed over Kate's silvery head toward the hill where the Glick walnut orchard grew. *I will lift up mine eyes to the hills, from whence cometh my help.* But help hadn't come, had it? The Pearsons had come, and changed their lives forever. "But now I know it's not. The law will go forward without us, and they will reap what they've sown."

"If there's vengeance in your heart, it also means there is no forgiveness, *Dochder*. Be careful."

She had forgiven. Seventy times seven, she had forgiven. And every time she thought she had succeeded, there would come a night where she would lie sleepless, silently weeping with fear and despair, and know she had not.

And she would have to do it again.

"As you always say," she said with a sigh, "forgiveness is the longest road."

"But it is the shortest distance between two hearts," her mother-in-law finished softly.

THE LONGEST ROAD

She had no desire to be anywhere near Janet Pearson's heart, and it wasn't likely she'd ever get the chance. But still ... how far would the vengeance hidden in her own heart, her unforgiveness, take her from the heart of God? Would there be a fourth soul wandering lost from Him? Would that be laid at Janet's door, too? Or at her own?

"You must forgive, *Liewi*," Kate said softly. "I speak from experience. Because if you don't, it will wound you far worse than the pain you've known up until now."

How could that be possible?

But Rebecca knew what Kate referred to—a story not even Jonathan knew. It was the kind of story women shared when they were close, meant to help in time of need. When Kate had been young and restless, she had been special friends with Timothy Riehl, now her husband. But even though he had asked her to be his wife, she hesitated. He went away to work for the summer and she waited for him, because it hadn't taken long for her to realize that life without Timothy was a bleak place, and she had been a fool to make him wait.

Except he had not. Months passed and he became engaged to someone else in another state, and the first she heard of it was when the wedding invitations began to arrive and her best friend brought hers to show her. Their family would have been a completely different one if the girl in Ohio had not changed her mind and Timothy had not come back to Whinburg Township.

It had taken Kate three years to forgive him—including the year after their wedding day. But once she did, they could have a real marriage, one where both hearts were fully in tune with one another—and with God. That had been nearly five decades ago. But the message Kate meant to give her applied just as much now as then.

Rebecca, like her son Samuel, had a choice. Forgive. Obey. Restore. Because if she could not, then she could not sit in Council Meeting and publicly affirm her ability and willingness to take communion two weeks later. And if she could not take communion with a pure heart, she could not be Amish.

Blindly, her gaze fell on the poor brown lettuces, cast out of the garden in a harsh harvest.

Mammi Kate saw the direction of her glance. But in her wisdom, she said nothing, only made her slow way back across the lawn to the *Daadi Haus*.

Rebecca gathered up the heap and carried it over to the compost box. Then she started on the sunflowers, who had managed to seed themselves here and there in her orderly garden, but which she loved too much to yank out of the ground. They were so optimistic, their big heads becoming heavier and heavier with seed until they couldn't follow the sun anymore, but drooped and ripened until they were ready to give themselves up for usefulness in the autumn.

"Mamm!" Timothy and Paul came running across the grass, home from school. "Are you pulling out the sunflowers for the birds?"

"Can you help me?" she asked. "Look at these big heads—as big as you, I'm sure."

While she held the stalks and cut the heads off, and they chattered about their first day at school, the twins, their knees bending with the weight, carried the huge heads one at a time into the barn, where there was a drying loft. There they would dry until the snow flew, and then Jonathan would nail a head to all the bird feeders. The twins and Melinda loved the birds, watching them through the window as they wrestled the seeds out of their casings and ate them. The ground birds, the juncos and sparrows, would come along afterward and clean up.

Even the humblest of God's creatures had their part, and they did it not only because they had joy in it, but also because it meant their survival.

Does forgiving Janet Pearson mean my survival? Are you asking this of me, Lord?

As though in answer, a wren swooped down on a head of seeds and picked one out of it, then flew off with its prize in its beak.

She picked up the last two heads and carried them into the barn to meet her little boys on the steep stairs. "Here you are. Set these out and then we'll take the stalks over to the burn pile."

The stalks were so tall the boys had to carry one at a time between them, but it kept them busy long enough for Rebecca to come to a decision.

Yes, she could forgive. But hers was only one of the two hearts in the equation. In order for forgiveness to have the effect God intended for it, one heart must give, and the other receive.

She had never seen Janet Pearson in her life, nor ever wanted to.

But thanks to the conversation with Deputy Prinz, she had her address.

*

ADINA SENFT

Dear Janet,

My name is Rebecca Riehl, and I am the mother of Hannah and Leah, whom you call Megan and Ashley.

I have struggled with the writing of this letter. My husband's mother has a saying she is fond of— "Forgiveness is the longest road, but it is the shortest distance between two hearts." I believe it is God's will that I try to bridge this distance. To try to forgive. I hope you will let me.

Leah will be back with you by now, and will perhaps have told you a little about us. She has remembered a few things about the time before, but she does not have as many memories of us as we have of her. Hannah has more, and tells us she hopes to stay for another week, possibly two. This is a gift for me—though having her for two weeks when you have had her for thirteen years does not seem like a very fair bargain. But since God has brought the girls back to us, we cannot complain, only rejoice that they are alive, and healthy, and willing to be in relationship with us.

They have an older brother, Samuel. Next to Leah is Barbara, almost seventeen; Melinda, thirteen; Katie, ten; and my six-year-old twins, Timothy and Saul. They are teaching Hannah a little of what it means to be Amish. I do not know what she thinks of it, or what her plans might be eventually, but I hope in her heart she will feel the love that we have for her and her sister. If that is all we share, then that is enough.

I spoke of what it means to be Amish. Part of that is to love, and to be humble, and to obey the will of God. Part

286

of it is to be in harmony with those around us. And that means that I can no longer carry around this spirit of unforgiveness if I am to stay within God's will—and within the church.

So I want you to know that I do forgive you for taking my children and raising them as your own. I hope you will forgive me for the thoughts I have had about you all these years. For the sake of my daughters, and for my own soul's sake, I want there to be peace between us.

With sincerity,
Rebecca

23

On Wednesday morning, after Melinda, Katie, and the twins had left for school, it was clear that Hannah was a bundle of nerves about going to Amanda Yoder's house with Barbie and Priscilla and Sallie.

Everyone seemed to be a little on edge since the deputy's visit on Monday.

Rebecca tried not to think about that, instead thinking back to her *Rumspringe* years—had she ever been nervous about going places with friends? She honestly couldn't think of a single time—unless there were boys involved somewhere. Boys had always made her nervous. She knew now that they were just as unsure and self-conscious as she had been, but at the time, she'd been convinced that she was the least attractive of her buddy bunch, and that somehow she was on display at volleyball games and at singing, feeling awkward and yet hoping that someone would notice her for her good qualities and not just the surface ones.

Rebecca leaned on the door jamb of the bathroom as Hannah brushed her teeth. The toothbrushes of all the children were lined up in a row on the back of the sink, a different color for each person. Barbie kept them all straight, but Rebecca never could, even though she took them to the dentist and saw the hygienist give them out.

"Don't be nervous," she said as Hannah spat and rinsed her mouth. "You already know these girls, and you have something in common with them—quilting."

"Who says I'm nervous?"

Rebecca smiled at her daughter's reflection in the mirror. "At least there won't be any boys there. That always used to make me feel nervous. In our district, there weren't as many boys as there are here, and they knew they could pick and choose."

"But Jonathan chose you."

"Ah, but I didn't meet him back home. I was visiting relatives here, and I met him at a singing. After that, my relatives saw far more of me than they ever did before." She smiled at the memory. In the end, they'd invited her to stay. "I got a job here for two years as a *Maud*—a housemaid to an *Englisch* family—and we were married in the fall from my home. Jonathan was already planning to farm the home place, so we've been here ever since."

"I'm not nervous," Hannah finally said, "but I was wondering if this was good enough." She waved her damp hands at her jeans. "Or if I should put on Amish clothes."

"What do you want to do?"

Hannah's face scrunched. "They'd probably laugh at me if I turned up Amish. They'd know I was just playing a part."

"They'd know you were trying to be respectful. No one is judging you, Hannah. If you want to wear a dress instead of jeans, then you should. If you don't, then that's fine, too."

"I just don't want people to think I'm trying to be something I'm not." Her voice lowered to a mumble. "I did enough of that before."

"The only people who might think you were Amish are the tourists, and there aren't any at Corinne Yoder's, as far as I know."

At last Hannah smiled, which chased away the lines in her forehead put there by self-doubt. "Will you help me? Barbie's out waiting for Priscilla."

Would she help her do something she'd done with all her daughters from the day they could walk? Joy trickled into Rebecca's heart like a blessing from *der Herr*. "Of course."

In her room, Hannah stripped off her jeans and her black T-shirt. She'd stopped putting black lines on her eyes and coloring her lips when Leah had gone, so her face was bare and natural. She had put on a little weight, too, so her cheeks were fuller and healthier looking.

Malnourished. Not now.

"I don't think any of my slips will fit you, but for today probably no one will notice if you don't have one on under the dress."

"What's a slip?"

What was a slip. Goodness. Rebecca hid her surprise by turning to pull the purple dress off the hanger. "It's an undergarment, a bit like a sleeveless dress."

"Oh, I get it. They have slip dresses in the stores. Kind of satiny, right? With little straps?"

The *Englisch* wore slips as dresses? Whatever next? "Probably not as fancy—just white polyester, mostly. Here, arms up." She put the dress on over her head, settled it on her shoulders, and eyed the length. "That's pretty good. Do up the snaps, and leave your running shoes and socks on. If Priscilla's mother wants the cart after all, you might be walking over."

"We could take the market wagon."

"Not ours, I'm afraid. I need to go to town a little later. You'll enjoy the walk. Barbie has her own secret paths to get places. There's a woman named Carrie Miller on the other side of the highway who does the same. I'm sure they compare notes on Sundays after church."

Hannah pulled the black bib apron over her head and tied the strings in a bow in back.

Rebecca shook her head. "Not a bow, *Liewi*." The endearment slipped out so naturally that if Hannah hadn't turned to look, she wouldn't have realized she'd said it.

"What does that mean? *Liewi*?"

"It means dearest." When Hannah's gaze dropped as though she didn't know what to do with that, Rebecca cupped her cheek in one hand. "You are my dearest girl, and I can't tell you what it means to me to have these few minutes together, doing just what Amish mothers and daughters do."

Hannah's lips trembled, and Rebecca couldn't help herself. She took her in her arms and hugged her, rubbing her back. And what a world of relief it was to feel Hannah's arms come around her waist to hug her in return!

"Mamm," she whispered.

"Dochder," Rebecca murmured back. The moment was so sweet she never wanted it to end. If only she could freeze time—the midmorning light at the windowsills, the blue sky outside, the warmth of her daughter's body, well and unharmed, safe here again.

Hannah sniffled and drew away a little. "Why not the bow?"

It took a moment for Rebecca to realize what she meant, and time started up again. "We don't tie the apron with a bow—it's fancy. Just a simple granny knot does the job and doesn't draw attention to itself. Here, let me."

It only took a couple of seconds, and the strings lay in a flat, unobtrusive knot.

"Do you want your hair up, and a *Kapp*?"

"May as well go all in, I guess. But I don't really know how to do the hair."

"It's easy. Hand me your hairbrush."

Her hair felt coarse and stickier than hair should feel. The dye, she supposed. She wrapped the shortish length into a little knot in the soft spot at the base of Hannah's skull. "Hold this and I'll get a couple of pins and a *Kapp* from my dresser."

She showed her how the pins went in to hold the hair, and then took her into the bathroom. "See? Almost Amish."

Hannah made a face. "Not quite. The dress does go well with the purple hair, though—Pris was right."

The shades were pretty close, true enough.

"Let's see what this does." She settled the *Kapp* on her hair. "Now, we use straight pins to hold it on. One goes here, at the top of the band, and the other two here and here, on either side. This little string at the back gets tightened under your bob—that's what we call a bun. And see? Nice and secure."

Hannah stared at herself in astonishment. "It covers up nearly all the purple. I look … Amish … ish."

Without the makeup, the worldly clothes, and the hair dye, she could almost pass for the girl she would have been. Almost.

But there was something in her eyes, in her face, that was not Amish. The effects of how hard the world could be had stamped themselves permanently on her features, erasing the humility and innocence that were in the faces of the other girls. And in their place was a knowledge that Rebecca would have given her life to have prevented.

"Mamm? Are you all right?"

Once again, their gazes met in the mirror, and Rebecca forced her face to soften into a smile. "More than all right. Come. Pris should be here any time."

"I just need to do one thing and I'll be right down."

As Rebecca went into her room to return the unused pins to their dish, she heard a tiny click, like the sound the tourists' cameras made.

*

To Hannah's relief, Priscilla rattled into the yard in the most adorable little two-seater cart—not a buggy, but something like what ladies might have ridden in a century ago. Pulling it was a pony with glossy caramel hide and a creamy mane and tail.

Pris dropped the reins and stared when Hannah came out of the house. "Holy smokes!" she exclaimed.

Hannah had to laugh. "Watch your language, young lady."

With a wry twist to her mouth, Pris nodded and said quite seriously, "I'm glad the *Kinner* weren't here to hear me. But look at you! You look almost Amish."

"That's what Mamm said. See?" She bent her head so Pris could see the top of it. "Only a little bit of purple."

"Good for you." Pris's dress was a pretty raspberry color and on top of it was a bib apron. "Where's Barbie? Is she ready to go?"

"Right here." Barbie came around the corner of the house with two black sweaters and a square bag that had thick insulating sides to keep things cool. "It might get chilly on the way back so you can borrow one of my sweaters. And we're bringing cake and the raspberry pie we made yesterday, for later."

"The twins won't appreciate that," Hannah said.

"I know. But being the eldest has its privileges." She put the bag and sweaters under the seat, and squeezed in next to Pris and Hannah. "We might not fit after we eat that pie."

Pris shook the reins, and the pony started off. "If we don't, you two are walking home. Being the driver has its privileges."

As it turned out, even if they did eat the whole pie themselves, she and Barbie wouldn't have too far to walk. It was about two miles to the Yoder place, and the time went fast, between the pony's spanking pace and the chatter and laughter of her two companions. Pris was one of the most cheerful people Hannah had ever met, with observations about the things they passed that made them laugh. Barbie, she already knew, had a slightly more serious outlook on life, probably because of what the family had gone through, but still, she knew how to appreciate a joke.

When had she laughed like this in Pitt Corner? Oh, sometimes when one of Qu'riel's crew said something funny online, and once in a while at the coffee bar when her boss started in with his puns, but she could count those times on two hands.

Maybe the real question was, when was the last time she'd honestly been happy? The real kind, that didn't depend on getting something for a present or someone giving something to her, like a compliment? Not that that happened very often, either.

But today, with the sun shining and a pie under the seat and the pony's rump bouncing ahead of them, and the giggles of her companions making her want to giggle, too ... well, happiness was like a warm ball inside her that pushed its way out into a smile.

Even if she was doing what amounted to Amish cosplay.

Even if she was constantly waiting for one of the straight pins to poke her in the scalp.

Even if she was the only one in this cart who had no idea what she was doing with her future. Couldn't she still be happy, just because she was Hannah and she was here?

They turned into the Yoder lane, which wound among some maple trees and past a garden almost as big as Evie Troyer's, and Pris brought the pony to a halt in front of a patch of grass and a rail.

"Here you are." Amanda Yoder came down the front steps, smiling. "I've been waiting for ages."

"I hope you got some seams done while you were waiting," Pris said. "Hi, Corinne. *Wie geht's?*"

"I'm very well." The woman coming down the stairs behind Amanda must be her mom—there was the same great smile, the same dimple in her cheek, the same blond hair. "I'm so glad you girls could come. And Hannah—goodness me!"

"I hope it's okay," she said a little uncertainly as she climbed down from the cart. Sometimes people smiled when you tried to make friends and you thought things were okay—until they weren't and you realized your mistake when they turned their backs. Because you were new. Because you were different.

"It is very okay." Corinne reached out and hugged her, and in sheer surprise Hannah hugged her back. Who ever said the Amish were a dour bunch of folks? She'd racked up more hugs in a week than she had in the whole previous decade. "Words can't express how glad I am that you're here."

Hannah followed the girls in to a big living room where a quilt was stretched on a rack between two rollers. "I unrolled it so you could see the pattern," Amanda said. "We haven't got very far with the quilting because I only just finished it yesterday and we've been going crazy putting up the vegetables from the garden, but I thought that since you liked this pattern, you might want to see the whole thing."

Hannah let out a long breath. "It's so beautiful," she said softly. "You did this all by yourself?"

From what she knew of Amish colors, this one wouldn't be going on a bed upstairs, but was being made to sell. In the middle was a mix of spring green and gold, and as the pattern propagated outward, the golds merged into yellow and cream, and ended in a border of green and blue and gold. Oh, if only she had the money to buy it!

"Yes," Amanda said. "This pattern doesn't take long to go together."

"That's what I said," came a voice from the door. Sallie Troyer smiled as she maneuvered her work bag through the door. "I brought the top of mine so that Hannah could try her hand at the piecing if she wanted." Sallie walked over and slipped an arm around Hannah's waist to give her a squeeze. "You look very different from the last time I saw you. From the back, I thought you were Amish."

"The hair is a dead giveaway." Awkwardly, she squeezed her in return. "Isn't this quilt something? I think it looks like a summer day—like a field with the sun on it. Don't you?"

Amanda glowed. "That's what I'm calling it, then. *Blooming Summer Day*. It's for the volunteer firemen's auction in Whinburg—if I can get it finished in time, that is."

Wow. She, Hannah, had helped to name a quilt. How cool was that? "You guys will probably do better if you don't have to teach me. I can lay out squares on Sallie's."

Pris steered her toward the frame, where Amanda and Sallie manned the rollers and carefully rolled a section up, leaving a long strip a couple of feet wide for quilting. "You're not getting out of it that easily."

"You can't be worse than my sister-in-law Sarah." Amanda pulled up chairs and everyone took a needle and some thread. "She never comes to a quilting frolic but she goes home with holes poked in her poor fingers and has to doctor herself. She doesn't like sewing one bit."

"God gave her other gifts, and we're grateful He did," Pris said. She had her needle threaded already, and Hannah had barely sat down.

"Okay, if you're sure," she said doubtfully.

It didn't take long for Sallie to demonstrate threading the needle, then rocking it through the layers of fabric and batting, following the lines marked on top in some kind of chalk. "This is called loading the needle. It goes a lot faster than taking one stitch at a time, especially on the straight seams, like the ones you have in this section."

At least on the green parts maybe her mistakes wouldn't be noticed. She got into the rhythm of it, though tiny stitches like Sallie's were completely impossible for Hannah. If she got five on there before she poked herself, she considered herself lucky.

Two hours later, though, when Corinne suggested they break for lunch, they'd stitched a lot more than she ever thought six women could. What was that old saying? "Many hands make light work," she said aloud, surveying the stretch of quilt with a kind of amazed satisfaction. "This was fun."

"Sometimes when we're in a hurry, we can stitch the straight seams in the ditch by machine, but I like hand quilting," Barbie said. "Especially all together like this. It is fun. And now you know how, so you can do it at home."

Hannah's sense of satisfaction faded just a bit, as though a cloud had passed over the sun. Home. Where was that now?

No, she wasn't going to let anything spoil the day. There was raspberry pie to look forward to, and learning how to piece Sallie's quilt top. There was talking with these girls, and learning about what it was like to live here. There was probably even a little gossip about boys for entertainment.

She didn't need to think about serious stuff today. Not when she was having fun.

24

Because a couple of the guys on the graveyard shift were down with the flu, Samuel and Ben had volunteered to work a double shift—swing and then graveyard. They'd got off work at eight this morning and had splurged on a second breakfast in one week at the Dutch Rest Café, with plenty of coffee for the drive home. It had been a while since Samuel had felt this tired—almost loopy with it, in fact—but the extra money on his paycheck on Friday would make up for it.

"I've been thinking," he said to Ben once they'd paid the bill and were lingering over their last refill of coffee.

"Yeah?" Ben didn't even make a joke about how often this might or might not happen. He must be too tired to do anything except gaze out at the parking lot and the Amish Market, which was in full midmorning swing.

"What do you think Hannah is going to do?"

Ben's gaze swung back to him in surprise. "I don't know. She hasn't said much except that she wanted to stick around the farm for a few days."

"She didn't say anything about moving here?"

"*Neh*. Not a word. But I can tell she's confused about where she's going—or not."

"Can't blame her. Who would want to go back to those people after finding out the truth?"

"She can't stay on the farm, though, can she?" Ben savored his coffee. "Not without joining church, and I can't see that happening."

About as much as he could see himself going back. "So A and B are out," Samuel said slowly. "But what if there was a C?"

"Emigrate to Australia, like your cousin Jesse?"

Samuel snorted. "Maybe she could go on that show, *Shunning Amish*, like he did, and make fifty thousand. Maybe we both could."

With an eyebrow raised in appreciation of this idea, Ben said, "Why couldn't you? We should call them. They'd be all over it. I'm kind of surprised the TV stations haven't gotten wind of the girls coming back, myself."

"Ben Troyer, I swear, if you do—"

Ben waved him back into his seat, and slowly, Samuel relaxed. What an outrageous idea—a good one, but it would never happen. Samuel had been around last year when the crews had come to film *Englisch* Henry and had wound up with Jesse instead. Talk about a way to make a fast fortune—but as Samuel saw it, his young cousin had paid a high price. He'd never see his family again, and now he was on the other side of the world, rich and completely alone.

Samuel shivered. "Goose walked over my grave," he said to Ben's questioning look.

"So, you were thinking?" He reminded Samuel of what he'd been going to say.

"*Ja.* What if I was to move to Lancaster or someplace and get my GED? Hannah could go to the college there and we could get a place together."

Ben wasn't a guy who was easily surprised, but he sure was now. "Are you serious? You mean quit the RV factory? What would you live on?"

"I don't know, but there must be something. People get loans, don't they?"

Ben was already shaking his head, already rejecting the idea as nuts. "No way, man. You'd have to pay rent, utilities, food ... with nothing coming in. And it's not like you have any savings."

"Right ... but see, I only have a Plan A. Working at the factory. What if I wanted a Plan B or C or even D? What if I want something more than this? Don't you?"

"I want a new truck, so I don't have to borrow your beater and get stranded out in the boonies once a week." But there was more to him than that. There had to be.

"I'm just tired of doing the same thing and getting no-where," Samuel said, turning his empty mug around and around. "*Englisch* kids go to college. Why shouldn't Hannah and I go, too?"

"I think you mean Ashley. Except she's already gone and left you and Hannah behind."

Which was painfully true. But that gave Samuel another idea. "We could go down there, to wherever she is. Go to

302

school in the same town. Be all together, like we were meant to be."

"You'd have to run that by them, man. I didn't see Ashley wanting to play house with you all."

Dang it, why couldn't Ben rejoice with those who rejoiced? Why did he always have to point out the downside to things?

"Of course I would. Maybe I'd even—" Samuel stopped, distracted. "Hey, isn't that their car?"

Ben's gaze swung to the parking lot of the Amish Market, which was pretty much all you could see out the window. Sure enough, a silver Subaru crept in slowly, as if it wasn't sure where it was going, and nosed into a parking spot. "Is that Ashley?"

Samuel squinted, trying to see through the glare on the passenger window.

But the woman who got out of the car was a complete stranger. "Who's that, and why is she driving the girls' car?" Ben was on his feet now, leaning to look out.

"Maybe the girls were driving *her* car," Samuel suggested. "Maybe that's her. Their *Englisch* mother. The one who—" His breakfast turned into lead in his stomach.

"I don't know," Ben murmured, his gaze riveted on the woman, who was approaching Gracie Lapp's whoopie pie stand as if she wanted to ask directions. Behind the counter, Gracie shook her head, and the *Englisch* woman took a few steps away, staring at the market entrance as though she were debating going in.

"Come on." Samuel made up his mind. "I'm going to ask her."

"Whaaaat?"

303

But Samuel was already on his way out the door. By the time she made her way back to her Subaru with its familiar New York plates, he was standing next to it waiting for her. "Good morning," he said politely.

She flicked a glance at him, her car keys already in her hand. "I don't want any, thanks."

"I'm not selling anything. I just wondered if you needed help."

"You're not Amish, so I doubt you could help me. Of course, she is—" She jerked her chin at the whoopie pie stand. "—and she pretended not to understand English."

"Some don't," he said. "I used to be Amish."

"Then maybe you know where the Riehl farm is."

He'd been expecting her to say something like that, but still, when she really did, it felt like a push in his already tense stomach. "Are you interested in buying a quilt?"

That only made her even more annoyed. "Why would I do that? I'm looking for someone, if it's any of your business."

"Well, there are a number of Riehls around here. Which one are you looking for?"

With a sigh, she raised her eyes above his head as if she were imploring strength from heaven. "That's right. I forgot they breed like rabbits."

He blinked. Wow. Had he made her mad?

"They might have some visitors from New York. But I suppose you wouldn't know about that."

Definitely the *Englisch* mother. Definitely the woman who had stolen his sisters thirteen years before. Janet Pearson was her name. Now he was beginning to understand why one sister had fled to college and the other didn't want to go home.

The question was, should he tell her where the farm was? Would that be a little too much like abandoning Hannah to this woman the way he had once already? A chill shuddered through him. That same goose, walking back across his grave? Or his intuition telling him that pointing her to the farm would be a mistake?

But Hannah was a grown woman now, not a little girl. She'd already chosen to stay behind when Ashley left. It wasn't likely that this woman would change her mind, and if Janet had come looking for a confrontation with her, who was he to get in the way and complicate everything? It wasn't his business. It was Hannah's.

So he gave her the directions, and stood there watching as her car pulled out and Ben came up behind him.

"That her?"

"*Ja.* Funny, I never saw them. That day. But when she got out, I just knew."

"The car was a good clue."

"Hey, you were the one who thought Ashley came back, which would never happen. Come on."

"Where to? Home? I'm so tired I could fall down, but my mind is all jacked up after that coffee."

"Mine too. Which is why we're going to do this now, before she gets too far."

"Huh?"

Samuel practically pushed him into the passenger seat. "We're going to talk to the sheriff."

*

Samuel hadn't seen the deputy in about five years—not since he'd gone through that dark time and been arrested for drunk driving, then for reckless mischief when he'd been caught driving the old beater across someone's field as a shortcut. Unfortunately, he hadn't chosen very well and its crop of beans had just begun to come up. He'd had to make restitution to its Amish owner, which had been the thing that had finally compelled him to apply at the RV factory, which paid as well as anything could around here. That had turned out to be a good thing, but his bank account was still not very healthy, though the debt had been paid for a couple of years now.

The deputy happened to arrive just as they were asking for him at the reception counter, and he couldn't conceal his surprise. "Well, I'll be. Samuel Riehl, isn't it?"

To Samuel's surprise, he offered a hand, and Sam shook it automatically. "This is my friend, Ben Troyer."

Another handshake, and the deputy ushered them into a room with a table and four chairs that Samuel knew all too well.

The deputy must have seen his face, because he pulled up a chair first and sat, instead of standing with his arms folded like he had before. "I'm assuming you're here about your sisters. Sorry about the interrogation room. It's the only place we have around here where I won't be interrupted by the phone or by people needing something."

"How did you know we were here about my sisters? Did you know they were back?"

Deputy Prinz nodded. "The whole township is buzzing with it. One of your folks stopped me in the parking lot at

Schroeder's Dry Goods on Monday to tell me the good news, so I went out to your folks' and spoke with your sister myself."

"You did?" Samuel could hardly believe it. "What did she say?"

"Among other things, it was pretty clear that she has no hard feelings toward her—toward the Pearsons. That's their name. Pearson."

"I know. She told me." He leaned forward, resting his elbows on the Formica tabletop. "That's what I came here for. We just talked to her. The mother. Janet Pearson. She was over at the Amish Market asking directions. She didn't know who I was when I gave them to her."

"Janet Pearson is here?" Samuel couldn't read the expression on the deputy's face. Surprise? Elation? Shock? "Are you sure? I thought you didn't see them the day your sisters disappeared. How do you know it was her?"

"I've seen her car. It's the same silver Subaru the girls were driving—it's got New York plates on it."

Deputy Prinz used an expression that would have got Samuel's mouth washed out with soap if he'd used it in Mamm's hearing. "She can't be stable. Coming back here is not the act of a rational woman. How did she seem?"

"Ticked off," Ben offered. "She thought Sam was trying to sell her something."

"And you say she didn't know who you were?"

Samuel shook his head.

"Good." He got up and pressed a button on his shoulder radio. "Linda, I'm going out to the Jonathan Riehl place. Apparently Janet Pearson is on her way out there."

"Roger that. Do you need Jim for backup?"

"No, I don't want to alarm the family—they've been through enough. Just ask him to stand by on Red Bridge Road, all right? I may need help taking her into custody." He glanced at Samuel and Ben. "She was alone, you said?"

Again, Samuel nodded.

Deputy Prinz pressed the button. "Apparently she's alone, so I'm not expecting any trouble."

"Ten-four. That's a bit weird, right?"

He didn't reply to that, only said, "Thanks, Linda." He keyed it off and went to the door, holding it open. "Thanks for coming by, boys. I appreciate it."

"You're going to arrest her?" They'd been dismissed, but Samuel wasn't ready to go yet. He followed the deputy outside to the black and white police car parked in front of the building. "Right now?"

The car beeped as the deputy popped the lock with his key fob. "She and her husband kidnapped your sisters and took them over the state line to New York. Your parents don't want to press any charges, and neither does Hannah, but it's out of their hands. If she's back in my jurisdiction, it's my job to bring her down here and get the process started."

He got in, but then the window dropped so he could lean out. "Thanks again, Samuel. I guess you'll be glad to see this case closed, won't you? I only know a little of what you've been through, but it can't have been easy."

Samuel was still a little winded at the speed at which the deputy had believed him and then acted on it. Before he could even answer, the other man had backed out of the lot and rolled off in the direction of the farm.

Ben grabbed his arm. "Come on. What are you waiting for?"

"Huh?"

"We're going to go see. We can take Zooks' harvest track in and come through the orchard. If we step on it, we can probably beat him there."

25

Rebecca so rarely had the house to herself that it must be a gift from *der Herr*—Hannah and Barbie had gone to Yoders', the little ones were at school and Jonathan, of course, was out in the fields. So there was not a soul to see her go into her bedroom and close the door, or to ask questions as she sank into the rocker by the window and pressed a hand to her mouth.

The tears came welling up as though the closing of the door had given them permission. She pressed her apron to her face as she sobbed—the grief welling up, too, and the happiness, and oh, she didn't know what she felt. But it all had to come out or she was going to burst.

Hannah in Amish clothes!

The years her daughter had lost when she could have been growing up in faith, learning the ways of *Gelassenheit* and joy in service to God and her family!

THE LONGEST ROAD

Maybe that was the root of this sweetly edged pain—to see in the flesh what could have been if not for the dangerous selfishness of a worldly woman and a husband too weak to refuse her.

And yet, there had been happiness in Hannah's face as she'd driven off with girls whom she'd known long ago. She wouldn't remember them, of course—Pris had been only a toddler in a pinafore when the girls had been taken. But from things Hannah had let slip over the last couple of days, it almost seemed as though she had no real friends in her *Englisch* life. How could she? *Nine homes in thirteen years,* the deputy's voice said in her memory. You couldn't really make lifelong friends when you weren't around long enough to see friendships bloom and grow.

Would these girls be her friends? How could they, if she didn't join church? Friendship was only the first step—for true fellowship, for the communion and unity a person needed to live a godly life among others who had chosen the same, there had to be a spiritual commitment. Would Hannah be willing for that someday?

It was so rare for *Englisch* people to join the Amish church, especially the Old Orders. Some of the liberal Mennonite churches and the Beachy Amish welcomed people born outside, but people attracted to the Amish life who didn't realize the deep spiritual foundation it required often got discouraged and left, taking the families they had formed with them.

Rebecca took a deep, shuddering breath and let it out slowly while she scrubbed at her face with the apron. If Jonathan came in and saw her all tear-streaked, he would want to know what was wrong. While she could share nearly anything with him, his was a practical nature. He would tell her that the future belonged to God, and she must leave it in His hands and not think these things that made her cry.

Of course he was right. But still …

She got up and blew her nose, and was splashing her face at the sink when she heard the sound of rubber wheels crunching in the driveway. Not a buggy. An *Englisch* car.

Leah, come back to take her sister away again?

No, that couldn't be. Hannah had been clear that nothing was going to keep Leah from her college plans, and she would be on the campus by now.

The deputy again? It must be.

She dried her hands, smoothed down her bib apron, and went to the door. Peeping out the window in the top, she sucked in a breath.

There sat the silver car the girls had first arrived in. Had Leah decided not to go to college after all? What—

The driver's door opened and a woman got out, hanging onto the top of it as though she couldn't decide whether to get out all the way or get in again and close it.

And Rebecca knew.

Way down deep in her bones, she knew she was looking at her. Janet Pearson. The woman who had taken her girls thirteen years ago.

Rebecca fought the irrational urge to run straight out the back door and hide in the drying cornfields. But Jonathan would see her out there and know something was dreadfully wrong. No, she could not run. She must face her, this woman she could not successfully forgive. Had the letter brought her? But the mail wasn't that fast—surely it had not arrived yet.

She had said she wanted peace between them, but she didn't mean face to face!

Oh, Lord, you are a very literal God, aren't you? You've brought her here and made sure I was alone. I must do as my husband would tell me, and put myself in Your hands. Because there is nothing else I can do if I want to survive this day.

She opened the front door and walked out onto the verandah. If she had been walking to her own death, it would have been easier. She was prepared for the end of her life on this earth. But nothing could have prepared her for this.

She stood there, silent, until the woman noticed her. "Is this the Riehl farm?"

This made the second time in a week that someone had asked that. And for the same reason.

"Ja." She was surprised that her voice worked. "You are Janet Pearson, aren't you?"

The woman nearly closed the door on herself in surprise. As it was, she shut the hem of her skirt in it and had to open it again to extricate it. "How do you know that?"

"Because this is the car that Hannah and Leah arrived in last week. Leah got back to Pitt Corner safely, then?"

"If you mean Ashley, then yes, she did."

She still stood by the car, fussing with the strap of her purse on her shoulder. Maybe she thought Rebecca would attack her somehow, like a watchdog, if she came any closer. But Rebecca didn't want anyone to feel that her home was not a place of welcome.

At the same time, the sooner this woman drove away, the better. Why was she here? What—

And then the second lightning bolt of knowledge struck.

She was here to take Hannah away again.

No, Lord. Please, no. This cannot be Your will—to do this to us a second time, out in the open and in broad daylight. Please don't. Please don't let this happen. I cannot bear it. I can bear up under many things—I can trust in Your promise that You will not tempt us past what we can bear—but I know I cannot bear this.

The woman gazed at her, shifting from one foot to the other, as though the silence was making her uncomfortable.

"Has she gone off to her college?" Rebecca finally asked, her mouth so dry the words clicked on her tongue.

"Yes, she left yesterday with Keenan. That's her boyfriend."

"I know."

"She told me, you know. That's why I'm here."

Twenty feet still separated them, Rebecca on the stairs and this woman in the yard next to the silver car. Wrens and sparrows twittered in the trees, having recovered after its noisy arrival. The buggy horses nodded over the pasture fence on the far side of the garden, interested in something different in their day. It didn't seem fair that the animals were not sounding the alarm when inside her head, a crazed dog was barking and snapping with fear.

"Told you what?" she managed.

"That Megan was going to stay here. She's not Amish. This isn't her world. She needs to come home."

The certainty inside her had not been wrong. Rebecca latched on to the only truth she knew. "She prefers to be called Hannah, instead of a name that belongs to another child," came out of her mouth.

The woman gasped. "How dare you!"

"I'm not daring anything. I'm simply telling you what she says."

"Where is she?"

"With some of the girls at a quilting frolic."

The woman's whole face went slack with shock. "That's impossible. Megan doesn't know the first thing about quilting. I certainly don't sew. She doesn't even know how to boil water. All that girl knows is how to play video games and make coffee."

"Maybe in your world that's true, but here, she helps make bacon and eggs and biscuits for breakfast, and she's learning how to quilt."

Out of the corner of her eye, Rebecca saw the back door of the *Daadi Haus* open—*not Daadi Riehl, please not him, he'll run her off the place before I convince her not to do this*—and Mammi Kate walked down the two shallow steps. She made her slow way over to the car and put out her hand, the sun shining through her spotless *Kapp* and turning it into a nimbus over her white hair. "I am Kate Riehl, Hannah's grandmother."

Automatically, the woman gave it a single shake. "Janet Pearson. Her mother."

Kate didn't even blink. "Why don't you and Rebecca come in the house? I just put the frosting on some cherry bundt cake and I need some help to eat it."

"I can't—"

"Mammi, neh, ich—"

And then Rebecca realized what her mother-in-law was doing. Despite all the traditions of hospitality—*Be not forgetful to entertain strangers: for thereby some have entertained angels unawares*—Rebecca could not, *could not,*

315

invite this woman into her home. It would be like inviting the wolf in among the sheep. Like asking a cancer to come and take up residence in your body.

But in her unassuming, humble way, Kate was offering her neutral ground. A kitchen that wasn't Rebecca's, food she hadn't made, so that no memories would be attached to them once Janet had gone.

"Please," Kate said. "Do you like cherries?"

"Well, yes, but—"

"We had such a good crop this year." Somehow she had maneuvered herself so that she was beside the woman, walking around the car and then across the lawn with her. "We had to ask my other son's boys to come and help pick them—which is a little like asking the crows to come and do it—but even so, we canned cherries for weeks. Our shelves look good, though. I like a full pantry well before winter, don't you?"

Rebecca's feet unfroze themselves from the porch steps and she followed.

Kate didn't stop talking until they were all three settled at her small kitchen table—the one where she and Daadi Riehl ate breakfast and sometimes entertained their grandchildren with a puzzle or a book. She handed cherry bundt cake around as though they all had been friends for years, and poured coffee into the special mugs that she'd bought from *Englisch* Henry Yoder.

"These are nice," the woman said, turning the mug around. Its handle was a pair of slender daffodil leaves that spread to cradle the rim.

"One of our men here in Willow Creek is a potter," Rebecca managed. "You might have seen his things on the television last year."

"I don't watch television."

So much for that topic. Rebecca was willing to talk about any ridiculous thing to keep her from revisiting the subject of taking Hannah away. But what? She couldn't imagine eating anything, but one glance from Kate made her pick up her fork and take a bite of the cake.

"This is *wunderbar*," she said hoarsely. "So moist."

Janet was already halfway through her piece. Maybe she didn't get much in the way of homemade cake.

Malnourished.

Rebecca put down the fork and picked up her mug of coffee.

"When will Megan be home?" the woman asked again.

"I don't know," Rebecca said slowly, when Kate made it plain her help could only go so far. She had given them a place to talk and a witness to it; the rest was up to Rebecca. "With the quilting, sometimes the work can be done in a couple of hours, sometimes a whole day. I expect they'll stay for lunch, then put in a little more work, and come home by the time the other children get home from school."

By which time you had better be gone, before you go getting ideas about my other little ones.

"You have other children?"

"Yes. I told you so in my letter."

"You sent me a letter? When?"

"I wrote it on Monday and sent it Tuesday. Maybe it will be there by the time you get home."

"But why would you write to me?"

Rebecca took a deep breath. This had been hard enough on paper. In person it was nearly impossible. *Lord, how oft shall my brother sin against me, and I forgive him? till seven times?*

"I wanted there to be peace between us."

"Peace!" Janet Pearson sounded as though she hadn't been expecting that at all. "I have nothing against you. I just want my daughter back before she gets too interested in your religion."

Rebecca reeled from the upside-down-ness of that. "Anything Hannah does is up to her, not me. Or you. She is nineteen and past the age of consent."

The fork sliced into the wide spine of the cake. "She may be nineteen on paper, but that girl knows less about taking care of herself than a baby in a crib."

"Maybe you should have taught her."

Just like that, Janet's mood changed again, and she glared at her. "I did my best! You don't know what it was like, moving from place to place, getting them into schools, parenting."

"Then you should have left them to me to bring up." Rebecca couldn't stop her tongue. Her brain said, *Stop!* and her mouth just kept flinging out words.

"Those kids were starving!" *Bang!* went the fork on the table.

First malnourished, now starving?

Kate put her hand gently on Rebecca's arm, the way she'd done many a time during those long years when they'd talked. "Hannah has told us what she remembers, and about her life moving from place to place," she said to Janet. "She has not said a word against you, but you have to realize how difficult this is for my daughter-in-law."

"It's just as difficult for me. I still don't have any proof you're her family, despite what Ashley told me when she got home."

"Would you like us to take a—what do they call it?" Rebecca looked at Kate. "A DNA test?"

"No!" Janet looked as though she was about to push away from the table. "No doctors. No hospitals. I've had my fill of that. I only meant that the memories of a child aren't much to go on."

"They are our children." Rebecca hauled back on the reins of her temper and tried to stay calm. "Hannah remembers things from her childhood that we know are true. Ashley remembers things about the day you took them that we also know are true. Even Hannah's interest in quilting isn't a surprise if you know what she was like as a child."

"It's a total surprise to me," Janet retorted. "She's always been a gamer. That's all she was ever interested in. Even when she was tiny, she'd make tic-tac-toe grids on pieces of paper." She laughed—a sound with no humor in it. "She didn't know what to do after she made the grid, but it didn't take long to teach her. I suppose that was the beginning. Now she's battling dragons with other kids from all over the world."

Rebecca had no idea how dragons came into it, but she felt starved for any small detail of the life of a child who still remembered her real home. She would take a crumb of memory even from this woman's hand. "What is a tic-tac-toe grid?"

The woman made an *Are you serious?* face. "Do you have a piece of paper?"

Kate fetched the grocery list and a ballpoint pen, and Janet drew a few swift lines on the back of it. "See? Then you take turns filling the squares with *X* or *O*. The first person with three in a row wins."

Rebecca gazed at the grid for a moment. "That is not what she was doing."

"Of course it was. What else do you do with a hash mark?"

Rebecca took the pen and made four fresh lines. Then she colored in two at the top, one in the middle, and two at the bottom. "This is a Nine-Patch block. A quilt square."

"Now you're going to have to explain."

Wordlessly, Kate got up again and went into the bedroom. When she came back, she had a quilt over her arm—a black Nine-Patch she'd made when she was a young married, with squares of green, burgundy, blue, and rust from her dresses and the shirts she'd made her husband. She'd made the quilt as a memorial of forgiveness, the way the Israelites had made piles of stones to mark events in the desert. Rebecca had had two children herself before she'd found out the meaning of that quilt.

"Oh," Janet said. She looked at the paper, then back up at the quilt. "But that still doesn't prove anything."

"Maybe not. But it tells you what she enjoyed then, and enjoys now." In her room in the other house, she had kept those squares carefully sewn together with basting thread. Even then, she had put colors together with more harmony and thought than Rebecca had ever seen in a child. But to make this point, she would have to invite this woman into her home to see the patches, and Rebecca couldn't bring herself to do it. Not yet.

Janet Pearson put down her mug. "I don't have to justify myself. Whether these are quilt squares or not, whether you have a DNA test or not, we did what we thought was right."

In what world was taking someone else's children right? And she didn't have to justify herself for having done it? Rebecca supposed she was right, there. No amount of justification was even possible.

Janet must have seen the question in Rebecca's face, because her cheeks reddened. "Some days that's hard to live with, but they were starving. That's what I tell myself, because it's the truth. And you can't deny we gave them a good home."

"Nine of them in thirteen years. That, I understand, is also the truth."

She shouldn't bait her like this. Confrontation was not the Amish way, and Kate's gaze was beginning to fill with alarm. But she couldn't help it. Thirteen years of fear and anger and grief had been stirred up inside her. She felt like a pot on the stove, about to boil over any second.

"Lots of people move around. With the economy the way it's been, finding work hasn't been easy. But I've always made sure the girls were in school and fed and clothed, no matter what."

"We do not go past the eighth grade."

"Yes, well, that's illegal everywhere else but here. I'm really proud of Ashley. From the girl who couldn't even speak English to a 587 on her SATs is pretty amazing. Frankly, in her case, settling for an eighth-grade education would have been a crime."

Rebecca didn't know what an SAT was, either, but she could respond to the first part.

"Our children speak *Deitsch*—Pennsylvania Dutch—in the home. They don't learn English until they go to school."

"That explains why only Megan spoke a little, then."

"Tell me about the other Megan," Kate said softly. "Your first child."

Clever Kate, deflecting the conversation before Rebecca lost her temper. She would have expected Janet to talk about her other child eagerly, but instead, her face settled into bleak lines, like a frostbitten flower.

"How do you know about her? Megan shouldn't have told you. That's private."

"She referred to herself as the replacement child."

Another sharp glance from Kate. She must stop throwing words like darts, or this woman would get even more upset and angry, and Rebecca didn't like to think about what might happen then—especially if Jonathan or even Hannah herself came home.

Too late.

Janet Pearson's eyes filled with tears, and her mouth shook. "How dare you!"

She'd never been a very daring person, but it seemed she was becoming one. Or perhaps simply speaking the truth was an act of daring.

Speak the truth in love.

Rebecca caught her breath at the rebuke in that still, small voice. Her throat swelled with tears, too—but not of anger. Of shame.

THE LONGEST ROAD

Forgive me, Lord. That is the part that's missing here. I can't seem to govern my tongue. Please help me heal the two of us, not hurt.

"I am sorry that you lost a child," she said at last. "That must have been very hard."

"It was." Janet sounded grudging, as though she would rather be outraged than accept sympathy. "The hardest thing I've ever been through, except—" She stopped. "She was beautiful, with blond curls that used to wrap themselves around my finger, and big eyes like Megan's—I mean, Hannah's—I mean—" She frowned. "Why did you change her name?"

"She changed it," Kate reminded her for the second time. "Back to what it was before. Hannah is Rebecca's mother's name."

"Megan Alice," she said, as if Kate had not spoken. "My mother's name was Alice. After Alice in Wonderland. She died."

Alice in Wonderland? That was a storybook, wasn't it? Rebecca couldn't remember if the character died or not.

"Everybody dies." Janet got up. "Everyone gets taken away from me. And now you want to take her away from me, too. Well, I'm not going to let you. You direct me to wherever this quilting bee is, please, so I can take her home."

Something in her face didn't look right. Normal.

"Are you all right, Janet?" Caution began to blossom into alarm. "Maybe you should sit down."

"Take me there, now. Come on. Get in the car. You Amish don't drive cars, do you? I'll drive you over there and you give me directions."

Rebecca wouldn't get in a car with this woman even if Kate had not made a murmur of dissent.

"Why don't we have another piece of cake while we wait for her? I'm sure she won't be long. I can phone over there, too, though the phone shanty is all the way at the end of the driveway and no one may hear it."

Janet shook her head as though Rebecca's attempt at soothing her was as annoying as a swarm of mosquitoes. "I have no idea what you're talking about. Come on."

She pushed back her chair and was outside on the lawn before Rebecca or Kate could stop her. Through the open door, Rebecca heard a sound that made her blood freeze in her veins.

Hooves, and the sound of a pony cart crunching down the lane.

26

Hannah saw the Subaru when they topped the little rise and headed into the yard, and her heart leaped. Ashley had changed her mind and come back! It seemed incredible, but maybe miracles still happened.

Then she caught sight of movement on the front steps of the little house where Mammi Kate and Daadi Riehl lived, and instead of leaping, her heart nearly stopped in her chest.

"Mom!" she said on a gasp.

Priscilla pulled on the reins, but the pony hadn't even come to a halt before Hannah flung herself out of the seat, stumbling a little in the gravel before she recovered herself.

The woman she'd thought was her mother for thirteen years stared at her with absolutely zero recognition.

"Mom!" she exclaimed. "What are you doing here?"

Janet's jaw sagged, and her eyes rounded. "You're not my daughter."

"Yeah, I know," Hannah blurted, before her brain could kick in. "Is Ashley all right?"

And then full recognition hit Janet Pearson as though someone had swung one of the bags of chicken feed at her. "Megan! What have they done to you?"

She'd forgotten she was still wearing Amish clothes.

"I knew it! I knew they were trying to get you back into their church! Well, it's not going to work. You go upstairs and change right now, and I'll take you home."

"Wait—what? Why?"

"You heard me." She sounded just the way she used to when she and Ashley were kids and had done something bad, like plug up the holes in the tub and flood the bathroom, or break an ornament that had somehow managed to survive all the moves.

"Did something happen to Dad? What's going on?"

"No, of course not. Come on. Stop talking and get moving."

"But I need to talk. I'm not going home yet. I'm staying for another week. Ashley said she was going to tell you. Is she okay?"

"How should I know? I haven't heard a word since she and Keenan left yesterday. What do you need to stay another week for?"

Hannah spread her hands to take in the yard, Rebecca, Mammi Kate, and the other girls, all of whom were frozen silent, as unmoving as the trees on the lawn. "To get to know everybody." She purposely didn't say *my Amish family* in case Janet got even more upset.

"You've had all the time you need to do that. Come on, now. Ashley said you were going to do this, and I couldn't call because your phone just goes to voice mail—"

"I can't charge it here, so I've been keeping it turned off."

"—so I had no choice but to come and get you myself."

"But why? What difference does a week make? Are you sure you're okay? Did you take your meds? Does the doctor know you're driving?"

Barbie flinched as Janet told her what the doctor could do with his meds—and his opinions.

Which told Hannah he probably didn't know she'd gotten behind the wheel on those medications when she wasn't supposed to. Maybe the rules about that were different in Pennsylvania, but still—

Pennsylvania. Janet was back in Pennsylvania, where Hannah realized now she and Carl had always been careful never to take a vacation or accept a job. Not that it would have done any good, if what Deputy Prinz said was true about the statute of limitations. The point was, she had to get her mother out of here.

"Mom, listen."

"No, you listen. You're coming home with me and that's that. Go and get your things, and for goodness sake, take that outfit off. You look like you're in a play."

"All right, all right. But Mom, it's not safe for you to be here."

"Why not? Are they coming out of the fields with hoes and scythes?"

"This isn't *Witness*. The sheriff was here on Monday and he knows about you. You have to go before somebody tells him you're here."

"Nobody's going to do that."

"You don't know the Amish telegraph. They usually don't have much to do with the sheriff, but he still found out. You've got to go."

"I'm not leaving without you."

Agonized, Hannah's gaze found Rebecca's, and what she saw there made tears spring to her eyes. If *she* was freaking out about Janet being here, Rebecca must be ready to have a breakdown. She'd never seen eyes like this—twin wells of despair and grief. She was suddenly sure that this was what her mother had looked like the day she and Ashley disappeared.

She couldn't leave. Not with Rebecca's stricken face the last thing she would see in the rear view mirror.

But if Janet wouldn't go unless she went with her, what was she going to do? Deputy Prinz would come and arrest her.

Whether it's here or there, he's going to make sure it happens. Your going with her won't accomplish anything except to hurt Rebecca even worse.

She couldn't bear it. Go, and add to Rebecca's burden of pain? Or stay, and risk Janet having a meltdown right here in the yard? Or worse—another suicide attempt? And she'd be responsible for it this time—directly responsible.

"Hannah." Rebecca crossed the yard to her and slipped an arm around her shoulders. "We don't want you to go, of course. But if it would bring peace, then I encourage you to do as Janet asks."

Hannah turned into her embrace. "The sheriff will come. I know he will. And I can't have that on my conscience."

"No one here will call him."

She lifted her head, her lips trembling as she tried to hold back tears. "You won't? But he said—"

"This is a matter for our family, not the law, despite what he believes to be true. The law says we should telephone him. But our faith says we must forgive and let go."

"How can you do that?" Hannah breathed. "I'm not even sure I can."

"I must," Rebecca said simply. "And today I have. We ate cake at Mammi Kate's table and talked a few things over."

Hannah pulled away a little in astonishment. "You did?" Maybe Janet wasn't as close to suicide as she'd thought. Maybe this would all come out right, if she could just keep calm.

"We didn't get very far before we heard the pony, but—"

"Megan, come on," Janet said impatiently. "Say your good-byes and get in the car."

Gently, Hannah stepped out of Rebecca's hug, but didn't leave her side. "I wasn't saying good-bye. I really want to stay for a little while, Mom. But you have to go. I don't want you to be arrested."

"Arrested! No one's going to arrest me if you'll just do as you're told and get your things."

"I need a week. I want to stay for a week, okay? Then I'll catch the bus home and call you from the station, I promise."

Janet's face set in the way Hannah knew meant it was her way or the highway. "If you would rather stay here in a religious cult than come home to be with your father and me, then you'd better get used to wearing those clothes, because you won't be welcome at our house anymore. I'll mail all your things here—except your computer. That you'll have to live without."

"Aw, Mom, come on—"

"I mean it, Megan. Make up your mind."

It's not fair! wailed the little kid in her head.

She's manipulating you, said a cooler, more rational voice. *A mother who loved you would want the best for you. She wouldn't put you in the middle, like the rope in a tug of war over a giant mud puddle.*

A mother who loved her would want her to be happy, even if that meant going with the other mother. Wasn't there a story about that somewhere? The baby had wound up almost getting sliced down the middle, which was pretty much what was happening inside her.

Don't let her do this to you.

"Hannah—" Rebecca began, but stopped and turned.

Hannah heard it, too. The sound of a car coming down the drive. No, not down the drive. Across the field. In a moment, two doors slammed.

"The sheriff?" she asked.

"Not on the Zooks' harvest track," Barbie said, thawing abruptly and pointing across the yard. "Mamm, look. In the orchard."

Now Hannah could see them—Samuel and Ben, running through the orchard like a pair of men on a mission, instead of driving up the lane like normal people.

"Samuel," Rebecca breathed. "Oh, Samuel, your father—"

330

"Hannah," Samuel called when they came around the corner of the house.

"What are you doing here?" Didn't he know how upset their father would be if he saw him?

"We came to tell you. To stand by you if no one was here. The sheriff—"

Hannah gasped. "I knew it!" She whirled to Janet. "You've got to go, right now."

"Not without—"

"Oh, for Pete's sake! Fine!"

She ran up the steps into the house, then up the staircase to the bedroom. She stuffed everything she could get her hands on into her gym bag in frantic haste, grabbed her phone off the dresser and stuffed it in the pocket of her dress, and slinging the bag over her shoulder, ran down and outside again.

"Fine, let's go."

"Not like that, you're not. What will people say?"

"What did they say the last time you had Amish girls in your car?" Hannah snapped, completely losing it. "Mom, either we go right now or all of us are going to have to watch you getting arrested. Is that what you want?"

"Nobody has arrested anybody in thirteen years, so it's not likely they're going to start now. Get those clothes off before I start taking them off you."

Take that dress off before I take it off you myself.

Like an echo from the past, Hannah heard almost the same words in exactly the same exasperated tone. History was repeating itself.

Or it would, if she didn't do something about it. Because now she had the ability to change things. To stand up and do what was right.

Janet Pearson had so little sense of self-preservation that she was willing to risk her own freedom to have her back. To have a daughter. Even if Hannah wasn't her own. Even if she broke another mother's heart in the process.

And here was poor Samuel, risking his father's wrath to come here and stand by her if she'd been alone.

What kind of a life did she have to go back to? No kind of a life, that's what. Ashley had the guts to make her own, but all Hannah had was what she was holding onto by her fingernails, right here. This was worth taking a risk for.

Family. Love. Home.

Even if she eventually had to leave it, right now she wanted to stay with every cell in her body. Hannah opened her mouth to tell them she'd changed her mind. That she'd made a different choice.

And then they all heard the crunch of gravel as a car turned into the lane.

Janet spun to look up the drive as the black and white sheriff's car nosed over the rise and rolled to a stop behind Priscilla's pony trap. The pony whuffed and sidestepped, its reins loose in Priscilla's limp hands, and the trap clattered on the gravel. Without a word, Ben walked around the frozen group of women and patted the pony's nose, then led it over to the fence. Priscilla climbed out, and she and Ben stood next to the horse, as unwilling as witnesses could be, but still … they, too, were standing behind her if she needed them.

Her big brother walked quietly to her side.

Deputy Prinz got out, speaking into his shoulder microphone in a low tone, searching the yard. When his gaze connected with Hannah's, he seemed to relax. "Hannah, is everything all right?"

She couldn't get any words out of a throat constricted by anxiety, but she nodded.

"Is this your other mother, Janet Pearson?"

"How do you know my name?" Janet demanded. "Megan, what have you been saying? What do you mean, other mother? I'm her mom. That's a title a woman earns, you know. Mom. It doesn't come just because you have babies."

Deputy Prinz had been approaching slowly, looking as calm and unthreatening as a man could who had a big utility belt and handcuffs and a gun in a holster on his hip. "Mrs. Pearson, my name is Deputy Prinz of the Whinburg Township Sheriff's Department. I would like you to come with me."

"What for? I certainly can't go anywhere now that you've blocked me in."

"I want to talk with you about the events of thirteen years ago. If you don't mind stepping over here, we can go down to the office and you can tell me what happened."

"I don't get into cars with strange men," Janet snapped. "And I certainly don't have anything to say to a sheriff, unless wanting to take my daughter home is a crime. I'd appreciate you moving your car so we can go."

"I can't do that, ma'am. Hannah is staying here, and I'd like you to come with me."

"She is not! Look, she has her bags packed and ready to go. If she wasn't so slow, we'd have been gone already."

"Is that true, Hannah?" He asked her, but he kept a watchful eye on Janet. "Were you going to leave with her?"

"Only because ..." *Only because I was deluded for ten minutes too long. Only because I wanted her out of here before you came, so my family wouldn't have to witness this.* She cleared her throat. "No, I wasn't. I changed my mind at the last minute."

"Hannah!" And there was that look on Janet's face again, where anger and hurt mingled, where pain and selfishness stared out of her eyes. That look that said, *Why don't you do what I want you to? Why aren't you who I want you to be?*

"I'm not going back," she said to the woman she'd thought of as her mother, but who had never mothered her. Not really.

Ben stepped a little closer, and Samuel's sleeve brushed her arm. He was trembling, but still he stood beside her.

Two subtle movements, two silent young men, but they gave her the courage to say, "You should go with Deputy Prinz. I'm going to stay here for a while, long enough to figure out what I'm doing with my life."

"No." Janet shook her head, as if Hannah had told her she wasn't going to eat her peas. "No. You're coming with me." Before the deputy could move, she marched across the grass and grabbed Hannah's arm. "You tell him nobody's done anything wrong, that you're perfectly fine, and you're coming home."

Hannah tried to pull her arm out of Janet's grip. "No."

"Don't say no to me!"

"Mrs. Pearson, let Hannah go, please." The deputy said something into his shoulder microphone and started toward them.

"Megan, I said now!" And she slapped Hannah full in the face.

Rebecca cried out, and Samuel and Ben both stepped forward to take Janet's arms, as though the three of them were going for a walk together. Hannah stumbled back, her hand pressed to her stinging cheek.

"Let go of me! Deputy, these boys are assaulting me!"

In a blink of an eye, the deputy had her arms behind her and was clicking the handcuffs closed.

"Megan!" she shouted as he pulled her with him and put her in the backseat of the car. "Megan!" But the windows were rolled up, and the sound was muffled behind the glass.

Deputy Prinz nodded to Hannah. "You're all right?"

"Yes," she managed.

"Do you want me to charge her with assault?"

"No. Oh, no. I just want this to be over."

"You did right. Don't forget that. I'll be in touch." He got in, wheeled the car in a neat three-point turn, and accelerated up the lane. They could hear the powerful engine racing away up Red Bridge Road.

Hannah turned to find herself enveloped in Rebecca's hug. The rapid, heartbroken words were *Deitsch*, but Hannah had no trouble translating. "Oh, my daughter, my sweet girl. Are you all right? Did she hurt you?"

"I'm okay," she whispered. "I'm fine."

It had hurt. The shock of it had hurt more. But it would fade, like the memories of living another girl's childhood would fade. Even now, the sweetness of her mother's embrace was taking over and erasing the sting.

All that was left was the love. All that was left was her brother, and her mother, and her sisters and her friends, and in the distance, the urgent figure of Jonathan, charging across the field toward his family. He'd clearly just seen the sheriff's car leaving. Hannah lifted her tearstained face and met her mother's wet gaze.

"It's okay. She didn't hurt me. And she can never hurt us again."

It wasn't over by any means. The sheriff had been straight with her about that on Monday. Hannah would have to make decisions that wouldn't be easy, and would probably hurt. She didn't even want to think about explaining this to Ashley, but that had to be done, too. She'd probably have to go back to Pitt Corner and pack up her things … and face Carl Pearson. Or maybe the police would get there before she did, and she'd be spared that, at least.

Oh yes, it was far from over. But right now, the only thing that mattered was reveling in this unfamiliar feeling of safety and knowing she was exactly the person her mother most wanted, right there in her arms.

Rebecca's chest heaved as she struggled not to cry.

"It's all right, Mamm," Hannah whispered, holding her tightly. "Don't cry."

"They are tears of joy," Rebecca told her softly, her voice scratchy with emotion. "They are tears of happiness that you have chosen to stay." She drew a deep breath. "And what is it that you called me?"

"Mamm." Hannah somehow knew exactly what she meant. "Spelled the Amish way."

And as Jonathan ran up, his face creased with alarm, he found the two of them weeping together, their faces shining like the sunlight through the rain.

Epilogue

Jonathan was an upright man but not a cruel one—Rebecca had told Hannah that he had the strength of his convictions and a spirit that worshipped reverently at the feet of God, from whom came all good gifts. So her father could see how much it meant to Rebecca that Samuel not be sent away the following evening.

Another day, maybe, but not tonight. Not after the events of yesterday in which Samuel had played such a huge part to make right what he'd always thought of as his mistake.

As if a bunch of little boys horsing around and losing track of their little sisters could be a mistake. The mistake had been all in Janet Pearson's actions, and in Carl's for falling in with them. Maybe Sam would never get over feeling guilty for not being there to stop them, but with time and love, and having Hannah around to show him she hadn't been broken—messed up a little, maybe, but not broken—he would get over his shame in time.

And speaking of shame ... not that he was ashamed of his *Englisch* kids, but Jonathan did ask them to have their dessert on the lawn at the back side of the house, where they couldn't be seen from the road. The silver Subaru was parked once again next to the barn ramp, out of the neighbors' view.

Baby steps.

So here was Hannah, with Samuel and Ben, Barbie and all the little ones, and Rebecca and Jonathan and Mammi Kate and Daadi Riehl, and a couple who'd been introduced as Onkel Orland and Aendi Ruthie and their kids, sitting on lawn chairs and all over the grass in the twilight of a warm Indian summer day, with a giant piece of blueberry pie that had homemade vanilla ice cream melting on top of it.

"I never thought this day would really come," Barbie said, wonder in her voice. "Only Leah is missing—but at least you were able to talk with her. All the rest of us are here. God has been good to us."

"It's been a very long road, but he has had the reins the whole time," her father agreed.

"In some ways, we're not at the end of the road yet," Rebecca murmured. "We still don't know if Hannah will have to go to this worldly court and speak against her other mother."

"Deputy Prinz said he'd do what he could so I didn't have to." It was one thing to be glad that Janet was in the hands of the justice system, and Carl about to be as soon as they located him ... and another thing to actually have to face that system and be a part of bringing a sentence of some kind against them. She didn't want to be the one raining vengeance down on their heads, the way she'd once played in video games. She didn't even want to sit across a courtroom and see their faces. Didn't want to imagine what was going on in their minds. Didn't want to see what was in their eyes, whether that was love or accusation.

No, what she wanted to do was exactly what she was doing now—sitting here in her jeans and T-shirt with Ben on one side and Barbie on the other, scarfing down the best piece of pie in the universe.

She was still weighing her options, of course. Just because Jonathan had made a concession tonight didn't mean he'd make the same one tomorrow. Neither could she stay here indefinitely, the *Englisch* cuckoo in the Amish nest.

As if she'd been listening to her thoughts, Rebecca said, "It's *gut* to have peace again. We may not have tomorrow, any of us, but at least we have tonight."

"Peace in the heart is a gift from God," Mammi Kate agreed. "Whether that comes from the end of pain, or from forgiveness, or from submitting to His will."

Rebecca smiled at her mother-in-law as if they had a secret they weren't planning to tell anyone else. But it was a good smile. It went all the way to her eyes, and Hannah was glad to see it. If she had her way, nothing would ever hurt Rebecca again. So, okay, maybe that was out of her hands. But maybe she could get the hang of how to put in a good word with God and He would take care of it. Everybody around here sure thought He could.

"When God allows us to see the working of His will, it is a marvelous thing," Onkel Orland said. "That sheriff coming just at the same time the Pearson woman came for Hannah, now—only God could have caused that to happen."

Samuel choked on his pie. His mother thumped him on the back. "Samuel! Drink a little milk."

"It wasn't God," he finally gasped. "It was me."

Her hand stilled on his shoulder. "What?"

"She asked for directions at the Amish Market and I told her. Then me and Ben drove straight over to the sheriff's and told him she was coming out here."

"You did that?" Hannah said. "It was you?" Not the Amish grapevine at all. Had Janet known she was talking to the boy whose life she had ruined? She'd probably never know, now.

She would have asked Samuel, but he was not looking at her. He was looking into his mother's face, looking for something. Forgiveness? Approval?

"Mamm. I did it for us. For you."

"Oh, Samuel—" Rebecca said brokenly, touching his face, his sawed-off hair. "That was not our way. Not that *Englisch* vengeance."

"It would have happened anyway. And I don't regret it."

And Hannah understood that Samuel had done the one thing she had been too afraid, too steeped in misplaced loyalty to do. He had needed to close that case file in the sheriff's office—the one where the first piece of paper in it was probably a little boy's statement about losing his sisters in an orchard.

Over his mother's shoulder, his gaze met Hannah's. He didn't smile, but she saw something in his eyes that she had never seen in all the hours they'd spent together. Not triumph, not revenge, not even happiness.

She saw peace.

Rebecca saw it, too, when he straightened out of her hug. "Maybe the *gut Gott* used you to work out His will," she said at last.

"Maybe," he said quietly. After a few moments, he got up, as though he didn't want to dwell on that thought for very long. Surely he wasn't going to go, was he? But no, he was only lighting the lamp that used to stand in the kitchen window, so that he could see to cut himself another piece of pie.

"So, Hannah," he said, settling back into his chair with his plate, "do you have any plans?"

She shook her head. She couldn't blame him. This was getting a little intense. But at the same time, did they have to talk about her right now? "Your tongue is purple. You know that?"

The little kids stuck theirs out for inspection and yup, they were too.

But he wasn't going to let her get away with dodging the subject. "I was thinking that maybe I'd look into getting my GED."

Jonathan drew a breath and laid down his fork. Rebecca put a hand on the back of his, and he turned it over to grip her fingers, hard.

"And if you were thinking of going to college, too, maybe we might do that together."

She gazed at him, a little amazed at his bravery, saying things like this in front of his parents, who would never approve in a million years. "I don't know, Sam. Do you know how bad my GPA was? I don't think any college would accept me."

"It can't be more awful than mine will be," he said with the self-deprecation that seemed to be part of his personality. "I've got four years to catch up on." He glanced at his dad. "If I do it. If I don't decide to go away and work at something else."

"Like what?" Ben asked. Mr. Strong and Silent, who hardly ever said anything. All the same, she was glad he had been there yesterday, and was here now. This might not be his family, and maybe there was no hope with his dad the bishop, but she was glad that Rebecca and Jonathan had included him in theirs. Even if it was just for tonight.

Sam shrugged. "I dunno. Maybe go out to Colorado. See if I can get work on that ranch that hired on Simon Yoder and Joe Byler."

"The tourists and hunters go home in November, after turkey season, and they shut things down," Jonathan told him.

"With the horses and hunters, maybe. But they might have winter work, like construction or something."

"Not much construction going on at twenty below," Ben said. "Maybe you could be a ski instructor."

Melinda and Barbie giggled.

"Very funny. In the spring, then. I want to do something different. The factory was okay when I needed money, but I can't see myself spending my whole life there."

"If you joined church, you could spend your life here," Jonathan said quietly. "Take over this farm, like I did from Daed."

Daadi Riehl nodded at him.

Hannah wondered if they were going to fight about it in front of everybody. Would Jonathan kick him off the place, just when they were feeling sort of like a family for the first time in, well, almost her whole life?

"I don't know, Dat," Samuel said at last. "Hannah doesn't know her plans right now. Maybe she and I and Ben could figure out some things together, *nix*?"

"Du und Hannah und Ben und der Herr," little Katie told him firmly.

Out of the mouths of babes. Hannah laughed and put her empty plate on the grass, then pulled the little girl into her lap. She kissed her hair, done up in a bob but bare of either *Kapp* or *Duchly*. Just a little blond sister who was cute as could be—and very firm about deep things that even Hannah didn't have the wisdom for.

"It's been a long road back, but I think this is as far as I'm going to go for a while. It's a good place."

"Ischt Heem," Katie corrected her, the little bossypants.

Hannah grinned, and even Samuel and Ben shared it. She gazed around her in the gentle lamplight, at Rebecca and Jonathan holding hands, at the twins and their cousins lying on their backs counting fireflies, at Daadi Riehl with his hand protectively on the back of Mammi Kate's chair, and her uncle and aunt each holding one of their kids in their lap. She didn't know much, but she did know one thing.

"You've got that right, *mei Schweschder*," she said to Katie. "No matter what else happens, this is home."

THE END

Watch for *The Highest Mountain*, the next novel of the Whinburg Township Amish, to find out who goes to Colorado and what happens there...

glossary

Achting gewwe!	Pay attention!
Auch gut.	Also good.
Bohnesuppe	bean soup
Boppli	baby
Daadi Haus	grandfather's house
Demut	humility
Denki, denkes	thank you, thanks
Deitsch	Pennsylvania Dutch
Dochder, Dechter	daughter, daughters
Dokterfraa	female herbalist or healer
Druwwel	trouble
Duchly	headscarf
Eck	corner
Englisch	Someone who is not Amish, the English language
Gediere	animals

THE LONGEST ROAD

Gelassenheit	letting go of the world
Gott	God
Gmee	congregation
Guder mariye	good morning
Gut	good
Gut. Und dich?	Good. And you?
Hochmut	lit. highness; being proud
Ischt Heem.	It's home.
Ischt okay? Du bischt engschderlich	
	Is it okay? You're trembling.
ja	yes
Kapp	The heart-shaped organdy prayer covering worn by the Amish women of Lancaster County
Kinner	children
Kumm mit.	Come with me.
Liewi	dear, dearest
Maedel	young girl
mei Schweschdere	my sisters
neh, nix?	no, is it not?
Onkel	uncle
Ordnung	rules of the church community
Rumspringe	lit. running around, the time of freedom for Amish young folks between age 16 and marriage
Snitz	sliced apples
Uffgeva	giving up one's own will
Was ischt, Mamm?	What is it, Mom?
Wie geht's?	How is it going?
Wo bischt du?	Where are you?
Wo is dei hut?	Where is your hat?

| *wunderbar* | wonderful |
| *Youngie* | unmarried young people |

about the author

Adina Senft grew up in a plain house church, where she was often asked by outsiders if she was Amish (the answer was no). She holds an M.F.A. in Writing Popular Fiction from Seton Hill University in Pennsylvania, where she teaches as adjunct faculty.

Writing as Shelley Bates, she was the winner of RWA's RITA Award for Best Inspirational Novel in 2005 for *Grounds to Believe*, a finalist for that award in 2006 with *Pocketful of Pearls*, and, writing as Shelley Adina, was a Christy Award finalist in 2009. Three of her books have shortlisted for the American Christian Fiction Writers' Carol Award for book of the year.

A transplanted Canadian, Adina returns there annually to have her accent calibrated. Between books, she enjoys traveling with her husband, playing the piano and Celtic harp, quilting, and spoiling her flock of rescued chickens.

ADINA SENFT

also by the author

The Smoke River series:
Grounds to Believe
Pocketful of Pearls
The Sound of Your Voice
Over Her Head

The Whinburg Township Amish novels:
The Amish Quilt trilogy:
The Wounded Heart
The Hidden Life
The Tempted Soul
The Healing Grace trilogy:
Herb of Grace
Keys of Heaven
Balm of Gilead

The Longest Road
The Highest Mountain (coming soon)
The Sweetest Song (coming soon)

CPSIA information can be obtained at www.ICGtesting.com
Printed in the USA
LVOW07s1617010916

502833LV00001B/90/P